STALKED

STALKED

ROBERT WANGARD

To Emma —

Hope you enjoy it !

Robert E Wangard

AMP&RSAND, INC.

Chicago • New Orleans

ISBN 978-0-99056039-5

Design
David Robson, Robson Design

Published by
AMPERSAND, INC.
1050 North State Street
Chicago, Illinois 60610

203 Finland Place
New Orleans, Louisiana 70131

www.ampersandworks.com

———

www.rwangard.com

Printed in U.S.A.

For Frank Albrecht, who saved my life

ONE

Pete Thorsen clicked off the lamp and leaned back in his recliner to take a break from reading. He listened with eyes closed as Johnny Cash's gravelly voice drifted softly from the Bose music system, and as one old favorite followed another, he couldn't help but smile. Sometime after the Man in Black went to Jackson to mess around, he nodded off.

A couple of hours later, he was wakened by a *Thud!* that came from somewhere in the darkness. He sat up in the recliner and stared straight ahead, feeling momentarily disoriented. The only light came from the dying embers in the fireplace. Everything was quiet, too. No music, no more strange sounds.

Pete listened a while longer and then turned on the light. The book he'd been reading about General Patton had slid from his lap and lay on the floor open to a random page. On the end table next to him, the ice cubes in his vodka and tonic, his first of the season even though the weather really wasn't right for that drink yet, had dissolved into a quarter-inch of clear liquid in the bottom of his glass. A twist of lime floated lifelessly in the liquid. The clock on his fireplace mantle read 1:37 a.m.

He walked to the window and looked out. Even when he shaded his eyes, all he could see was his reflected image staring back at him. He turned off the light again, and when his eyes had readjusted to the darkness, he felt his way back to the window. Night hung over the area like an inky shroud. Any moon that might have been visible earlier had vanished from the sky and the lake and the trees and bushes around his cottage blended with the blackness.

Pete inched back toward the end table, using the embers as his guide, and turned the light on again. It had been ten minutes since the sound—like someone had slapped the outside of his cottage with an open hand—had disturbed his sleep, and since he heard nothing more, he wrote it off to a dream.

He rinsed his glass in the sink and tidied up the kitchen. After checking to make sure the front door was locked, he was about to go up to bed, but the nagging voice inside wouldn't let him. He switched on the porch light and unlocked the door. When he eased it open, he saw a large plastic bag on the stoop with reddish fluid oozing from the opening where the slide closure had popped open.

He looked up and scanned the area in front of his cottage, but saw nothing. He bent down to get a closer look at the sheet of paper that lay under the bag. There were words on it, but they were upside down and the bag covered most of them.

Most of the fluid had leaked from the bag and the pool was now nearly three feet across. That made hopping over it tricky and he decided to go out the mudroom door so he could see the message and everything else from the other side. The whole thing puzzled him, because in his experience, April wasn't the time when vandals were likely to be cruising around.

His outside flood lights illuminated a broader area than the porch light, but before stepping out, he thought about how he'd protect himself if the person responsible for the mess were still lurking around. All the cottages near his were shuttered for the winter and he knew no one would be around to hear him if he called for help. After considering the limited options, he grabbed the nicked-up Louisville Slugger bat he kept in the umbrella stand by the front door.

The calendar said April, but damp cold hung in the air like the icy talons of winter hadn't let loose yet. He zipped his jacket tighter and looked around his cottage, casting his flashlight beam on the surrounding trees and bushes and bramble as he went. He continued to watch for signs of movement as he walked out the driveway, but saw nothing. When he came to M-22, he flashed his light up and down the deserted highway. A mausoleum at midnight would have had more activity.

He went back to his cottage and examined the front door and stoop from the outside. The door had a splash mark near the top where the bag had hit and the rest of it looked like macabre stalactites had been painted on the wood. The fluid didn't look like paint. Or smell like paint. He sniffed the air again and inhaled the same tinny odor he'd noticed before. Maybe it was the way the light hit everything, but the pool of fluid also looked darker than it had when he'd first opened the door.

He squatted and was able to read the first two words on the paper, *Is this . . .* He was tempted to move the bag so he could see the rest of the message, but knew better than to tamper with the scene, whether the incident turned out to be a prank or something more serious.

Pete went inside again, and after making sure both doors were locked, called the county sheriff's office. When the dispatcher answered, she mumbled something unintelligible into the phone and punctuated that with a lengthy yawn, signaling that she'd been sound asleep when the phone rang. He gave her a moment to collect herself, then identified himself and explained the reason for his call. After assimilating what he'd told her, the dispatcher said his situation didn't sound like an emergency. She suggested he wait until morning when all of the deputies would be in.

That led to an argument when Pete insisted on having someone come out sooner. The dispatcher finally sighed as though she thought Pete were making a case of good old fun into a biological warfare threat in the heart of Manhattan. She said she'd *try* to get a message to the night duty deputy and took down Pete's address and contact information. Her parting shot was that she couldn't guarantee the deputy would be able to come out even if she were able to reach him because he might be involved in a matter that was *truly* pressing.

Pete left the outside floods on and went upstairs. He pulled a chair over to one of the windows in his bedroom and waited for someone from the sheriff's office to arrive. Jumbled thoughts bounced around in his head.

He saw movement among some of the bushes near the lake. His pulse quickened and his eyes immediately focused on the spot. Minutes passed and he saw nothing else. Then he saw movement again and strained to see what was making it. It wasn't wind because none of the other bushes near the lake were moving. Something finally came into the illuminated area. He breathed out when he saw that it was a deer and chided himself for being so jumpy.

It was past 3:00 a.m. when a SUV with red and blue lights flashing pulled into his driveway. Pete exited through the mudroom door and walked to where a reed-thin uniformed deputy was leaning against his vehicle writing in a small spiral notebook. He looked up as Pete approached.

"Mr. Thorsen?"

Pete nodded.

"I understand you called to report an intruder."

As Pete got closer, he saw that the deputy was not more than thirty years old. He had a brush cut and a hatchet face that fit the rest of his body. The firearm on his hip looked like it would have been better suited to a man twice his girth.

"I don't believe I used the word intruder when I talked to the dispatcher," Pete said.

"That's what she told me," the deputy said owlishly, checking his notes again.

"Someone threw a plastic bag filled with some kind of fluid against my front door."

"Paint?"

"I don't believe it's paint. It looked reddish at first, but now seems to be darker."

The deputy shot Pete a look and flipped to a new page in his notebook. He used a stubby yellow pencil to write the words, "Reddish fluid that turned darker," repeating them aloud as he wrote. He looked up with a quizzical expression and said, "What made you think this event is so important that it couldn't wait until morning? Sounds like garden-variety vandalism to me," apparently reading from the same play book as the dispatcher.

Pete tried to remain patient and smiled. "With all respect, I don't think this is just vandalism, Deputy," he said.

"What else could it be?" he persisted. "We must get twenty, twenty-five reports like this every year."

"At 1:30 a.m. in cold spring weather? With a note?"

"What's the note say?"

"I couldn't read it without disturbing the scene, which I didn't want to do. Come around to the front and I'll show you."

"First, let me get some information," the deputy said. He flipped his spiral notebook to another new page. "I'm Deputy McGruder, by the way."

Pete stewed while McGruder asked him a lot of questions, many of which he must have already had answers to because he'd talked to the dispatcher and managed to find Pete's cottage. He spent an inordinate amount of time trying to understand why Pete called the lakeside of his cottage the front and the side facing M-22 the back.

When McGruder finally finished, he followed Pete to the front door and shined his flashlight on the mess on the stoop. After studying the scene, he said, "Just as I suspected. Vandalism. Probably some delinquents driving around bored out of their noggins looking for chuckles. I'll write up a report. If I were you, I'd get some sleep and clean things up in the morning. We'll talk to a few of the bad apples around town and let you know if we come up with anything."

"I hate to sound like a broken record, but I don't think we're talking about vandalism here."

The deputy's world-weary look made his hang-dog face seem longer. "Every time something like this happens," he said, "the homeowner thinks he's the victim of the crime of the century. I ask you again, what makes you think this is something other than vandalism?"

"Everything," Pete said. "I've already mentioned two of them — the note and the time of the year. The substance also doesn't look like paint to me and I didn't hear anyone peel rubber away from the house after the bag was thrown at my door."

McGruder busily recorded what Pete had just said in his small notebook.

Pete kept prodding him. "Smell the air. Do you smell paint fumes?"

"Paint dries. It doesn't smell after it dries."

"Aren't you even going to *try* to check out the fluid?" Pete asked, his frustration beginning to show.

"Look, Mr. Thorsen, I'm the only deputy on duty at this time of the night. Our people who do forensics are all sleeping. Do you want me to call them at 3:15 a.m. and get them over here to look at your problem?" When he said problem, he raised two fingers of each hand to signify quote marks.

"I'm not asking you to get anyone out of bed, but since you're already here, I thought maybe you'd want to satisfy *your own* curiosity."

McGruder rolled his eyes and walked closer to the stoop. He sniffed the air a couple of times, then knelt and reached out with his index finger, obviously intending to take a smear of the fluid. Pete saw what he was planning to do and said, "Don't you have a pair of latex gloves in your vehicle? I wouldn't get that stuff on my hands until we know what it is."

The deputy seemed unhappy with being told how to do his job by a mere civilian. He scowled and walked to his cruiser and returned with a latex glove. He put it on his left hand and knelt by the pool of fluid again and sniffed a second time. He swiped his protected forefinger along the edge of the pool. He looked at his finger and muttered, "This stuff is hard already." He swiped at the fluid again, seeming to press harder this time. He looked a second time and opened and closed his thumb and forefinger several times, as if testing for tackiness, and sniffed a third time.

He looked up at Pete with an expression that suggested he'd just discovered the key to a centuries-old mystery entirely on his own and proclaimed, "I think this could be blood."

TWO

Pete was thinking the same thing. "How sure are you?" he asked.

"Not positive," the deputy said, "but it damn sure isn't paint. Doesn't smell like paint. It's not tacky like paint would get after an hour or two. This happened about 1:30 a.m., right?"

Pete nodded. He pressed the deputy for more information. "With the vandalism situations you've seen, I assume paint is most common."

"Almost always. The perps want to mess up the place. Usually with red or yellow or some other bright color. They want something that calls attention to their deed."

Pete thought back to his college days and the red door of his fraternity house. He couldn't count the number of times the brothers woke up in the morning and found that the door had been repainted chartreuse or white with pink polka dots or some other garish color or combination of colors. But that was all in good fun. This, he feared, was something else.

"Can you read the note?" Pete asked.

McGruder got down on his hands and knees, careful to stay out of the pool of fluid, and shined his flashlight on the note. He looked up at Pete and shook his head. "All I can read is two words. I can't make out the rest."

That's all Pete could see, too.

McGruder put on his take-charge mantle and said, "I'm going to tape this area. In the morning, I'll have our detective and his team come out for a closer look. You have another door you can use, right?"

Pete avoided rolling his eyes. Ten minutes earlier, McGruder had seen him come out his back door. He just nodded.

The deputy went to his vehicle and returned with a roll of crime scene tape that he proceeded to string around the handrails leading to the front door. When he was finished, he stepped back and admired his handiwork. "All right, Mr. Thorsen," he said, "you can expect someone out here first thing in the morning. Sorry for the disturbance. We'll get to the bottom of this," he said with a grim air of certainty.

After Deputy McGruder left, Pete stared at the mess some more and scanned the trees and bushes around his cottage again, then went inside.

He left the outdoor floods on as a precaution and tried to sleep, but kept checking the alarm clock on his nightstand. Finally he got up because he wanted to be ready when the crew from the sheriff's office arrived. He was out of the shower by 7:15 a.m. and stepped on the scale to check his weight. He grimaced when he saw the digital numbers creep up to two hundred and four pounds. That wasn't terrible for a middle-aged man who was six-feet-two, but it wasn't great either. Harry McTigue was always prodding him to join him at the fitness center. Maybe he needed to take him up on it more often.

He heard tires crunch across the gravel driveway and glanced out the window to see Detective Joe Tessler get out of his unmarked car. Pete took another swipe at his damp hair with a brush, pulled on a pair of jeans and a flannel shirt, grabbed his jacket, and went out to meet him. Tessler was standing with his hands in his pockets and a spiral notebook tucked under one arm, sizing up the scene at the front door. He glanced Pete's way as he approached and said, "You had an uninvited visitor last night."

"Yes," Pete said dryly, "rude of him not to knock and say hello. Did you see the deputy's report?"

Tessler nodded. "From what I understand, the perp threw a bag of crap against the door of your house and left a love note." After a moment he added, "Excuse me. I meant to say door of your *cottage*. I keep forgetting that you people around the lake have your own lingo for things."

"Your deputy says he believes that what you call 'crap' might be blood."

"That's what his report says." Tessler continued to look at the bag and the pool of fluid on the stoop which was now dark brown and hard.

"Have you touched anything?" he asked Pete.

"No. But McGruder did. I had to coach him to put on a latex glove before he put his finger in the 'crap,' to use your word."

"Rookies," Tessler muttered, shaking his head. Then he said, "I know this might sound like a dumb question, but do you have any idea who might have done this?"

"Not offhand, but if this is blood, it strikes me as a pretty sick thing to do."

"Amen."

"Have you ever seen anything like this before?"

Tessler's brow furled and he appeared to think. "Not exactly like this. When I was with Chicago PD, I worked on a case once where a guy left freshly killed chickens smeared with their own blood on another guy's front step three days in a row. But they were Haitians and into voodoo and all that stuff."

"What kind of blood do you think this is?"

"I don't want to even hazard a guess. We'll have to test it."

Another unmarked car pulled in Pete's driveway. "That's Amy Ostrowski," Tessler said. "I think you met her last year when you were trying to figure out what happened to your girlfriend who was involved in that accident on the Leelanau Peninsula. I asked her to stop by when

I found out the substance in the bag might be blood. Besides forensics, she's our back-up photographer so she kind of does double duty for us."

After they shook hands and exchanged greetings, Amy positioned herself in front of Pete's cottage door and stood motionless for a few minutes while she studied the scene. Finally she said to no one in particular, "I better take my pictures."

They watched her photograph the scene from all angles and at various distances. While they waited for her to finish, Pete asked Tessler some more questions about the chicken case involving the Haitians. Finally, Amy called to them, "Okay, let's get a look at that note."

She pulled on latex gloves and handed a pair to Tessler. She leaned across the pool of dried fluid—blood or whatever—and tried to lift a corner of the plastic bag. It was stuck to the stoop. She got what looked like a putty knife from her car and gradually worked everything free. Then she concentrated on separating the note from the bag, and after a few minutes of careful work, was successful. She read the note and held it up so Pete and Tessler could see the words. It was in oversized print and read, *Is this what your blood looks like, Pete?*

Pete stared at the paper.

"Now that you've seen all of the words," Tessler said, "do any thoughts come to mind that you didn't have before?"

Pete shook his head, but didn't say anything.

"Nothing?" Tessler persisted. "You can't think of anyone who might have done this? An old enemy? Anyone?"

"I need to think about it," Pete said.

Amy Ostrowski, who'd been quiet, said, "The note puts to rest the notion that this might be something other than blood. It sounds like a threat, too."

Tessler appeared to study Pete for a long moment, then said, "You've been involved in a couple of situations in the past few years. Do you think someone you've crossed swords with could be behind this?"

Pete didn't say anything, but he'd been thinking the same thing. He watched them put the plastic bag and note in evidence bags and scrape samples of the dark substance from the door and stoop into vials. Amy said a few words to Tessler, bid goodbye to Pete, and left.

Tessler said, "I'm going to have a fingerprint check run on the bag and note and we'll test to confirm that the substance is blood and see if we can determine where it came from. We should know more when the results are in."

Pete continued to stare at the taped-off part of his cottage.

"This is ghoulish as hell," Tessler said.

Pete still didn't say anything.

"Getting back to what I asked," Tessler said, "you're telling me that you can't think of a single soul who might have done this?"

"Joe, for the tenth time, I need to think about it."

" Well I think you have to sit down with paper and pencil and write down the name of everyone who comes to mind as the possible perp. Then we should get together and go over your list."

Pete nodded.

"Do you still have that security alarm system you installed a couple of years back?"

"I keep paying the bills from the alarm company. I don't arm it very often."

"Until we know what's going on here, I'd change my ways and start arming that sucker every night before you go to bed. I agree with Amy. The note sounds like a threat and not a very subtle one."

Pete saw a county sheriff's department vehicle with a light bar on the roof pull into his driveway. Through the windshield, he recognized the face of his old nemesis, Sheriff Franklin Richter.

THREE

Richter got out and adjusted the wide leather belt that held his holstered sidearm and some other tools of his trade. He didn't wear a jacket in spite of the chilly weather, and most strikingly, his uniform shirt had short sleeves. His muscular torso was disproportionate to the rest of his body and was shoe-horned into a shirt that looked like it had been tailored for some eighteen-year-old marine boot camp warrior on his first off-base pass. Unlike most of his deputies, Richter didn't wear a hat, either. Pete had long suspected that was because he feared it would mess his carefully groomed hair.

Richter swaggered across the dormant grass and stood in front of Pete's cottage with thumbs hooked in his belt and surveyed the taped-off area. Like he was an Old West lawman about to enter a saloon filled with bad guys. A smirk creased his face.

"It looks like someone doesn't much like you, Thorsen."

"Now how could you possibly get that idea, Sheriff?" Pete asked. His voice dripped with sarcasm.

"Intuition," Richter said in a jaunty manner.

"Happened last night, Frank," Tessler said. "Someone threw a plastic bag with some unknown substance in it against Mr. Thorsen's door in the middle of the night. About 1:30 a.m., right?" He looked at Pete for confirmation.

Pete nodded.

"Did you see who did it?" Richter asked Pete.

"I was sleeping."

"If you were sleeping, how do you know it happened at 1:30 a.m.?"

"I woke up when the bag hit my door."

Richter looked at Tessler and asked, "Any idea what this unknown substance is?"

"Blood," Pete said before Tessler could answer.

Richter raised his eyebrows. "Where's the bag?" he asked, looking at Tessler again.

"In my car. I'm taking it in to have it tested and processed for evidence."

"If you're having it tested, you must not be sure it's blood."

"We're pretty sure. We want to confirm what everyone who's been out here believes."

Richter digested everything for a minute. "As I see it," he said to Tessler, "this could be an act of vandalism or it could be something else. And until we have proof it was something else, we can't spend a lot of time on it with these drug cases we have to worry about."

Pete had been trying to stay even-tempered, but now was about to earn time in the Big House by punching the chief law enforcement officer of the county in the face.

Tessler rescued him by chiming in, "We're pretty sure it wasn't just vandalism, Frank. Amy Ostrowski was here earlier and—"

"You involved Amy in this matter?" Richter said. "We pay her by the hour, you know."

"I know, but—"

"I was just reviewing our numbers for last month. We were over budget by ten percent for Ostrowski and that other freelancer we use. It's no wonder if we use her for stuff like this."

"I called you twice this morning and left messages," Tessler said defensively. "I didn't hear back so I involved Amy because of the report McGruder wrote up. I thought we should treat this as a crime scene."

"Okay, okay," Richter said, "I must have been at the gym or something and I haven't had a chance to check all of my messages. What did Amy think?"

"She agrees with the rest of us that the substance looks like blood. When put together with the note—"

"Whoa, whoa, slow down," Richter said. "What note?"

"There was a note attached to the bag. It was specifically addressed to Mr. Thorsen."

"What did the note say?"

Tessler told him. "Amy and I agree that the note constitutes a threat against Mr. Thorsen that we need to take seriously."

Richter looked at Pete and his jaw worked. "You know, Thorsen, before you moved up here, this county used to be a beautiful, quiet place. A great community for people to live and raise their children. Have a picnic on Sunday afternoons, maybe hit a few golf balls, go skiing in the winter at Crystal Mountain. Now it's one incident after another."

"I see," Pete said dryly. "It's my fault if a body shows up in the lake or a developer is killed on his own golf course, is that what you're saying?"

Richter ignored his comment and continued. "And when something did happen, we knew we could count on the cooperation of our citizens and be confident that none of them would interfere in law enforcement matters."

Pete stared at him.

"That's all changed," Richter concluded.

He looked at Pete and seemed disappointed when he didn't fire back. He finally said to Tessler, "I've got to get to the office and get some things done. And we need to get together this morning so you can bring me up to date on the Cusak case. If we don't do something about those drug kingpins operating up here, we'll all be in trouble. That's got to be priority one."

"I'll be right behind you, Sheriff," Tessler said.

When Richter was gone, Tessler looked embarrassed and said to Pete, "Think you two will ever learn to get along?"

"Not as long as he does things like gloat about what happened to my house and show absolutely no interest in finding the people responsible. Or any concern for my personal safety."

"I don't know if he was *gloating*."

"Bull, Joe, he was gloating. We both know it."

"Just between you and me and that birch tree," Tessler said, "Frank can be a bit of an ass at times. To patch things up, though, sometimes one person has to make the first move. You catch the drift of what I'm saying?"

"How could I miss it?" Pete said. "You want me to make the first move to mend fences with a guy who sees my redecorated house and hears about the note and all but laughs in my face."

Pete thought about how his relations with the sheriff had gotten worse in the five years since he was treated as a suspect in the drowning death of Cara Lane merely because he'd had dinner with her the night before her body had been found in the lake. He didn't like his bully tactics or his tendency to try to pin crimes on the first suspect he was able to latch onto.

"In Frank's defense," Tessler said, "he thinks you're always second guessing our department and sticking your nose into things you should stay out of."

"Second guessing," Pete said disgustedly. "I'm a lawyer whether he understands that or not, and just about everything I've gotten involved in has been in that capacity." He looked at Tessler and added innocently, "Or something his chief detective wanted to pick my brains on."

Tessler's head jerked around and he looked at Pete with wide eyes. "Jesus, don't let on to Frank that we talk now and then. He'd send me packing faster than I could spit."

"I don't know," Pete said. "If I'm going to try to try to patch things up with him, I'm going to have to throw him a bone, right?"

"I know you're just yanking my chain, but if you get tempted to sample the truth serum, just keep in mind that I've bailed your ass out of some real bad trouble a couple of times."

"I'd have to weigh that along with the other considerations, of course, but at the same time ..."

"Boy, you don't stop even when someone threatens to drain the blood from your carcass." He shook his head. "Well, I've got to get back to the office and think of something I can report to my boss to get him off my tail about these drug cases."

"Question before you go. Can I clean up this mess? I assume you have everything you need for your investigation."

"Yeah, clean it up. I'll let you know about the lab tests and whether we find any prints."

After Tessler left, Pete went to town for a bite to eat and to get some cleaning supplies to scrub the blood off his front door and stoop. He was just finishing his breakfast sandwich at Ebba's Bakery when Tessler called to tell him that two alpacas had been killed the night before on one of the farms south of town and there was better than an even chance that the blood that messed up his cottage came from those animals. Tessler said he couldn't talk more because he'd stepped out of a meeting with Richter and two deputies to pee and had to get back. He promised to call again later in the day.

Pete gossiped with Ebba for ten minutes and then stopped at the hardware store. After he finished buying what he needed, he headed for the alpaca farms instead of going directly back to his cottage. There were two—Crystal Lake Alpaca Farm and a newer operation,

Heavenly Meadows. Tessler told him the alpacas that had been slain were part of the new farm's herd.

He found Heavenly Meadows and pulled into the driveway and parked near the long, low-slung barn that was painted lavender and decorated, at least on the front side, with a giant mural consisting of colorful flowers in a bucolic field and birds tweeting happily under fluffy white clouds. He stared at the barn's splendor for a full minute.

Pete looked around for someone to speak to, and seeing no one, was about to head for the house when a woman came out of the barn and waved at him. The woman looked about his age, maybe a few years older, and had gray-streaked hair pulled back in a ponytail. She wore a plain blue dress with a long skirt and a wide-brim straw hat that he normally associated with July.

"Are you from the sheriff's office?" she asked hopefully.

"No, I'm Pete Thorsen. I live on the lake." He extended his hand. "I stopped because a detective in the sheriff's office told me about the incident involving your animals. Someone threw a bag filled with blood at my cottage door last night. They're testing it now to see whether the blood came from your alpacas."

A second woman walked out of the barn and came over and grasped the hand of the one he'd been talking to. It wasn't hard to see her dependency. Her eyes were red and face was streaked with tear marks. The first woman said, "This is my life partner, Sunshine Warrick. I'm Higgie Brown. We were just discussing the memorial service we're going to have for our babies, Jane and Virgil."

Pete saw the grief on their faces, and with all the empathy he could muster, said, "I'm very sorry for your loss."

"They were part of our family," Higgie said. The women sobbed in unison while Pete stood by feeling uncomfortable.

"I understand your alpacas were killed last night," he said after Higgie, at least, had regained some of her composure.

"Yes," Higgie said, "After 10:00 p.m. That's when Sunshine and I said goodnight to all of our babies like we do every night. It was the last time we saw Jane and Virgil alive." They began to cry again.

Pete gave them a few moments. "Did it happen in the barn?" he asked.

"No," Higgie said between sniffles. "It was outside. We never lock our babies in. We believe that all of God's creatures are entitled to freedom and should be able to come and go as they please."

"Mmm," Pete murmured. "I gather from what you said that someone from the sheriff's department is coming out again."

"They said they want to take pictures and ask us some more questions, but we haven't heard from anyone. Do you think we should call?"

"If they said they'd be out," Pete said, "I'm sure they will. Again, I'm sorry for your loss."

As he turned to leave, Higgie said, "You said someone threw a bag with our babies' life fluid against your house?"

"Yes. They're not sure it came from your alpacas, but they're testing it now."

"Oh my."

"A few hours after you said Jane and Virgil were killed."

"This is terrible," she said. "To have the devil loose in our community like this."

FOUR

P ete had a spray bottle of all-purpose cleaner in one hand and a scrub brush in the other, working on his front door and listening to Fats Domino croon about blueberry hill, when he heard a vehicle with a muffler badly in need of replacement clattering along M-22. The trees and bushes were still without leaves and he saw an old red pickup slow to a crawl near the mouth of his driveway. Pete recognized it as the one Calvin Seitz drove and his mind shifted into overdrive as he recalled his confrontations with Seitz the previous fall.

"Sonofabitch," Pete muttered when the picture came together. He dropped the scrub brush and cleaner, leaped off the porch, and ran toward the highway. Seitz must have seen him coming because he pulled away and his pickup's engine backfired and spewed black smoke as it picked up speed. Seitz had rounded a curve and was out of sight by the time Pete reached the highway.

Cursing, Pete ran back toward his cottage, stripped off his latex gloves, and jumped behind the wheel of his Range Rover. His tires spun gravel and dirt as he tore out his driveway onto M-22 without pausing to look for other vehicles.

Pete stomped on his accelerator to catch up with Seitz. He careened around curves and glanced in every driveway he passed in case Seitz had pulled off the highway to evade him. He was going almost double the posted speed limit and braked for a curve, then accelerated again and shot down a straight stretch of road. He still didn't see Seitz. Another curve loomed in front of him and he took it at a reckless speed. He entered a straight stretch again and caught a glimpse of Seitz's pickup just before it rounded the curve ahead.

He gave the accelerator more foot and rocketed down the straight-away. He slowed for another curve and then accelerated again. His Range Rover lurched and his tires squealed as they bit on the asphalt. He clutched the steering wheel firmly with both hands. Like he had when he was in Charlotte, North Carolina for a client conference, and as part of the entertainment, took his turn cruising around the Charlotte Motor Speedway with Richard Petty riding shotgun. Only the curves on that legendary race track were banked at twenty-four degrees and the banking on M-22 was close to zero.

He rounded another curve and saw Seitz's pickup a hundred yards ahead of him. He accelerated some more and closed the gap. Fifty yards. Twenty-five yards. Through the pickup's small rear window, he saw the yellow cap Seitz had worn every time he'd seen him. When he was five yards behind Seitz, he swerved into the oncoming lane and pulled even with him and lowered his passenger-side window. Seitz was leaning forward in his seat and clutching the steering wheel with both hands. He shot a glance Pete's way and loosened his grip with one hand long enough to give him the middle finger salute.

Pete dropped behind Seitz because of an oncoming car and then got back in the left lane and pulled even with Seitz again. He screamed at him to pull over. Seitz gave him the middle finger again and re-gripped the steering wheel, eyes glued to the road ahead, as if willing his ancient vehicle to go faster. Pete jammed his accelerator some more, and when he was ahead of Seitz, he swerved into the right-hand lane and slowed down. Seitz slowed as well. Pete saw this and braked even more.

The red pickup's brakes squealed and gravel flew as Seitz veered toward the side of the road to avoid the Range Rover. Pete knew his actions were reckless, but he didn't care. Seitz was the one who'd messed up his cottage and left him the threatening note and he was beyond mad. He looked in his rear view mirror and saw Seitz's pickup in the ditch, listing sharply to the right. Like it was about to topple sideways.

Pete backed up and jumped from his Range Rover. The odor of overheated engines and burning rubber filled his nostrils as he ran toward the pickup. He wasn't worried that Seitz might be hurt; he wanted to pound him for what he'd done.

Seitz had what was possibly the only vehicle left in the county with manual crank windows. He was frantically winding up the window on his side when Pete came up. He looked at Pete, seemingly paralyzed for a nanosecond, and then hastily slid to his right. Seitz leaned back to depress the pickup's door lock, but he was too late. Pete wrenched the door open. Seitz groped behind the seat for something and Pete grabbed his ponytail and yanked him from the vehicle. He fell on his back on the shoulder's gravel and mud and clutched his head with both hands in obvious pain.

Pete got his emotions under control as he stood over him and said, "Driving past my cottage to admire your handiwork, Calvin?"

Seitz's jaw worked, but words didn't come out. He continued to rub his head. Finally he mumbled weakly, "I don't know what you're talking about."

"Like hell," Pete said. "Why did you stop when you got to my driveway?"

"I didn't stop. I just—"

"Bull! You stopped! Did you think I wouldn't see you?"

"You're nuts, Thorsen!" Seitz showed signs of regaining his feistiness.

"If I'm nuts, maybe you can explain why you just happened to be driving past my cottage the day after someone messed up the place."

"I don't have to explain nothin' to you!"

"You slimeball! I should jam your head up the tailpipe of that piece of crap you drive!" Pete reached for Seitz's ponytail with his left hand and cocked his other fist.

Seitz cowered, raising his arms to protect his face like a boxer would do. He lowered his arms when he apparently realized that Pete wasn't going to hit him and said, "You think you own the highways, too, Thorsen? I heard in the food store that you had some kind of incident at your house and I drove by for a look-see. That's it! It's still a free country, ain't it?"

"Sure you heard about it in the food store."

"You're just on my case because you're pissed about what happened last fall. *I'm* the one who should be pissed."

Pete heard another vehicle coming and looked down the highway. When the vehicle got closer, he saw the light bar on its roof. *Crap,* he thought.

Seitz saw the vehicle, too, and his bewildered look disappeared. "Now you're in trouble, asshole," he crowed. "The law's here."

The county sheriff's department vehicle pulled up behind Seitz's pickup and its light bar began to flash. A uniform got out and started toward where Pete was standing over Seitz.

"What's the problem here?" the deputy demanded. He looked at Pete, then down at Seitz, then at Pete again. Finally he said, "Mr. Thorsen, Calvin, what's going on?"

Pete recognized him. His name was Varga or something like that. He'd been with Tessler when Joe dropped something off at Pete's cottage a couple of years earlier. He had on a Smokey Bear hat and a hip-length uniform coat that looked heavy enough to keep him warm in a January blizzard.

"Deputy," Pete said in an even voice.

Seitz rose to his feet. His eyes rattled around in their sockets like he was unsure of whether to hurl more curse words at Pete or seek protection behind Varga. Finally he cut loose with another verbal tirade.

"Officer, this here yahoo run me off the road!" He stabbed a finger at Pete. "I was driving along the public highway like I'm entitled and he comes up behind me and runs me off the stinking pavement! Probably wreaked my truck, too!"

Varga frowned and then shifted his gaze to Pete. "That true, Mr. Thorsen?" he asked.

Pete scoffed. "No, it's not true. Last night, this guy threw a bag of crap against the front door of my house in the middle of the night and—"

"I heard about that," Varga said. "It was blood, right?"

"Joe Tessler thinks so. Anyway, this afternoon, I was cleaning up the mess and who do I see driving past my house at about a mile an hour? Good old Calvin Seitz. It was obvious he was hoping to admire his handiwork."

"I understand there was a note with the blood, too," Varga said.

"A *threatening* note would be a better way to describe it. So when I saw Mr. Seitz, I got in my vehicle and followed him with the intent of asking him about the incident. He must have seen me coming because he floored his pickup and when I got close to him, he flipped me off a couple of times. Then he ran off the road. Must have taken his eyes off the highway while he was giving me the finger."

"You friggin' liar!" Seitz screamed. "I didn't run you off the road! You *run me* off!"

Pete ignored Seitz and continued, "When I parked and came over to his truck, he reached behind the seat for that old smoothbore he hunts with. That's when I hauled him out of the truck to protect myself."

Varga was furiously recording everything in a spiral notebook. Seitz's eyes were fiery and his freckled face was flushed. He started to say something, but Varga held up a hand to silence him. When Varga looked up from his notebook, he said, "Let's take this one step at a time. Calvin, you said Mr. Thorsen ran you off the road. Mr. Thorsen denies it. Did any third party witness this alleged act?"

"No," Seitz said, visibly frustrated. "It's April and there ain't many people around at this time of the year. But that's sure as blazes what happened."

"But you didn't see any witnesses, right?" Varga persisted.

Seitz just glared at Pete with fiery eyes and didn't say anything.

Varga asked, "Did you see anyone pass by who might be a witness, Mr. Thorsen?"

Pete shook his head.

"Okay," Varga said, "we have an incident where you say one thing, Calvin, and Mr. Thorsen says another. So it's one man's word against another's."

Seitz continued to glare at Pete.

Pete resisted the impulse to smile. Things were going better than he expected.

Varga turned to Pete and asked, "Now you said you believe Calvin threw a bag of blood at your door and left you a threatening note. Why would he do that?"

"This ass—" Seitz started to say.

"Quiet, Calvin. I asked Mr. Thorsen a question."

"That's easy, Deputy," Pete said. "Remember that shooting at the Civil War reenactment last fall?"

"Of course. It was big news in these parts."

"Thomas Edinger was killed with a smoothbore weapon. I discovered that Calvin hunts with a smoothbore and reported it to the sheriff. I guess the sheriff sent someone out to talk to him and he's been honked at me ever since. He blames me for trying to finger him for the murder."

Pete glanced at Seitz and saw his eyes still scorching holes in him.

"Kind of a revenge motive," Varga said.

"Right."

"What evidence do you have that Calvin is the one responsible for what happened at your house?" Varga asked.

"I told you what I think," Pete said. "The investigation by your office will prove I'm right."

Varga nodded and said, "There will be an investigation. I know that." He made some more notes in his notebook. Then he looked at Seitz and said, "I'm going to have a look at that piece you have behind the seat of your pickup, Calvin."

Seitz erupted again. "You can't go in my truck! You need one of them warrants!"

Varga shook his head. "The plain sight rule, Calvin, the plain sight rule. If I stop at the scene for legitimate purposes, which I did, I can examine anything I see in plain sight. I don't exactly need my bifocals to see the stock of your smoothbore sticking up behind the seat. Are you saying this truck isn't yours?"

"Sure it's mine!" Seitz sputtered.

Varga gave him a disgusted look and pulled the weapon from the truck. He examined it and looked at Seitz again. "Is this thing loaded?"

Seitz stared at the ground with a surly expression and didn't say anything.

"Well, is it, Calvin? If I pointed this weapon at you and pulled the trigger, would there be a click or a bang?"

Seitz's head snapped up and he held a hand palm out toward Varga. "Jesus, officer, don't point that thing at me. It's loaded, okay? It's loaded."

Pete smiled.

Seitz apparently saw him and took a step his way. "This is all your fault, Thorsen!" he screamed.

Varga blocked his path and said, "So you're not denying you've been driving around with a loaded weapon in your vehicle."

"I was going squirrel hunting," Seitz fumed.

"*Squirrel hunting*," Pete said in a disbelieving voice. "He just told me he was driving past my place because he heard about the blood incident from someone in the food store. Now he tells you he was going *squirrel hunting*? I know where he hunts squirrels. It's on somebody else's property close to where he lives, not ten or fifteen miles away. He's lying, Deputy."

"That true, Calvin? Are you lying?"

"I ain't lying." Seitz shook his head several times and turned his fiery eyes on Pete again.

Varga eyed him suspiciously for a moment but didn't say anything. He closed his notebook and said, "I need to inform both of you that if you want to file any charges against the other party, you'll have to come to our office and go through the proper procedure."

"Damn straight I'm going to file charges against this yahoo!" Seitz said, waving a hand in Pete's direction. "Idiots like this shouldn't be allowed to drive around on public roads and assault law abiding citizens!"

"You'll have to do that in our office like I just said."

Seitz continued to glare at Pete and didn't say anything.

Pete shook his head. "You know, Deputy, I was planning to wait until your investigation is complete before doing anything. But after hearing the garbage this nut just spewed out, I'll probably file charges against him for threatening me with a loaded firearm and get the ladies at Heavenly Meadows to file against him for slaughtering their alpacas. I'm sure other charges will follow after the investigation is complete."

Seitz looked ready to explode.

"Okay," Varga said, sighing, "I can't stop either of you for doing what you feel you have to do. One other thing, Calvin. I'm going to give you a pass just this one time on carrying a loaded firearm in your vehicle. But if I ever catch you doing that again, you'll be spending the night in the county jail. That clear?"

Seitz's hate-filled eyes were trained on Pete again.

Varga walked around the old red pickup and inspected it. "Mr. Thorsen, if you'll give me a hand, I think we can push this truck back on the road. Kind of a goodwill gesture. Calvin, you get behind the wheel."

With Pete and Deputy Varga pushing and Seitz gunning the engine and enveloping the area in a cloud of smoke that would cause the Greens to writhe in agony, they finally got the pickup back on the pavement. Seitz clattered away without stopping to thank his help crew. Pete half expected him to flip both of them the bird as he drove off.

FIVE

"I'm glad you decided to join me," Harry McTigue said as he puffed and wheezed and his stubby legs churned to keep up with the treadmill's belt.

"I—"

"Just a minute."

Harry shut down his machine and squinted at the controls with an intensity he normally reserved for restaurant menus. Pete smiled as he watched. His friend didn't look like the same man without his trademark half-glasses, which Pete had long suspected were already perched on his nose when he pushed out of his mother's womb. Harry found a setting he liked and turned the treadmill on again. The belt resumed moving, although at a pace the average octogenarian would find too leisurely. Harry's legs began to work again.

"You were saying?"

"I was saying that after my right arm got a workout taking seven telephone calls from you," Pete said, "I felt the rest of my body needed some exercise to restore my equilibrium."

"You'll be surprised how much better you feel after working out," Harry said, gasping for air again. "I'm a fixture here these days. I've never felt better in my life." The fringe of gray hair that ringed his bald head dripped sweat.

"You *are* looking buff."

"Glad you noticed," he said. He gave Pete a sly look and switched off the treadmill. "Let's take a break. I'm scheduled to start working with my personal trainer in fifteen minutes. I don't want to leave my entire game on the practice field."

They sat at a table in the corner of the lounge area. Pete unscrewed the cap on his bottle of spring water and took a swallow. Harry gurgled down half of a tall, slim container of Jamba blueberry pomegranate juice which according to the neon script that screamed from the bottle's label, was "the energy drink that's naturally boosted."

"That stuff good?" Pete asked, bumping the Jamba container with his water bottle.

"Not just good, great. My trainer put me onto it. After I drink a bottle of this, I feel like I can run for two hours. All of the professional athletes are drinking it."

"Umm," Pete murmured.

Harry took another swig of Jamba juice and stared out at the workout floor with a look that always telegraphed he was thinking. "So the blood in that bag was traced to those animals on the farm south of town, huh?"

"Alpacas."

"What?" Harry said, taking another swallow.

"The animals were alpacas."

"Oh, right. That's where the blood came from, though, right?"

"According to Tessler."

"Alpacas are expensive animals, you know. Fifteen, twenty thousand dollars each, I'm told. Their hair makes wonderful sweaters. I have one that I've worn for years."

Pete nodded.

"Who would want to kill nice animals like that?"

"The same psycho who messed up my door and left me a threatening note."

"And they didn't find any fingerprints," Harry said, going right on and continuing to look thoughtful.

"Not on the plastic bag *or* on the note."

"It doesn't sound like just a prank to me."

"You're so prescient, Harry. No wonder you're a great newsman."

"No need to be sarcastic about it."

"Sorry. I'm still ticked off."

"I understand, but the point I was making is that a couple of vandals wouldn't have had the foresight to wipe everything clean of prints."

"Everyone seems to agree with that. Except, possibly, Sheriff Richter."

Harry ignored Pete's slam at the local sheriff and added, "Plus the fact the note names you makes it personal."

Pete didn't say anything.

Harry mopped his brow with a paper napkin and looked at his watch. "Jesus, I've got to hunt up my personal trainer. My session starts in three minutes. Are you going to hang around for a while? We can grab a sandwich after I'm done."

"I'll be here." He wasn't about to leave before he had a chance to observe Harry's session with his trainer. He finished his water and found an open stationary bicycle that gave him an unobstructed view of the exercise area. After adjusting the bike's controls, which had been set at a resistance level suitable for someone training for the Tour de France, he started peddling and watched for Harry.

He also thought more about his encounter with Calvin Seitz. Pete had always viewed Seitz as an eccentric, unbalanced character, but now that he focused on him, it wasn't hard to visualize him slaughtering two alpacas, collecting their blood, and using it to mess up his cottage out of hatred for him. Hopefully, his bull-in-a-china shop manner would result in him leaving evidence behind that Tessler could glom onto.

Harry emerged from one of the rooms in back with a towel draped around his neck chattering animatedly with the dark-haired woman at his side. She was at least Harry's height, maybe five feet-nine or ten, and was clad head-to-toe in black Lycra. A red headband with a zig-zag black pattern held her hair back. She had long legs, and from the look of her, about minus two percent body fat.

Harry scanned the exercise area and finally made eye contact with Pete, obviously wanting to be sure he saw him with the trainer. He looked like a contented Cheshire cat about to start on a fresh bowl of warm cream.

For the next hour, the personal trainer put Harry through his paces. First they spent time on the treadmill. The Jamba juice apparently didn't produce the advertised effect, because after five minutes, Harry looked like a runner who was near cardiac arrest after completing the first mile of the Chicago half-marathon. Next they moved to the lifting area, and while Pete couldn't tell how much weight the trainer was trying to coax Harry into pressing, the tortured expression on his face confirmed that it was beyond his physical capacity.

The climbing wall was the final stop. The trainer scampered half way up the wall, communicating technique over her shoulder to Harry below as she went. His chest was still heaving and he looked more mesmerized by her skill than eager to emulate her. The trainer clung to the wall in mid-climb, demonstrating how to use the feet by letting one foot dangle free, then finding a new foothold and continuing upward. Once she was at the top, she talked to Harry some more, then snaked smoothly to the floor again.

Now it was Harry's turn. He tried various places for his hands and tested about ten different footholds. Finally he found a combination he liked and put his weight on one leg and hoisted his body upward. One foot up the wall. He found new places to grip with his hands and repeated the process with his feet. Two feet up the wall. Pete saw the trainer peek at her watch as Harry tried to flatten himself against the wall, which wasn't easy given his girth. After a few minutes more, he was three feet up. Pete saw Harry glance over his shoulder at the safety of the floor as he clung to the faux rocks with chalk-white knuckles.

Finally the trainer showed mercy and talked him down again. She clapped enthusiastically as Harry stood there sucking air, his look of terror slowly morphing into a triumphant grin.

Pete pulled over to the side of the highway to take Joe Tessler's call.

"I got your message about Calvin Seitz."

"I think you have to question him and find some basis to search his shack before he cleans up the evidence or it grows stale."

Silence, then Tessler said, "I read Deputy Varga's report. I understand you had a confrontation with Seitz on the highway. You suspect him of killing the alpacas and using the blood to mess up your house, huh?"

"No question. He all but stopped at the end of my driveway, obviously hoping to see the result of his handiwork the night before. Plus it's clear he still hates my guts because of what happened in the Edinger case last fall."

"Mmm, that's something."

"*Something.* There couldn't be a clearer motive. He's a hunter and uses a knife to skin animals all the time. He lives in the area. He's certifiably nuts. What more do you want?"

"Frank would have to okay it. I might need something more tangible to convince him."

Pete rolled his eyes. "Tangible! I just gave you eighteen things. The guy's a psycho."

"I don't think you understand. We can't just scribble out a warrant and then run out to someone's place and search his house and car. A judge has to sign off on it."

"I know that. So get him to sign off on it."

"Pete—"

"Would my dead body give you what you need?"

"That's a little melodramatic."

"Is it? You saw my cottage. The thought of him slaughtering alpacas in the dead of night and skulking around my place and using the blood to mess things up and leave me notes threatening to gut me like he did those animals makes me nervous as hell."

"Just because a man is a little different doesn't mean he's insane."

"You've talked to him exactly once, when you questioned him about the Edinger shooting. I've seen the guy in action. He confronted me on the street over the questioning and raved like a madman. He'd just come from the hardware store and I thought he was going to bury his new garden tool in my chest. A few days later, I was in the woods looking at the reenactment site and he shot a few feet over my head. Ten would be a generous estimate. You know what his excuse was? He was aiming at a squirrel and didn't see me. Now we have this blood incident. He's both nuts *and* dangerous."

"This is the first time I've heard about the street confrontation or the shot over your head."

"You've heard about them now. You need to work on Richter."

Silence again, then, "I'll see if I can catch him in the right mood."

Pete was still fuming over his conversation with Tessler when he walked into *The Northern Sentinel's* office. Harry was ripping away at his club sandwich like a famished wolf that had just emerged from his lair after a winter that featured too much snow and too few animals to prey on.

"Did you watch the whole workout?" Harry mumbled with his mouth full of sandwich.

Pete tried to put the conversation with Tessler out of his mind and said, "Most of it."

"The part you probably didn't see," Harry said, taking another bite in mid-sentence, "was when Eve tested my body fat. She said I was down two percent from when I started the program."

"I assume Eve is your trainer's name."

"Yeah, she's something, huh? It'll probably take me six months to get in the kind of condition she's in."

Pete nodded soberly. "Conditioning takes time. What did she say your body fat was?"

Harry's brows knit together and he said, "You know, I don't remember the exact number, but the important thing is a person's trend and that's definitely down in my case."

Harry washed down the remainder of his sandwich with the final slug of his Jamba juice and tossed the empty bottle in the wastepaper basket. He got the faraway look in his eyes that Pete had seen before and said, "I wish Eve had changed the order of my workout, though, and gone with the climb first. Then I probably would have made it to the top of the wall instead of only halfway."

Pete just nodded and started on his own sandwich.

Harry hadn't finished recapping his workout. "You know," he said, "I don't suffer from vertigo or anything, but when I was up on that wall, I started to feel oozy."

"Maybe you should ask your friend Eve how she does it," Pete suggested.

"She's not really my *friend*. She's my personal trainer. We have a professional relationship."

"Sorry. Imprecise language."

"It's a good thought, though. Eve was up even higher than I was and it didn't seem to bother her. I wonder if there's a secret to it."

Harry got another Jamba from his small office refrigerator and settled in behind his desk again. He looked out the window at the street and said, "I was thinking about that incident at your house again. You ought to make a list of people who might have done it."

"Good suggestion, but I've already started."

"Any names on it yet?"

"Yeah, Calvin Seitz."

Harry frowned. "Seitz. Is he the crazy guy with the red hair who lives back in the woods?"

Pete nodded and reminded Harry that Seitz was a suspect in the reenactment murder. He told Harry about chasing him down M-22 after he saw him stop at the end of his driveway.

Harry's eyes widened. "You chased him in that old Range Rover of yours?"

Pete shrugged. "Seitz drives a pickup that's even older than my vehicle."

"You could have been killed the way M-22 twists and turns through that area."

"I'm still here."

"Yeah, but you might not be."

Pete just looked out at the street and didn't say anything.

"What makes you think it might be Seitz?"

Pete went through the analysis he'd just given Tessler. He repeated his contention that Seitz was crazy.

"You seem pretty sure about Seitz"

"Is ninety percent sure?"

"I'd say it is."

"The problem I have is getting the sheriff's office to look into it before the trail gets cold."

Harry looked out the window again and appeared to be thinking. He repackaged his earlier comment and said, "I don't want to be preachy, but you weren't being very smart when you chased Seitz like that. He could have taken a shot at you, or at very least that deputy might have believed his story and run you in."

"I told you, I was mad."

Harry looked like he wanted to say something but held back.

"Besides, it worked out okay."

"Sure, it worked out, but it might not have."

Pete didn't say anything.

SIX

Pete arrived at his office the next morning dressed in dark clothes and wearing a pair of old hunting boots. He skipped his usual caffeine fix because he was already on edge. He found his county road map book, located the right section and figured out where he could park his Range Rover so it would be inconspicuous. After that, he plotted a course through the woods and committed it to memory.

He put the map book away and stared out at the bay. The first boat he'd seen that spring powered its way across the gray water toward Lake Michigan. In a month or so, the outlet would be filled with all types of craft coming and going. And the tourists would be converging. Hordes of them, forcing him to park two blocks away from his office.

His wall clock read 10:00 a.m. Three hours to go. To take his mind off the time, he decided to start on the article he hoped to sell to *The Fjord Times* about a relative who'd emigrated from Norway in the nineteenth century. He opened the file drawer with the family archive materials his mother had bequeathed to him when she died and took out the red manila folder labeled "Ottar Jacobsen."

Ottar was on his mother's side of the family and had come to America together with his parents and siblings in 1854. Seven years later, when he was fifteen, he joined the First Minnesota Norwegian Volunteers to fight on the Union side in the Civil War. Age wasn't scrutinized too carefully in those days, particularly in the case of immigrants. If a boy looked capable of handling a rifle and said he was seventeen, that pretty much settled the issue.

The young Ottar occupied a storied place in family annals for two reasons. He fought in fifty battles of the war and the only injury he suffered was when he had the lobe of one ear shot off during the Second Battle of Bull Run. And when he was discharged, he was given a parchment certificate that was signed personally by President Lincoln commending him for his uncommon valor in battle and his exceptional service to the Union cause. Ottar's legend grew as later relatives such as Pete's grandfather told stories about him that lavishly embellished the already impressive truth.

Pete's desk and credenza were soon covered by yellowed photographs, old newspaper clippings, handwritten letters in the style of the time, military commendations, and a smattering of other documents, all protected by individual plastic sheaths. Pete read the translated version of one letter Ottar had written home telling of the many hardships the troops had to endure. He closed with a burst of excitement and pride that literally exploded from the page, saying he'd been selected to receive one of five new Henry repeating rifles that had been allocated to his unit.

Pete checked the time again and began to outline his article, using the chronology he'd developed. He tried several punchy alternative openings, always his favorite part of writing, but didn't come up with anything that really grabbed him. He wasn't satisfied with the flow of the story either, and started over from scratch.

As the time drew closer to 1:00 p.m., he found it impossible to concentrate any longer. He straightened his desk and walked down the street for a sandwich before he headed south on M-22.

As Pete trudged through the woods towards Calvin Seitz's shack, an inner voice kept reminding him of how reckless what he planned to do was. But he couldn't get Seitz out of his mind. He didn't *regret* confronting him on M-22, but when he thought about it without anger driving him, he started to be concerned that the incident might further fuel Seitz's rage and prompt him to do something even more violent.

Pete's telephone conversation with Joe Tessler the previous day reinforced his anxiety. Even if Tessler managed to talk the sheriff into letting him question Seitz and seek a warrant to search his shack and vehicle, he was concerned that the passage of time would make the likelihood of finding something practically nil.

He hadn't researched the issue, but suspected that killing the alpacas and slopping their blood on his cottage might be misdemeanors rather than felonies. Still, if Calvin were convicted of those offenses, it would put him in the crosshairs of law enforcement and might deter him for the future. The note . . . That might be different.

The forest floor was soaked from the recently-melted snow pack, and Pete could feel the moisture seep into his old boots as he walked through the woods. Through the barren trees and bushes, he spotted Seitz's shack a quarter mile away. He trained his binoculars on it and watched for a few minutes, but saw no signs of movement. He moved from tree-to-tree and closed to within a hundred yards. He stood behind a large oak and watched. And hoped his dark clothes blended into the landscape.

The shack had slabs of plywood nailed to the exterior in place of regular siding. Moisture had caused the slabs to curl, giving the place an even rougher look, and with age the red paint had faded to a washed out pink. Seitz's claptrap pickup was parked in front of the shack. Another truck that looked even older rested on blocks with its wheels off. Twenty feet from the front door, an ax leaned against a chopping block and freshly-split firewood that hadn't been stacked lay nearby. Wispy gray smoke drifted from the shack's chimney.

All Pete could do was wait to see if Seitz left to run some errands, or maybe took his ancient smoothbore out for a little spring squirrel hunting. Then he'd decide if he was willing to take the risk and enter the shack to look around.

No one came or went and it occurred to Pete that Seitz might already be outside. Possibly skulking silently through the woods, searching the trees for his quarry. Pete hadn't seen anybody and certainly hadn't heard the bark of his old smoothbore, but that didn't mean he wasn't out there. Every few minutes, he glanced over his shoulder in the direction he'd walked in from.

After an hour of waiting and watching, Pete heard a vehicle approaching on the road leading to Seitz's shack. Road was too grand a description. Unimproved path would be a better term. A newish black Chevy Silverado came into view and splashed water and kicked up mud as it lurched from pothole to pothole. It stopped behind Seitz's pickup and the driver got out and banged on Seitz's door. After a minute, he banged on it again. Using his binoculars, Pete could see the Silverado's license plate number and jotted it down.

Seitz opened his door. He was tucking his plaid shirt into a pair of baggy camo pants and hitching up his suspenders, as though his guest had caught him sitting on the can. They conversed in voices Pete couldn't hear, then went inside. Pete stood by the tree and felt the damp cold knife deeper into his body with each minute that passed.

He was about to abort when the door opened and Seitz and his friend came out. The two men exchanged more words Pete couldn't hear, then the second man got in the Silverado and drove out the one-lane bumpy, muddy road. Seitz watched him go and went back inside.

Pete's watch read 3:30 p.m. He waited some more, and to take his mind off his discomfort, thought again about what he'd look for if he got inside the shack. A knife with traces of dry blood. Blood-stained clothes. Plastic bags with blue slide closures like the one that had been thrown against his door. Maybe a computer and printer since the one-sentence note had been typed.

When Seitz didn't appear again, he gave it up and retraced his route through the woods to where his Range Rover was parked. He was chilled to the marrow, but also relieved that he hadn't been forced to make the decision he'd been agonizing over.

Pete turned up the volume on his Bose, which was playing a Chuck Berry CD, and moved his chair closer to the fire to soak up the warmth. He unfolded the slip of paper with the Silverado's license plate number and dialed Joe Tessler's cell phone number.

"What's going on over there?" Tessler asked when he answered. "It's early for a party, isn't it?"

Pete chuckled. "No party," he said as he turned down the volume again. "I wonder if you could do something for me."

"If I can. What is it?"

"I have a license plate number for a black Chevy Silverado. I'm interested in knowing who the owner is."

Silence, then, "Does this have something to do with Calvin Seitz?"

"It does."

"You haven't been following Seitz around, have you?" Tessler asked suspiciously.

"No, just being observant."

More silence, then, "You're going to get sued for harassment if you don't watch out. I talked to Varga and he told me that Seitz is already hotter than a firecracker about that incident on the road. If he finds out you've been following him around . . ."

"I told you, I haven't been following him."

"Where did you see this Silverado?"

"In town. The driver was talking to Calvin Seitz." He wasn't about to say anything about being at Seitz's shack, or what he was thinking about doing there.

"Which town? There are four within a small radius."

"Frankfort, okay?" he lied. "I saw them in Frankfort."

"What were they doing, just talking?"

"Oh for crissakes, forget that I asked. I'll find some other way to get the information."

"No, no, I'll run the trace. I'm trying to get a full picture is all. I don't want you to get in trouble again."

"The trouble I'm worried about is the guy who wrote that note and is threatening to gut me like he did those alpacas. I can't seem to get that through to anybody."

"I'll check in the morning."

"Early in the morning? Late?"

"Pete . . ."

Before Pete went to bed, he checked the doors and windows to make sure they were locked. Then he set the alarm. He'd armed it every night since the blood incident, but hadn't broadcast that fact to anyone, not even to close friends like Harry McTigue.

SEVEN

After spending the morning revising and fleshing out the outline for his article about Ottar Jacobsen, Pete was considering wrapping things up and heading out to Calvin Seitz's shack again when his outer door opened and Higgie Brown and her life partner, Sunshine Warrick, walked in. They were dressed like twins in long black dresses, sensible shoes, and broad-brimmed black hats with veils that extended below their eyes. To complement their identical dress, they had charcoal grey knit stoles draped around their shoulders.

In the few seconds it took them to cross Pete's waiting room, two questions flashed to his mind. The first was how was he going to finesse their request that he investigate the slaying of their alpacas, which he was sure was the reason they'd come to see him. And second, he wondered how many people had seen the two women parade down Main Street dressed in their finest mourning clothes, arms linked and a certain resoluteness tempering their looks of sorrow. In particularly, he hoped Harry hadn't seen the procession because if he had, a picture of the women entering his office would be on the front page of the *The Northern Sentinel's* next edition.

"We're sorry to intrude without an appointment, Mr. Thorsen," Higgie Brown said with an air of formality, "but we've just come from a private burial ceremony for Jane and Virgil and we'd like to discuss an important business matter with you. If you have time, of course."

"Higgie, Sunshine," he said. He almost wished he'd had a hat on himself so he could have doffed it in a display of respect for their loss. He settled for, "I know this must be a sad day for you."

Sunshine Warrick took Higgie's hand in hers and squeezed it. Both of them sniffled.

"We'd like to see justice done," Higgie said. "Our babies didn't deserve to die like that."

"I can certainly understand your feelings," he said. "I know from what you said earlier that the sheriff is investigating," he added, hoping that would help deflect the request he saw coming.

"That's what he said," Higgie replied. "But we have the feeling that the deaths of Jane and Virgil aren't priorities with him."

"In fairness," Pete said, "it's only been a couple of days." It galled him to be an apologist for Frank Richter, but . . .

"Mr. Thorsen," Higgie said as Sunshine continued to weep, "we've been asking around and people told us we should talk to you. They said you have a certain . . . *reputation* for solving situations like ours."

Just then his telephone rang and he saw from his Caller ID that it was Joe Tessler. He decided not to take the call even though he was eager to hear who owned the black Silverado. He wouldn't feel comfortable speaking freely in front of Higgie and Sunshine, and if he did, he feared it would undercut his suggestion that they should let the sheriff's investigation run its course.

"You can answer that," Higgie said. "We don't mind."

Pete waved a hand and said, "It's just a friend. I'll call him back." He let Tessler's call go to voicemail.

"To get back to your point," Pete said, "I've had the misfortune of getting tangled up in a couple of murder situations as part of my law practice, but I'm a lawyer, not a private investigator. The people you talked to might not understand that."

Higgie and Sunshine looked at him with what he was sure were mournful eyes if he'd been able see through their veils. Higgie began to sob, joining Sunshine who was already dabbing at her face with tissues. "We feel we don't have anyone to help us," Higgie said between sniffles.

Pete put on his most empathetic expression and said as gently as he could, "Believe me, I know how you feel about the loss of Jane and Virgil, but I also know that in real life, police investigations take time. It's not like *Law & Order* on television."

"We don't have a television set," Higgie said, sniffling again. "We've never seen *Law & Order.*"

Pete nodded sympathetically and said, "It's a police show where even the most serious crimes seem to be solved in a jiffy. Real life isn't like that."

Higgie and Sunshine sat across from him and continued to cry softly. Pete pushed a box of Kleenex their way since they'd exhausted the supply of tissues they had with them.

"I'll tell you what," Pete said, eager to wrap up the emotional scene, "I do know about one thing that's going on in the investigation because I passed the information on to the sheriff's department and I'm waiting to hear back. If that turns out to be relevant to your situation, I'll let you know right away."

"Could you share it with us?" Higgie asked hopefully. "We won't tell anyone."

"I'm sorry," Pete said, "I can't do that. Police confidentiality." He felt bad about the half-truths, but felt he had no choice.

They weren't completely satisfied, but agreed to leave it on that basis. Before departing, they engaged in a group hug with Higgie clinging to his left side and Sunshine clinging to his right. Pete was hesitant to break the emotional embraces until they were ready and endured the brims of straw hats sawing against his neck from opposite sides.

When they were finally gone, Pete called Joe Tessler back. He didn't answer and Pete got his voicemail. He waited impatiently for Tessler to return his call, periodically checking the clock.

It was nearly 3:00 p.m. when Tessler called back. "I called earlier," he said.

"I know you did. I was with a client."

"A law client, huh? I thought you just chased killers."

"Oh, ha ha. Who's the license plate registered to?"

"A guy named Randy Seitz."

Pete paused, then said, "Calvin's brother."

"Brother or cousin or something. Anyway, it looks like there's a family connection. The most current address the DMV has for Randy is in Detroit. I don't know whether he still lives there or has moved up here to be with Calvin. Calvin has a shack in the woods off M-22 as you no doubt know. Maybe Randy moved in with him."

"Possible, but I don't think so," Pete said, recalling how Randy had appeared at Calvin's place and then left again.

"And you say that because?"

"When I saw the two of them in town—and I assume the guy Calvin was talking to was Randy—they were both driving their own trucks. Like they'd just met up rather than staying together."

"You said this was yesterday?"

"Yes."

"Umm," Tessler murmured. "I also did a database search on Randy Seitz. He has a record for drug-related offenses. Small time dealer. Then it gets interesting. He spent a couple years in the joint for carving up a guy in a knife fight. I don't know the details. Before that he was booked on a domestic violence charge involving a girlfriend."

"What did the domestic charge involve?"

"The usual from what I understand. An altercation of some kind in the woman's apartment, Randy lurking outside her building at all hours of the day and night. Calling her repeatedly and then hanging up."

Pete was silent for a moment. "He sounds worse than his brother."

"A real sweetheart. It's another reason you need to stay away from those guys. If you experience another incident, report it and let us handle it."

Pete was thinking as they talked and said, "Someone obviously used a knife on those alpacas."

"Unless it was Dracula and he regurgitated the blood into a bag," Tessler said dryly. "But to be serious, the fact Randy was convicted of a knife crime in Detroit doesn't mean he had anything to do with our situation up here."

"I understand that. But Randy is here now and might have been here when the alpacas were killed and my door was done, which raises questions. Have you talked to Frank yet about questioning Calvin and going for a search warrant? I know you haven't done anything with Randy yet because you just found out about him, but I think you should question him, too."

Tessler sighed and said, "I floated the idea with Frank after I found out about Randy, and he just about threw me out of his office. He isn't taking the incidents at your house and the alpaca farm that seriously. He thinks they were one-time incidents. To make sure I don't do anything on my own, he calls me every hour for a progress report on the drug cases."

Pete shook his head and said, "Okay, thanks for running the trace."

After he got off the phone with Tessler, he spent another hour on his article, then locked up and took the scenic route home. The days were getting noticeably longer and when he crested the last hill on Bellows Road, the lake spread out before him. He turned west and admired the familiar scene. The ice had broken up two weeks earlier and the sun was low in the west and glinted on the choppy water. He'd gotten used to the quiet offseason. No one was on the road and the boat hoists and piers were still stored upside down opposite the water. Across the lake, a few house lights winked at him in the gathering dusk.

He grilled a burger and heated some frozen vegetables in the microwave, then sat in the dining alcove and ate and listened to a Don

McLean CD that featured "American Pie" and other memorable tunes. After he cleaned up, he moved to the living area, started a fire, and sipped a weak vodka and tonic made with his trademark Thor's Hammer vodka. It was his second of the season, as though he were willing warm weather to move into the area.

He listened to the Don McLean CD again and mouthed the words and reflected on the lives and deaths of Buddy Holly and the other musicians who had supposedly inspired McLean's song. He freshened his drink and hummed along with the lyrics. "Bye, bye . . ." A great song, and one that had endured over the generations. He wondered if anyone would remember a Lady Gaga song in ten years.

He got up to freshen his drink again, but caught himself. He had to get back to his old days of self-control when he limited himself to two drinks. Besides, there were calories in alcohol and he remembered what the scale had told him a few days earlier. He vowed again to make visits to the fitness center a part of his regular routine and not just when Harry pestered him.

EIGHT

eep! Beep! Beep! echoed through Pete's cottage. He was awake instantly and rolled out of bed and grabbed the baseball bat he'd moved from the umbrella stand near the front door to his bedside. He listened but couldn't hear anything over the insistent chirping of the alarm. He gripped and re-gripped the bat handle as he stood flattened against the wall.

After a few minutes, he moved quietly to the bedroom door and reached around and clicked on the bank of light switches. The interior of his cottage came alive with light. He made his way slowly down the stairs and wished he'd had the foresight to install an alarm control panel on the second floor. As it was, there could have been six thugs in his living room having cocktails and he wouldn't have heard their merriment over the din of the alarm.

Pete gripped the bat handle tighter as he reached the bottom step and peered around the corner. He saw nothing. The alarm continued to beep as he went from room to room and checked the entire downstairs. He tried the mudroom door leading outside and found it still locked. He passed through the living room to the front door. It was locked as well. He turned off the alarm and then checked the windows in each of the rooms. They were all locked, and inside at least, he saw no signs of tampering.

The front door was solid and he couldn't get a good look at the stoop from an adjacent window. He turned on the outside flood lights and opened the door slowly, bat at the ready. He didn't see anyone on the stoop or standing along the wall, but he did see a piece of paper tacked to the door. He scanned the trees and bushes between his door and the lake, but saw nothing. He opened the door wider and read the message: *My, my, an alarm system. You must be nervous Pete.*

He re-read the message, then studied the area around his cottage again. He closed the door, dropped the deadbolt lock, and stared into space. *Who the hell is this?* He debated calling the sheriff's office again, but decided against it when he thought about the reception he'd get if he called in the middle of the night for the second time in a week and insisted that someone come right out.

Pete re-armed his alarm system and decided to leave the outside floods on again as an additional precaution. He went back upstairs and hit the bank of master switches. He sat in the darkness in the same chair by the window he'd watched from the night the bag of blood was thrown against his door. *This isn't going to go away* his inner voice told him again. He thought about Randy Seitz's rap sheet and his crazy brother, Calvin.

After a sleepless night, Pete called the sheriff's office to report the incident promptly at 8:00 a.m. Tessler arrived at his cottage an hour later.

"Another wakeup call, huh?" Tessler said when Pete came up. He must have noticed Pete's bloodshot eyes because he added, "I might have some eye drops in my Acura if you want them."

Pete shook his head. He'd already used Visine twice in attempts to rid his normally clear-blue eyes of the roadmaps of red veins.

"Front door same as last time?" Tessler asked.

Pete nodded and led him around to the lake side of the cottage. Tessler read the note and said, "Sounds almost like a taunt."

"I think the Seitz brothers or whoever scoped out my place before last night because they knew I had an alarm system."

"Maybe the perp noticed it the night he threw the blood at your door," Tessler volunteered.

"I don't think so. I don't have stickers on any of my doors or windows saying the place is protected by a security system. That may be good advertising for the security company, but it's an open invitation to a burglar because then he knows what he's dealing with. This guy has been here more than once. That's clear from the note, too. I doubt that whoever did this carries a laptop and printer around in his vehicle and types a note after he sets off the alarm."

Tessler examined the note again. "Do you have a camera? I'd like to get some shots before I take this down and have it dusted for prints."

"Isn't your forensics team coming out?

"If I got Amy or somebody else out to photograph a note on the door, Frank would ream my butt. You heard him the other day."

"Especially if the note you found was left for me," Pete said sarcastically. He went inside and returned with a digital camera. He handed it to Tessler and said, "Shoot away."

Tessler took a dozen photographs of the note pinned to the door, then donned a pair of latex gloves and removed the sheet of paper with the same oversized words as the first note and placed it in a plastic sheath. He walked around the cottage with Pete trailing behind. He stopped by a window and examined some marks on the wooden frame. "Were these here before?"

Pete looked at the wood and shook his head. "I can't say to be honest."

"Maybe the perp set off the alarm when he tried to pry open the window." Tessler took another ten photographs of the damaged wood from various angles. When he was finished, he said, "I'm going to take your camera along so I can transfer these pictures to my computer and print out some glossy shots. I'll get it back to you."

Pete just nodded.

"Who do you have on your suspect list besides Calvin Seitz? I assume you've made one by now."

They went inside and Pete showed him a piece of paper. He said, "The Seitz brothers are still at the top of my list for obvious reasons. Whoever killed the alpacas and messed up my door with their blood has to be a wacko. That fits Calvin to a 'T.' Now with brother Randy here . . . Well, I don't have to say more."

He'd drawn a line below the Seitz brothers and written two other names.

"Next I have Kurt Romer and Gil Bartholome."

Tessler's eyebrows knit together and he said, "Romer is the guy we sent to prison on drug charges a few years ago. Repeat offender. Had the meth mill near Thompsonville."

Pete nodded. "Romer and I have some history going back to when I was looking into the death of Cara Lane. I began to suspect that he might have had something to do with Cara's death and we sparred a couple of times. One night I —"

Tessler interrupted and said, "That was your investigation that wasn't really an investigation, right?" He rolled his eyes.

"Save the jokes for another time, Joe. As I was saying, one night I tailed Romer and stumbled onto his meth lab. I was trying to get a better look at the operation when his dog went crazy. Romer and his partner came after me and I had to take off through the woods. Later, I got Harry McTigue to call your office and tip you guys to the partner's plate number. That's how the feds caught them a couple of days later."

"So that's what happened," Tessler said.

Pete stared at him.

"Sorry, continue."

"Romer hates me. The thing is, though, he's in prison."

"Maybe he's out."

"If he is, I haven't heard about it."

"That's easy enough to check. The name across from Romer is Gil Bartholome."

"You must remember him," Pete said. "He's the member of the counterfeit immigration document ring that got away."

"I remember him very well, but I don't understand why he's on your list. The fact you helped break up that ring hardly seems enough to give Bartholome a motive to launch a vendetta against you."

"There's even more of a personal element with him. We both dated the same woman, Lynn Hawke. Lynn lived in our area for a few years and then moved to Seattle, ostensibly to be with her suicidal daughter, but in actuality to shack with Bartholome. A power struggle was going on within the ring and someone—probably Sandy Sandoval—killed Lynn by staging a fatal automobile accident. Alain Conti was head of the ring, and when I saw him in the hospital just before he was shot, he implied that Bartholome believed I had something to do with Lynn's death. Bartholome was obsessed with Lynn."

"Do you think that Bartholome might be back in this area?"

"I have no idea, but in the interests of being complete, I listed him."

Beneath Romer and Bartholome, Pete had drawn another line and listed Robyn Fleming.

"Remember that case five, six years ago when Robyn and a guy from Traverse City were convicted of sabotaging a hang glider's equipment and he wound up paralyzed?"

"I remember."

"Robyn was a business client of mine at the time. Before she was arrested, she was in my office one day and confessed to her part in the crime and asked me to get her a defense lawyer just in case, as she put it. She was arrested shortly after that and charged along with the Traverse City guy with attempted murder and conspiracy to commit murder. She blames me for passing on information to law enforcement that she told me in confidence."

"As I remember, the way we got onto her was we found her accomplice's prints on the hang gliding equipment, and when we arrested him, he turned on her."

"Right, but you didn't get anything from me. After Robyn came to see me that day, I was unsure of my professional responsibility in the circumstances so I researched it and concluded that since what she told me involved a crime that had already occurred, as opposed one she was contemplating, I had no professional duty to come forth and report it. I agonized about it for the next week or two and then my dilemma was solved when she was arrested independent of any action by me."

"She's on your list because she thinks you turned her in."

Pete nodded. "She sent me a bunch of hate letters from prison accusing me of unprofessional conduct and everything else imaginable. I felt terrible about what happened and finally went down to see her—she's in the maximum security women's prison in Indianapolis—to try to convince her I didn't have anything to do with her arrest. She refused to see me and a few days later sent me another nasty letter."

"Umm," Tessler murmured.

"The thing with Robyn, I'm fairly certain she's still in prison. Plus she's confined to a wheelchair because of an earlier hang gliding accident of her own. I doubt if she's capable of slaughtering two alpacas in the middle of the night and then coming over to my cottage to throw their blood against my door even if she's out of prison."

"So why's she on your list?"

"I don't know. Those letters she sent made an impression on me, I guess. She keeps popping into my mind."

"She could have hired someone to do her dirty work," Tessler volunteered. "She did that with the hang glider."

"I know, but it's harder if you're in prison."

Tessler looked thoughtful and said, "You've made your share of enemies, haven't you?"

Pete didn't say anything.

"This gives us something to start with at least."

"There are three or four people besides the ones on the list who might have grudges against me—a couple of former law partners, that sort of thing—but nothing that would provide a motive for murder."

Tessler stood. "I have to get back to the office. Can I take this list?"

Pete nodded. "Do you have a plan?"

"I'm going to tell Frank about this latest incident and try to talk him into launching a full investigation."

"Beginning with questioning the Seitz brothers and hopefully getting warrants, right? They're still at the top of my list."

"I hear you."

"My old boss in the CID always said that if law enforcement doesn't strike right out of the box, the chances of finding anything useful diminishes by the day."

Tessler sighed. "I'll do my best. I'll also verify that Kurt Romer and Robyn Fleming are still in prison. Then we can get together again and talk about where we're at."

Pete looked at him impassively.

Tessler must have noticed because he said, "I realize this isn't moving fast enough for you. Believe me, if I were in charge, we'd be all over these guys."

"Yeah, well, I'm not going to just sit around if I don't start seeing some action out of your office."

"What are you saying?"

"Interpret it any way you want."

NINE

ete worked on a hybrid trainer with the resistance set at a moderate level as he alternately watched Harry being put through his paces by Eve Bayles and brooded over why he hadn't heard from Joe Tessler about his meeting with the sheriff or his check with the prison authorities. He had his cell phone with him, which he didn't always remember to do, so he was sure he hadn't missed Tessler's call.

He switched from the Nordic track feature of the trainer to the cardio recumbent bike feature and continued to work. Sweat trickled down the side of his face and he mopped it with a sleeve. A youngish man in sweat pants and a tight tee shirt that showed off his biceps walked past with a stack of towels. He held one up without saying anything. Pete nodded and the man flipped a towel at his head. Pete caught it and mopped his face a second time.

Pete resumed pedaling. Exercise in a fitness center wasn't his favorite thing to do. He preferred to run or swim in the lake. But with all of the bells and whistles on modern exercise equipment, he could see the attraction in a way. There were cardio monitors and apps that showed how many calories you were burning and about eighteen different resistance levels on equipment like the device he was using. People who were regulars at the fitness center told him the routine took their minds off things and relaxed them. That wasn't the case with him. It brought out his aggressions and recently he'd been visualizing himself grinding the face of the guy who was stalking him into the gravel.

He was laboring on the hybrid trainer when Harry came over with his personal trainer. "Pete," he said, "this is Eve. She's the one who's whipping me into shape."

Eve looked at the machine Pete was working on and said, "You picked a good piece of equipment. These hybrid trainers give you a good workout. What level do you have it set at?"

Pete sheepishly said, "About the middle."

She glanced at the controls and said, "You ought to amp it up a bit. I always tell Harry that the goal should be to get out of your comfort zone and push yourself."

She was dressed in her familiar black from head to toe and had on just enough eyeliner to accent her dark, intense eyes. For a woman who'd already spent several hours in the gym, Pete thought she looked damn good.

"I can always count on Harry to push himself," Eve said, smiling and nudging him with her elbow. "He's doing well, don't you think, Pete?"

"He's becoming a real beast," Pete agreed. He watched the Cheshire cat grin appear on Harry's face again and added, "I particularly like the way he scampers up and down the wall."

Harry started to say something, but Eve beat him to the punch. "I have a few minutes before I begin working with my next client," she said to Pete, smiling. "Would you like to try it?"

"Yeah, Viking warrior," Harry said, "let's see how you do."

Pete sighed. "If I'd only known sooner. But as Harry likes to say, I've left my game on the floor already."

"Okay, boys, I've got to run. Harry," she said, winking at him, "time me."

She walked to the climbing wall, signaled to Harry that she was starting, then began her ascent. Harry's eyes widened as Eve effortlessly moved up the wall. He looked down at his watch, then at Eve again. She was already at the top. "Twenty-seven seconds," he called, sounding amazed. She shimmied down the wall and waved at them before disappearing into a room.

"Did you see that?" Harry asked. His eyes looked like they'd been propped open with toothpicks.

"I did. Like a jungle monkey. Or a tree snake."

"She doesn't look like any monkey or tree snake *I've* ever seen."

"Just a figure of speech."

"Now you see why I like working with her. She challenges me every time I'm here."

"Umm hmm. Are you sure you're not smitten by Eve the woman? She *is* something of a babe."

"I have a babe at home," Harry said. "Now you, you're the one who should be looking. You want me to fix you up?"

Pete laughed. "No thanks, Dolly," he said, referring to the legendary matchmaker. "I think I'm old enough to speak for myself."

"Seriously, I'd be glad to drop the word that you're interested."

Pete shook his head. "Besides," he said, pointing a finger belt-high in the general direction of the towel man, "the guy over there has been staring daggers at us. Maybe he's Eve's husband or boyfriend and doesn't like it when other men talk to her."

Harry looked toward the workout area. "I don't see any daggers."

"The towel guy."

Pete's cell phone burred and he saw that it was Tessler. He cupped his hand around the phone and said to Harry, "I've got to take this." He walked over to the window where he could get better reception.

"I've got good news and bad news, as the old saying goes," Tessler said. "The good news is that Robyn Fleming is still in the lockup and will be for the foreseeable future. The bad news is Kurt Romer is out."

Pete's stomach muscles tensed. "When did he get out?"

"February 14." When Pete didn't say anything, Tessler added, "Some Valentine's Day present, huh?"

"That means he was out when my door was messed up. Did he come back up here after he got out?"

"His parole officer said he's given an address in or near Thompsonville."

Pete was quiet for a moment, then he said, "Now we have another person you should question."

"Christ, Pete, I'm already working on Frank to get his okay on Calvin Seitz. If I suggest going after Romer, too, just because he's out of prison, I'll look like a carp flopping around on the bottom of a boat."

"What percentage of your cases have only one suspect?" Pete asked. "Ten percent? Twenty percent?"

"That's beside the point. I'm trying to be effective, not get a graduate degree in statistics."

"If you were effective, we'd have the asshole by now."

Tessler didn't say anything for a moment, then said, "That was a cheap shot, Pete."

Pete got a grip on his emotions and apologized.

"I know you're frustrated," Tessler said.

"I'm beyond being frustrated. Some lunatic skulking around my cottage in the middle of the night and leaving notes . . . You know me well enough to know that I don't hide under the bed every time a shadow crosses my path. But this has me worried."

"I understand. We'll get him."

"I'm in a public area and don't want to talk anymore," Pete said.

"Understand."

"And Joe, thanks for everything you've done. I'm sorry if I sounded unappreciative."

Pete walked back to where Harry was standing. Harry said, "I couldn't hear all of that conversation, but from the look on your face I can tell you aren't happy."

"Romer is out of prison."

Harry's eyes widened. "Already?"

Pete shrugged. "It's been four years. I guess even scum is released sooner or later."

Harry appeared to choose his words carefully. "Does this change your perspective on things? I mean on who might be behind what's been happening to you?"

"Romer was on my list. Not on top, but on the list. This muddles things."

Harry looked fidgety, like he was hesitant to say what was on his mind. "Now I've got something to worry about, too," he said slowly. "I'm the one who blew the whistle on Romer and his partner if you'll remember."

Pete and Harry had a history of giving each other grief over just about everything. It was part of the adhesive that bound them together. But Pete had thought about Harry's role in sending Romer away as well. Pete had nudged him into it and what Harry had done came out at Romer's trial. Pete was as concerned about his friend as he was about himself. If Romer were the guy after him, it wasn't unreasonable to conclude that he might want to even scores with Harry as well.

"We need to come up with a plan to make sure you and Rona are protected while I figure this thing out."

Pete sat across from Harry and Rona on facing loveseats in the living room of the old Victorian house on Forest Avenue that they owned together. A handmade antique walnut coffee table that had been rubbed to a fine luster occupied the space between the loveseats. A single object—a precisely-centered copy of the upscale magazine, *Architectural Digest*—rested on the table. Nothing else. No coasters for drinks, no clutter of any kind.

The table had been a present from Rona to herself the previous Christmas and had a certain history. Shortly after it arrived, Harry came home after a trying day at his newspaper and built a fire in the fireplace and settled in to relax on one of the loveseats with a scotch and water. His feet were propped up on the new table when Rona made an unexpected visit home from her restaurant. She saw Harry in his moment of relaxation and the explosion out of her mouth could be heard all the way over on Main Street. Now the three of them sat with their feet firmly anchored to the floor with their glasses nowhere near the antique table.

"Are you sure the two of you aren't being overly concerned about this guy?" Rona asked after Harry told her what he proposed to do. She tossed her thick brunette hair away from her face. Her hair still had traces of sun streaks from the previous summer and her eyes were like bottomless pools. Harry, who barely matched her five-nine height, seemed to shrink as she questioned them.

"Hon," Harry said, patting her hand, "someone has already attacked Pete's place twice and left threatening notes. We're thinking that the guy behind this could be Kurt Romer and that we could be on his target list, too, because of my part in sending him away."

"But you don't *know* it was him. You're just guessing. What I'm saying is that Pete is in one situation and we're in another. I can certainly understand Pete taking precautions after what happened, but nothing has happened to us even though Kurt Romer has been out of prison for two months. I repeat, *if* Romer is the one behind what's been happening to Pete."

"All we're saying," Pete said, "is that it might be prudent for you to install an alarm system in your house just in case. To be on the safe side."

"Yeah," Harry chimed in, "and the alarm system wouldn't just be to catch Romer if he should show up. Drugs are an increasing problem in this area, and there are lots of addicts around. Just ask the sheriff. You're at the restaurant most nights and I'm usually out, too. An addict could case our house during the day and clean us out while we're gone."

Rona sighed and said, "I know. It's just that the reason I live in a place like this is that it's peaceful and the people here are friendly. I don't want to start living my life like I'm in Chicago or Detroit or some other urban area where crime is rampant."

"I understand," Pete said. "But the reality is that this area has as much crime *per capita* as the big cities do. Maybe more."

Harry was sitting on the edge of his love seat now, looking at Rona with pleading eyes, obviously wondering what else he could say to make his case.

"Okay," Rona finally said.

"And it's not just Romer," Harry said. "As I said a minute ago —"

"Rest your case, Sweetie. As your attorney friend here would say, you've persuaded me."

Harry sat looking at her with his mouth slightly open.

"Stop while you're ahead, Sweetie," Pete teased. "Madam Judge has ruled on your motion."

Harry shifted his gaze to Pete, seemingly at a loss for a comeback.

Rona looked at them and shook her head. "Oh God," she said, "you two . . ."

TEN

While he waited for Amy Ostrowski to show up, Pete took his Viking longbow out to practice for the first time that spring. His army surplus silhouette targets had been buffeted by the winter winds and he righted them. He repositioned the targets at different distances among the trees and bushes, and pulled his bowstring back several times without an arrow to get the feeling back.

He nocked an arrow and visualized Calvin Seitz with his frizzy red hair tied back in a ponytail on one of the intermediate targets. He drew the bowstring back to his right ear and let the arrow fly and grimaced when it missed low left. He repeated the process. *Thunk!* Better. He launched a third arrow. *Thunk!* Dead center. And another. *Thunk!* Then it was brother Randy's turn and he peppered him with arrows as well.

He felt good and switched to another target. Kurt Romer's sneering countenance popped up. He drew the bowstring back and let go. *Thunk!* He developed a rhythm. *Thunk! Thunk! Thunk!*

Pete was hunting for an arrow that had gone astray when Amy arrived. She walked over to where he was searching and said, "Is this the fabled Pete Thorsen torture pit where he doesn't get mad, he gets even?"

"You got that mostly right," he said. "Only it's where Pete both gets mad *and* gets even. Want to try?"

Amy took the bow, and after admiring it for a moment, tested the pull. Her arms began to quiver when the bowstring was less than half-way back. She looked at him and said, "Do you have a woman's model?"

He grinned and said, "Give it a try. Aim for the close target." He showed her the basic mechanics.

She took her stance, held the grip with her left hand, and pulled the bowstring back until her arms began to quiver again. She let the arrow go and it fluttered to the ground short of the target. She shot an embarrassed glance Pete's way.

"Try another," he said encouragingly.

She did, with the same result. Then she tried a third arrow, and a fourth. Her fifth arrow hit the bottom of the target. "Yea!" she said, raising the bow triumphantly and prancing around in a circle. "Just like Mrs. Robin Hood."

"You did better than Harry McTigue," Pete said approvingly. "None of his first five arrows came closer than ten feet."

He collected the arrows and then showed her the window that Joe Tessler had identified as the one where the intruder might have tried to force entry. She looked at the window, then at the ground, and said, "It would have been better if I'd seen this before you two stomped around and messed up any footprints."

Pete shrugged and said, "Budget I guess. They pay you by the hour, don't they?"

She nodded and continued to examine the window.

"That's why I told you today is on my dime. I wanted your input even if the sheriff isn't willing to pay for it."

Amy turned to Pete and said, "I want to look at all of the windows and doors. But Joe could be right. This might be the window the perp tampered with. The marks you see could have been made by a tool of some kind."

They walked around the cottage, but didn't find any other places that looked suspicious. Amy examined the first window again. "Is your security system wireless?" she asked.

He looked at her blankly and said, "I suppose."

"Where's your control panel?"

They went inside and confirmed that the system was wireless. Outside again, Amy methodically worked her way around the perimeter of the cottage a second time. After she finished, she said, "It's possible that someone was trying to get into your head by leaving the note and then deliberately setting off the alarm either by jamming your window or using an electronic device."

"I understand the first, but you better explain the second."

Amy told him that most wireless alarm systems rely on radio frequency signals sent between door and window sensors to a control panel. An alarm is triggered when an entryway is breached. If a system doesn't encrypt or authenticate the signals it sends, someone with a fairly inexpensive device can intercept the data, decipher the commands, and play them back to the control panel.

"Which in plain English means what?" Pete asked.

"A person with the right device can set off the alarm even if he didn't intend to try to break into your cottage."

"Why would the perp, to use your term, want to do that? Why wouldn't he just leave the note? I'd see it the next morning anyway."

"Would that have had the same impact on you?"

He knew it wouldn't have.

"That possibility is consistent with the blood incident, too. The perp could have just left a note and threw a rock against your door to wake you in the middle of the night. But he didn't. He used a bag filled with blood instead. Again, greater impact."

Pete digested what she'd just said and immediately thought about Randy Seitz and the domestic violence charges against him that included lurking outside his girlfriend's apartment. It wasn't hard to visualize Kurt Romer doing something like that, either.

He was brought back to the moment when Amy asked, "Does your system alert the security company when the alarm goes off?"

Pete scoffed and said, "This is a rural area, remember? If an alert goes to a company in Traverse City and then someone calls the local sheriff, how long do you think it would take someone to get out here? I had the system installed to alert *me*, not someone who might come to my rescue the next day."

"I guess that's the reason so many people in areas like this have guns."

"One of the reasons, I suppose."

"But you don't."

"Not at the moment." Amy's spooking theory resonated with him. He said, "How can you tell if someone was or wasn't making a serious effort to get into my cottage?"

"I can't tell for sure. But windows lock from the inside. If someone really tried to force his way in, there probably would be more damage to the wood than you have. Or the perp would have had to cut the glass and reach in and unlock the window. Neither of those things happened here."

He thought about the blood and said, "Have you been out to the Heavenly Meadows where the alpacas were butchered?"

She shook her head. "I guess they thought that looking at some dead animals wasn't worth another charge to the department's budget."

"Want to go? I'll be happy to pay for another hour of your time."

"Sure. Don't expect me to find anything, though. The crime scene is probably trampled over by now, just like around your window, and I'm sure the carcasses have been hauled away."

They pulled into Heavenly Meadows and Amy's eyes widened when she saw the lavender barn adorned with colorful flowers and tweeting birds. Pete smiled to himself and let her absorb the idyllic splendor for a minute.

He saw Higgie and Sunshine peek out the door. He introduced them to Amy and explained that she worked part-time for the sheriff's office. He asked whether they could see where Jane and Virgil had been slaughtered. Sadness crept into their eyes and Higgie pointed to a roped-off area in the pasture, but didn't look that way. Like she couldn't bear the pain.

Baskets of flowers rimmed the rope-line as though it were the site of a child's tragic death. Pete explained in a low voice that the alpacas were free to come and go from the barn as they pleased, including at night. Amy ducked under the rope and looked at the places where blood stains were still apparent. Then she walked around the enclosed area and examined the ground.

When she was finished, she said, "Pretty much as I thought. The area has been so trampled that there's nothing here anymore from a forensics standpoint."

Higgie and Sunshine insisted on giving them a tour of their facility. Amy scratched the chins of several of the alpacas as she followed the two women around the barn. They came to a place with a sign that said, "Heavenly Harvest," which to less sensitive individuals might be called the shearing pen. Higgie explained the process reverently.

Before they left, Higgie delicately asked whether Amy had found anything that might be material to Jane and Virgil's murders. She said she hadn't, but promised to let them know if anything turned up. On their way out of the barn, Higgie sidled up to Pete and whispered in his ear a question: did the fact he brought Amy to see where Jane and Virgil had been killed mean that he'd changed his mind and would investigate after all? He shook his head sadly and explained that Amy was just a friend.

Before Pete and Amy departed, they had to engage in another group hug with the Heavenly Meadows ladies.

On the way back to pick up Amy's car, she filled him in on what she'd been doing since they'd taken a road trip together to the Leelanau Peninsula on that raw spring day a year earlier to examine the place where Lynn Hawke had been killed during an ice storm. The wedding planning business was brisk and paid the bills, she said, but forensic work was what really got her juices flowing.

Then she sprung the big news—she was planning her own nuptials. The lucky man ran a fishing guide service on the Boardman River south of Traverse City. It would be her fourth trip to the altar, she said, but this time it was "for keeps."

ELEVEN

A my Ostrowski's speculation about the two incidents at his cottage festered in his mind and elevated his anxiety level a notch. Cumulatively, he'd probably slept three hours the previous night, and during the day, he thought of little else.

He checked with Tessler to ask whether he'd questioned the Seitz brothers yet, and when Joe admitted that he hadn't, he threatened to confront them himself. Then he decided to take away one of Tessler's excuses for not questioning Kurt Romer.

After checking with bartenders at The Car Ferry and another bar in the local area that Romer used to frequent and being told that they hadn't seen him in years, Pete headed for Thompsonville. It was hard to imagine a guy like Romer, who'd made watering holes his second home, going celibate after he got out of prison. With his libido, it was more likely that he'd be making up for lost time.

Pete stopped at a station outside Thompsonville to gas up his Range Rover and to get information. He asked the pimply-faced young man behind the cash register about bars in town where singles typically hung out. The kid looked like a geek whose idea of a big night was to settle in with his keyboard and play Goat Simulator computer games for six hours.

He gave Pete the once over, eyeing him like he was some kind of pervert for looking for bars in the middle of the afternoon, and volunteered that there were two. Rosie's Tap in the heart of Thompsonville and The Nighthawk north of town. Pete thanked the kid, and on the way out, saw him shake his head.

When he walked in, there wasn't a soul in Rosie's except a man who was maybe forty years old with a shaved head and a tight tee shirt that showed off the tattoos on both arms. He was restocking the refrigerator behind the bar and looked up as Pete took one of the backless stools.

"Quiet afternoon, huh?" Pete asked in his friendliest voice.

The bartender ignored pleasantries and said, "What can I get for you?" From his voice, his first thought in the morning likely was of a pack of unfiltered Camels.

Pete ordered a Miller Lite. He wasn't much of a beer drinker any more, but ordering a Diet Coke didn't seem like the best way to build rapport with a bartender. Tattoo Man opened a long-necked bottle and plunked it down in front of Pete and went back to his stocking duties. Pete took a small sip of his beer, then another. The only sound in the place came from when Tattoo Man dropped an empty crate on top of another or banged the bottles together as he filled the fridge.

It was obvious there wasn't going to be any conversation unless Pete initiated it. He asked, "Who's Rosie?"

Tattoo Man was now moving bottles of liquor around so he could wipe down the glass shelves behind the bar. He said without turning, "My mother. She passed on six years ago."

"Sorry to hear that. She left the establishment to you, huh?" Pete used establishment rather than bar or tavern because an overhead sign listed burgers and nachos as the food choices.

Tattoo Man nodded and continued to wipe the shelves.

Pete decided no purpose would be served by being coy about his reason for being there. "I'm just passing through," he said. "I heard that a guy I used to know lives around here. His name is Kurt Romer. I'd like to say 'hello' except that I don't know his address or phone number. Any chance you know him?"

"Passing through. From where?"

Ah, two-way conversation. "Downstate. I move around."

"What's the guy's name again?"

"Kurt Romer." He spelled it for him.

"I don't think I know him. What's he look like?

Pete described Romer as he remembered him from before he went to prison.

"Sorry, pal, can't help you."

Pete left money on the bar to cover his beer and a tip and said good-bye to Tattoo Man. He got a grunt in return. Hopefully, the bartender at his next stop would be chattier.

He was still a couple hundred yards away when he saw a sign for The Nighthawk atop two tall poles with lights chasing each other around the perimeter. When he got closer, he saw a large bird of prey, a hawk of some kind, in the center of the sign. The bar itself was a low, rambling structure painted dark gray. It obviously wasn't two-for-one cocktail time because only three vehicles were in the lot.

Pete heard country music blaring on the jukebox as soon as he walked in. That set it apart from Rosie's which, allowing for the fact it was afternoon, had been like walking into a tomb that no one dared go near. He passed two men at the end of the bar drinking from mugs and a half-empty pitcher of beer between them. They were in deep conversation and didn't bother to look up when he passed. At the opposite end of the bar, an older woman with stringy gray hair who looked like she hadn't been home for three days sat hunched over her drink. Like Mrs. Nighthawk, waiting for nightfall. Her head swiveled Pete's way when he walked in and she continued to watch him, like she was sizing him up for the evening's meal.

He took a stool in the center of the bar. Across the room, a petite woman in a mottled blue top with spaghetti straps held up a finger to signal she was coming and then turned her attention back to the dart board. She leaned forward, threatening to split her painted-on jeans, and pumped her hand a couple of times like she was zeroing in on the bull's-eye. She let the dart fly. A clean miss. She slapped her thighs in frustration and readjusted her straw hat with the tightly rolled brim as she squeezed through the hinged opening to get behind the bar.

She gave him a thousand-watt smile and asked, "Whatcha drinking, hon?"

Pete ordered his second Miller Lite of the day. A little more of this and he might get in the habit of drinking beer again like he did in his army days and in college.

She put the bottle on the bar in front of him and leaned forward with her face in her hands and flashed that smile again. He assumed her pose was intended to give him an unimpeded view of her cleavage.

"I don't think I've seen you in here before, stranger," she said from beneath the brim of her hat.

He smiled and said, "Maybe that's because this is my first time."

"Well, a great big warm welcome to you. I'm Bonni. No 'e'. A lot of people get that wrong."

He didn't try to hide his real name. If word happened to get back to Romer that Pete Thorsen was looking for him, well, that wouldn't be all bad.

"Nice to meet you, Bonni. I'm Pete Thorsen."

"Pete, Peter, Pete," she said. "I had an uncle named Pete. Wonderful man. But he's gone now. Of course, he was older than you." She gave him her best ingénue smile.

He smiled back.

"Just a minute, Pete. I need to get some music going." She trotted over to the juke box and used a key to open a panel. "Do you like George Strait?" she called over her shoulder.

"Sure. Who doesn't?"

Soon Strait's classic, "All My Ex's Live in Texas," filled the room. Bonni worked her way back to the bar in a slow slither, snapping her fingers to keep time with the music. "I loooove George Strait," she said. "Did you know that he sang this song at his last concert appearance?"

Pete nodded again. "Along with about ten other stars."

Bonni either didn't hear his comment or chose to ignore it. When Strait's "Here for a Good Time" came on, she swooned again and placed a hand on her bosom to show her emotional solidarity with Strait.

Pete waited for her to regain her composure and then asked, "Bonni, you don't by chance know a guy named Kurt Romer do you?"

Bonni's eyes instantly turned wary and the wattage of her smile went down. "Why are you asking?"

"He's a friend of mine and I heard he lives in this area. I thought he might come in here. This looks like his kind of place. I'd like to buy him a drink if he's around."

"What's your last name again?"

"Thorsen."

"How do you know Kurt?"

"We used to bump into each other from time-to-time. I thought I'd renew our friendship."

"You aren't that parole officer guy, are you?"

Pete laughed. "No," he said.

"Oh for God's sake, Bonni," the woman at the end of the bar said, "why are you acting like you don't know the man? Everybody knows you've been shacking with him for the past month."

"Butt out, Irma! And don't you go walking out of here tonight without paying your bill, either."

"He ain't nothing but a convict. He's just hanging around you for your you-know-what and because he needs a place to stay. So there!"

"Pay up and get out!" Bonni screamed.

"Free country," Irma said smugly. "Besides, I ain't finished my drink."

"When Sam comes in, I'm going to have him throw you out!"

"Fat chance. Me and Sam went to grade school together. We got some memories between us, we do. He ain't going to throw me out."

Pete decided that he wasn't going to get any more information about Kurt Romer. He paid for his beer and gave Bonni a generous tip. She looked at the ten dollar bill and then up at Pete. Her manner softened. "I'm sorry I accused you of being the parole guy. You come back soon. Maybe we can talk some more." She flashed a murderous look at Irma and added, "Maybe we'll have more civilized company around by then."

He sat in his Range Rover and pretended to look at a road map. Just when he was about to give it up and drive back to the lake, Irma stumbled out of the bar and headed for her truck. It rivaled Calvin Seitz's pickup for age. He got out and walked over and grabbed her elbow. "Are you okay to drive, Irma?"

She looked up at him and said, "Well, hello young fella. I thought you'd high-tailed it down the road."

"Just making a cell phone call," he lied. "Are you sure you're okay to drive?" he repeated.

"Shoot, I ain't had but three drinks," she said. "I could drive all the way to Atlantic City if I had to. Play them slots when I got there, too."

"Okay, but be careful."

"You're a real considerate young man. You want to come over to my place and have a drink? I could whip us up something to eat. Mac and cheese or something."

"Gosh, I'd like to, but I have to meet a friend for dinner."

Irma's face twisted into a silly grin. "Now you're making me jealous. What's her name?"

"*His* name is Harry McTigue. He's the editor of the newspaper in Frankfort. We need to talk about an article I agreed to write for his paper."

"Well, you know where to find me if you want to come over some time. We could have a real pleasant time." She pinched his thigh.

"How about if I call you the next time I'm over this way?" he said, moving back slightly. "One other thing. What's Bonni's last name?"

"Oh that's Miz Calhoun," she said, drawing out the last syllable. "She claims she's descended from the owner of one of them railroads that used to be in this town. Shoot, my family came here in a covered wagon and owned half the town when her family was selling trinkets to the Indians."

Back at his cottage, Pete made something to eat. If mouthy old Irma knew what she was talking about, Kurt Romer was living with Bonni Calhoun in or around Thompsonville. Now he just had to find out Bonni's address. Then he'd be ready if Tessler said he couldn't question Romer because he didn't know where he lived.

He dialed his stepdaughter Julie's number to find out whether she planned to come to the lake over the Easter. She didn't answer and he left a message for her to call him. He put a Linda Ronstadt CD on the Bose, turned the sound down low, and settled in to read more of his book about Patton. It was a few minutes after 10:00 p.m. when his eyes told him he should call it a night. He tried Julie again, didn't reach her, and left another message. He set his house alarm and went upstairs to bed. His thoughts returned to his conversation with Amy Ostrowski about why the psycho might have set off his alarm system.

TWELVE

The next morning, Pete was in his office early puttering around and waiting for calls back from Julie and Joe Tessler. About 10:00 a.m. he called Julie for the third time, but was still unable to reach her. This was unlike her. Maybe school work had her under water he rationalized.

It was close to noon and his stomach told him it was time for lunch. Before heading down the street for a sandwich, he tried Julie for the fourth time. No answer again. If she didn't call back by the time he returned, he told himself, he'd call the school. He cringed at the thought that she might have gotten sick and been taken to the hospital.

He had his cell phone with him and checked his office voicemail when he got back. No messages from either Julie or Tessler. He found the telephone number for the school's administrative offices and dialed it. He identified himself as Julie's father, and said he'd been trying to reach her, but she didn't answer his calls. He asked the woman if something had happened to her. She asked him some questions and then passed him through to another woman who repeated basically the same questions. Finally his call was passed through to a third person.

"Excuse me, sir, what did you say your name was?" the man asked.

Pete was getting tired of the repetitive questions, but told him.

"And what's your relationship to Julie?"

"Her father. Or I should say, stepfather."

"One moment, sir." The man put him on hold. A couple of minutes later, he returned to the line.

"The contact information we have for Julie is a Mr. Wayne Sable, who's listed as her father. In Mr. Sable's absence, we have a Ms. Maureen Fesko shown as the alternative contact. You aren't on the contact list, sir. I'm afraid we can't release information about Julie except to an authorized person."

"You've got to be kidding. I've been at the school a dozen times to visit her. I pay all of her bills. What is this?"

"I'm sorry, sir. We have a privacy policy. It's intended to —"

"Screw your privacy policy. I want to know if something has happened to my daughter. Is she okay?"

"I really am sorry, sir. I'm just following policy."

He told himself that becoming belligerent wasn't doing any good. "Can you just tell me if she's gotten sick or something," he asked in a calmer voice. "That's all I'm asking."

"Again, sir, we can only talk to an authorized person about one of our students. Perhaps you should contact Mr. Sable."

Pete jammed the handset into the receiver and stared at it. Then he retrieved Wayne Sable's telephone number from his cell phone address book and dialed the number. A recorded message came on that said, "You've reached Wayne Sable. I'm out of the country for three weeks. Leave a message and I'll return your call after I return."

His frustration was close to overflowing and his apprehension wasn't far behind. He grabbed his cell phone and briefcase and headed for the door. He was about to lock up when he remembered the court order granting him visitation rights with Julie. He went back and found a copy and stuffed it in his briefcase and headed for his Range Rover again. He stopped at his cottage to grab his shaving kit and some clean clothes and headed for Julie's boarding school near Detroit.

It seemed to take a week for him to navigate the two-lane roads out to the Interstate. The clock in his car read 2:45 p.m. when he finally reached the I-75 entrance ramp and headed south. The traffic was light, but he knew that would change when he got closer to Detroit.

He gave the Range Rover more fuel and watched the mile markers fly past. His mind returned to his telephone conversations with the administrative people at Meadowbrook School and he got upset all over again. He believed in privacy, too, but the thought that they wouldn't give him *any* information about a girl who'd lived in his house since she was two and called him "Dad" infuriated him.

He thought about the incidents at his cottage and prayed that his inability to reach Julie didn't have something to do with them. Realistically, he didn't see how they could. Fewer than ten people outside the school even knew Julie was at Meadowbrook, so how likely was it that whoever had him in his cross-hairs would know where to find her even if he were inclined? Still . . . he pressed the accelerator again.

Just before he reached Saginaw, flashing red and blue lights appeared behind him. He glanced at his speedometer and saw he was going eighty-five miles an hour. *Damn,* he thought. He immediately eased up on the gas and pulled over on the shoulder. The flashing lights seemed so close they were almost in his rear seat. He hadn't had a ticket for a moving vehicle violation in more than twenty years. Hopefully, he could talk his way out of this one. The clock on his dash showed that it was after 4:00 p.m.

He fished his driver's license out of his wallet, found his registration and insurance card, and waited with window lowered. The state trooper he expected didn't come right away and he glanced at the clock again. Finally he arrived and asked him for the items he already had in his hand. He handed them to him and waited.

The trooper spent an inordinate amount of time studying his driver's license. He looked up and said, "Do you know how fast you were going sir?"

"I might have been going a few miles over the limit, officer. My daughter is—"

"Do you consider eighty-seven miles an hour a few miles over, Mr. Thorsen?"

"I didn't realize I was going that fast. I'm on my way to see—"

"Stay in your car." The trooper walked back to his cruiser.

Pete fidgeted and waited for him to reappear. He checked the time again. It was now 4:37 p.m. He knew traffic officers called the DMV to check licenses and registrations, but couldn't figure out what was taking so long. He thought about Julie again. *Hurry for crissakes!*

At 4:45 p.m., the trooper appeared again and handed him items that included a traffic ticket. "You're lucky you have a clean record, Mr. Thorsen. If you had some priors, you'd be following me down to the station. Now I've got two words for you and they're more than a request: Slow down."

78

THIRTEEN

It was nearly 7:00 p.m. when Pete reached Julie's dormitory. He ignored the signs and parked in one of the open slots reserved for students with cars who had parking privileges. The dorm's front door was still unlocked and students came and went. He walked through the lobby, trying not to seem like he was in a hurry, and passed the elevator.

He reached the door leading to the back stairs and wrenched it open and took the steps two at a time. As soon as he stepped into the second floor corridor, he saw the yellow police tape that spanned Julie's door. *Oh God, no!*

Panic tore at his insides and he looked around for someone who might be able to tell him what happened. He raced from room to room, frantically looking in every open door. Finally he came to a room with a girl sitting at her desk tapping on her computer keyboard.

"What happened to Julie?" he blurted out in a voice that may have been a few decibels louder than he intended.

The girl jumped and turned to look at him with her hands to her face. He could see the fright in her eyes and she seemed unable to speak.

"Sorry, I didn't mean to scare you," he said soothingly, modulating his voice. "I'm Julie Sable's father. Can you tell me what happened to her?"

The girl's composure slowly returned. She said, "Someone stuck a knife in her door. She had to leave school."

"A knife," Pete repeated incredulously.

"With a note," the girl said.

His anxiety was at the red level. "What did the note say?"

"I don't know, sir. I didn't see it."

"But she's okay? Julie I mean?"

"I think so. She was very frightened."

"Where is she now?" Pete asked.

"I don't know. Someone said a relative picked her up."

"Which relative, do you know?"

"No, I'm sorry."

He thanked the girl and bolted out of her room and thought about what to do. He knew it was useless to try the administrative offices because of the hour and the reception he'd gotten earlier. He headed for the campus police station. He'd been there two years earlier when Julie and another girl thought they'd been followed by two suspicious looking men who were lurking around campus.

He walked into the station and asked to see the person in charge. A middle-aged man in a blue uniform with a "Campus Security" patch on his sleeve came out of a glass-walled office and walked his way. Pete didn't recognize him from his previous visit.

"Can I help you, sir?" he asked.

"Yes, my name is Pete Thorsen. I'm the stepfather of Julie Sable, one of the students here. I understand she was the subject of some kind of attack. Someone stuck a knife in her door and left a note. I'm trying to find out if she's okay and get more details."

The security chief asked for identification and Pete gave him his state ID card because the highway trooper had his driver's license. He also showed him the court order granting him visitation privileges with Julie. The man studied the items while Pete waited impatiently.

He looked up at Pete and said, "From this, I gather you aren't Ms. Sable's legal guardian."

Pete nodded. "Julie was my late wife's child. She had sole custody and Julie lived in my house for twelve years. When Doris died, Wayne Sable was declared Julie's legal guardian because he was the biological father. But she calls me Dad," he hastily added, trying to sound calm.

"I see," the security officer said. "One moment please." He went to a nearby computer, logged on, and found what he was looking for. He looked up again and said, "Mr. Sable is listed as the contact person. You're not listed Mr. . . . ."

"Thorsen," Pete prompted him again.

"Right, Mr. Thorsen. You're not listed as a contact person."

"I know that because I talked to someone in the administrative office earlier. I just explained why Wayne Sable is listed and I'm not. All I'm trying to do is find out what happened and get assurances that Julie is okay."

"Sir, our privacy policy—"

Pete wanted to tell him what he could do with his privacy policy, but kept control. "Your privacy policy can't bar you from telling me if she's alright. That's all I want to know."

"Do you have another court document stating that she's your step-daughter?"

Pete almost let loose with a string of expletives but changed directions and asked, "Are you investigating this incident or are the local police? Or is that information protected by your privacy policy, too?"

"No sir, that information isn't subject to the policy. The investigation is being conducted by the Bloomfield Hills Police Department. A man by the name of, I've got it here, Mr. John Nowitzki." He gave Pete directions to the police department.

Pete apologized to the man for being testy and loped back to his vehicle. The Bloomfield Hills station house was a little more than a half-mile away and he had no trouble finding it. He parked in a slot reserved for visitors and walked in and asked for Nowitzki.

Five minutes later, a slim man with thinning gray hair and wrinkled pants came shuffling out. His stooped shoulders were a testament to having seen too much of an imperfect world. Pete introduced himself as Julie Sable's stepfather again, but this time also said he was her lawyer. He handed Nowitzki one of his business cards. He said the school had sent him over to get the details of the incident at Julie's dormitory room. Pete half expected to get hit with the privacy blockade again, but was pleasantly surprised. Apparently Nowitzki had grown up before schools adopted policies which let them accept tuition dollars, no questions asked, but then imposed a cone of silence when the payer had the temerity to make the most innocuous of inquiries.

"You're lucky you caught me," Nowitzki said. "I was about to leave for the day. Strange incident involving Julie. Frightening, really. A switchblade was jammed into her door with a note attached."

"What does the note say?"

"You said you're the vic's stepfather, right?" Nowitzki asked.

"Not in the sense that I've adopted her, but in every other sense."

"The note might have something to do with you then."

"Is it addressed to me?"

"C'mon, I'll show you." Pete followed him down to the evidence room and waited as he checked out what they had on Julie's case. Then he led Pete to a small conference room where he laid several items on the table.

"That's the note," Nowitzki said, pointing to a sheet of paper enclosed in a clear plastic sheath. Pete bent over so he could see it better. It read, *Too bad you have to pay for the sins of your scumbag father honey.*

Pete stared at the note. It was in the same oversized print as the two notes left for him at the lake. He could see the slit in the paper where the knife had pierced it. He looked up at Nowitzki and said, "No prints, I'll bet."

"Clean as a virgin's bottom."

"I think you're right," Pete said, "the note probably does relate to me." He told Nowitzki about the incidents at the lake.

"That explains a lot of things and puts all of this in a different light."

Pete's mind raced to figure out how the stalker knew he had a step-daughter and that she was at Meadowbrook School. *It had to be someone he knew.*

Nowitzki picked up a plastic bag and handed it to Pete. "Here's the knife. No prints on that either. Careful when you handle it. The blade's open, just the way we found it."

Pete stared at the sinister-looking weapon with the long sharp blade and slim curved handle and shuddered. He understood how Julie would have panicked when she opened her door in the middle of the night and saw it there.

"Here's a photograph of Julie's door," Nowitzki said. It showed the note pinned to the door by the switchblade.

Pete stared at the photograph for a few moments. "Can I get a copy of this?" he asked. "And of the note?"

"I guess."

Pete detected the uncertainty in Nowitzki's response and added, "I want to show it to the detective up north who's investigating the first two incidents." He didn't get into the internal politics of the office or say anything about his own investigation.

Nowitzki's comfort level increased and he said, "I think it's important that the investigations be coordinated if the incidents are related."

"I agree."

"Do you have contact information in case I want to talk to the detective?"

Pete gave him Joe Tessler's name and telephone numbers. He asked Nowizki whether he had any leads.

"None. The closest thing we have is the possible connection to the crime in your neck of the woods based on what you just told me."

Pete nodded. "One final thing. I've been trying to find out where Julie is. The school won't tell me that because of their sacred confidentiality policy."

Nowitzki waved a dismissive hand. "Let me get my notes," he said. When he returned, he said, "Here it is. Wayne Sable, her guardian, is out of the country so Julie's aunt picked her up. I guess Julie had to take a temporary leave of absence from school because of the trauma she experienced." He gave Pete the name of the aunt, Maureen Fesko, and her telephone number. "I'm sorry I don't have her address," he said.

He called Fesko after he left the Bloomfield Hills Police Department. She refused to tell Julie he was on the line and hung up on him. He thought about it for all of two seconds and then headed for Lincolnshire, the suburb north of Chicago where he knew she lived.

FOURTEEN

Pete parked in front of Maureen Fesko's house on Cambridge Lane. It was a modest Tudor with ragged bushes in front and a yard that still showed the effects of the area's harsh winter. A Toyota Corolla was parked in the driveway and he could see lights on inside the house.

He braced himself and pressed the doorbell and waited in the light drizzle. He was about to press it again when the door swung open and a short woman in a burgundy sweat suit and Adidas athletic shoes appeared. He hadn't seen Maureen in years and the passage of time hadn't improved her looks. Her black hair looked home-dyed even without the unforgiving glare of the sun on it, and rose-colored lipstick was smeared on her mouth as though it had been applied in the dark. A necklace with colored glass beads that could only have come from the local five-and-dime hung around her neck.

Her dour face darkened a couple of shades as she stared at him and she seemed momentarily speechless. Then she snarled, "What are you doing here?"

"I've come to see my daughter."

"Well she doesn't want to see you! And she's not your daughter!" She tried to slam the door, but Pete blocked it with his foot.

"Call her please," Pete said in an even voice.

"No, I won't call her! The way you live your life, you're a danger to everyone around you! I won't have my niece lying dead in an alley because of you!"

"That's ridiculous."

"Oh yeah? How about that knife in her door at school?"

"I'm as interested as anyone in catching whoever did it."

"It wouldn't have happened but for you! Now leave or I'm going to call the police!"

Pete shrugged. "Call them. I have a court order that entitles me to see my daughter."

"She's not your daughter!" Maureen screamed again. "I demand that you leave my house right now!"

"Dad?" a familiar female voice behind Maureen said.

"Yes, Julie," Pete called. "Your aunt won't let me speak to you."

"Aunt Maureen, please let him in."

"No! He's a bad man!"

"He's my Dad," Julie pleaded. "Let him in please."

"Your Dad is in Italy, honey. He'll be back in a few days. Now go back upstairs. Dr. Speidel said you need to rest."

"I'm not tired, Aunt Maureen. I want to see my Dad."

"No—"

"If you don't let me see him, I'm going to stand outside in the rain and talk to him." She pushed the door all the way open and shoved Maureen to the side and wrapped her arms around Pete and held him tight. Pete fought to keep the tears out of his eyes.

Maureen tried to pull her back into the house, but Julie elbowed her away and continued to cling to Pete. Maureen stood glaring at them. "Okay," she finally said, "he can come in, but only for ten minutes." She jabbed a finger at Pete and said, "If you don't leave after ten minutes, I *am* going to call the police." She stepped aside to let them in.

Julie led Pete into the living room where she sat close to him on the couch and held both of his hands. "I was so afraid, Dad," she said. Tears streamed down her cheeks.

Maureen stood in the arch with her arms crossed and glared at them. She all but counted the seconds until ten minutes were up. Pete glanced her way and said, "Would you mind leaving us alone?" She gave Pete a murderous look and left the room.

"So what happened, Sweetheart?" he asked.

Between sniffles she said, "It was *awful*. I'd been up late studying. I'd just gone to bed when I heard this funny noise at my door. Like someone had hit it or something. I thought maybe another student was pulling a prank on me so I jumped out of bed real fast in the hopes of catching the person in the act. You know how none of us locks our doors at night because we don't want to seem unfriendly and Mr. Tobin is downstairs watching to make sure nobody gets in? So all I had to do was turn the knob, but when I looked in the hallway, there wasn't anyone there. Then I saw this long knife sticking in my door. I got so freaked out." The tears became a geyser and he felt her body tremble.

Pete held her tight and said, "That's when you called Mr. Tobin."

"Yes," she said, sniffling again. "And he called the campus police and they came and . . ."

Fesko appeared in the doorway again. She had her arms crossed again and said in an imperial voice, "Time's up, Mr. Thorsen. Please leave right now."

Before Pete could say anything, Julie leaped off the couch and rushed toward her aunt. "Why do you always have to be such a bitch, Aunt Maureen? Can't you see we're talking?" She stood in front of Maureen with her arms hanging down and fists clinched and face thrust forward. Maureen seemed taken aback by Julie's outburst and retreated from the room again.

Julie nestled even closer to Pete when she returned to the couch. She was shaking and the tears started to flow again. "Can I go home with you, Dad? I don't want to stay here."

Pete squeezed her hand and said, "It's not that simple if you'll recall."

"I wish Wayne would *die!*"

"Now, now," he said as he held her. He didn't tell her that he'd wished the same thing many times. "To finish the story, you wound up here with Aunt Maureen because Wayne is out of the country, right?"

She nodded and continued to sniffle. "That note the awful man left, Dad? He called you a bad name."

"I know. I saw it."

She looked surprised. "How?"

"When you didn't answer my telephone calls, I got worried and drove down to school. The police showed me the note."

"Was I gone when you were there?"

"You were."

"Good old Aunt Maureen, again," she said in a low voice that dripped with disdain. "I was a total basket case that night. She drove up to school and convinced the administration that I was 'traumatized' as she put it. She told them I needed a temporary leave of absence from school to see a shrink. A shrink! I've never gone to a shrink! Then when we got here, Dad, she made me go see this weird little man who asked me a lot of strange questions. I'm fine now except when I have to relive the experience by talking about it all the time. I just want to get back to school again so I can be with my friends and get my life back to normal."

"Let me see what I can do."

"Do you think you'll be able to get me away from her, Dad?" she whispered. "I'll go crazy if I have to stay here and see that weird little shrink of hers every day."

"I'm going to work on it right now."

"Thanks. I feel so much better now that you're here." She squeezed him again.

"Do you have your cell phone with you?"

"No, when Aunt Maureen came, I was confused and she said we had to leave immediately. I forgot the phone. It's in my room."

That explained why she hadn't returned his calls, he thought. "Let me talk to your Aunt Maureen alone for a minute," he said.

Maureen appeared magically, like she'd been eavesdropping on their conversation.

He said, "I think the best thing is for Julie to get back to school and on a routine again so she just doesn't sit around and think about what happened that night."

"Oh, so now you're a psychiatrist?" she said sarcastically. "Dr. Speidel tells me that a person who has gone through the kind of trauma Julie experienced might need years of therapy to recover. I —"

"No, no, Maureen," Pete said, holding up his hand. "Julie tells me she's fine and I believe her. She's still a little shaken up, but I think the best thing we can do for her is to get her back to school so she can resume her normal life. The school has a psychiatrist on staff if she needs help."

"Dr. Speidel says —"

He moved a step closer and looked down at her. "I said no, Maureen. If you don't have Julie back to school by — let's see, this is Wednesday — by this Friday at the latest, I'm going into court and tell a judge that you're holding a person in your house against her will and that you won't let her communicate with anyone on the outside. I think I know what the judge will do. You have no authority over Julie and what you're doing probably constitutes criminal offenses under about six different statutes. Friday, is that clear?"

"I'm the official contact person for Julie if Wayne isn't around. I have authority —"

"You have *no* authority. Friday, or I'm going into court."

Pete knew he'd laid that on a little thick, but what the hell, the woman was a complete moron and an officious know-it-all to boot. He smiled to himself as he went to find Julie and assure her she'd be back in school by the end of the week. Behind his back, he heard Maureen hiss, "I really hate you." Pete waved mockingly over his shoulder and went to say goodbye to his daughter.

FIFTEEN

"That's unbelievable about Julie," Harry said, shaking his head. "And you think there's a connection between that incident and what's been happening up here?"

"Think? How can there be any doubt?"

"But it's you the guy is really after, right?"

"Christ, Harry, you *know* I'm the one he's after. By involving Julie, he's just raising the stakes."

Harry seemed taken aback by the vehemence of his reply. He waited a few moments and then asked tentatively, "So what are you going to do?"

"In the morning, I'm going to call Joe Tessler and tell him about the incident at school and put him in contact with that Bloomfield Hills police detective, John Nowitzki, so they can coordinate their investigations."

"Then you're thinking about going after whoever has been doing these things, aren't you?" Harry said nervously. "The Seitz brothers or Kurt Romer or whoever."

Pete didn't say anything and kept wiping water spots off the mahogany bar.

"I know you're tired of hearing this, but you ought to let law enforcement handle things."

"I have up to this point," Pete said, knowing that he wasn't being entirely truthful.

"Joe Tessler is an experienced, smart guy. I have a feeling he'll get to the bottom of this. He just needs time."

"Time?" Pete said. "The sheriff hasn't let him do squat so far except to dust for fingerprints on a couple of notes and verify that the blood came from the alpacas. I've pressed them to question the Seitz brothers and Kurt Romer and nothing happens. I've asked them to at least *try* to get search warrants and all they give me is eighteen excuses why they can't do it. I don't expect any of that to change. Meanwhile, the asshole behind this is after my daughter now. I don't need any more lectures about staying on the sidelines or continuing to be patient."

"I hope you don't think *I'm* lecturing you."

"This is all part of Richter's personal vendetta against me. He's using his precious drug cases as a convenient excuse to do absolutely zilch on my case."

"In fairness, drugs are a serious problem for the community."

"Of course they're serious, but my situation is serious, too, and now it's gotten worse. How the guy knows about Julie, I don't know, but he sure as hell does."

Harry licked his fingers after he'd finished the roast beef sandwich the Bay Grille's chef had prepared for him and asked the bartender for some extra napkins. He seemed to be grasping for alternatives.

"How about taking Julie away for a couple of weeks. Things might die down."

Pete looked at him incredulously. "There are ten reasons I can't do that even if I were inclined to, beginning with the fact I don't have legal custody of Julie. Wayne Sable would press kidnapping charges against me faster than I could blink. Plus, I don't believe the problem will go away even if Julie and I were to disappear for a while."

"Just trying to be helpful," Harry said.

"I know and I didn't mean to jump on you."

"All I ask is that you think about what I've said."

"Things change, Harry."

Harry seemed uncertain about what to say. He stared at his empty plate. "That was a great sandwich," he said, dragging a handful of bar napkins across his lips again. He looked longingly at the kitchen door. "I wonder if the chef would fix me another half. Or a whole one if you'll eat half."

"I think I'll pass," Pete said. Except for the two of them at the bar, the restaurant was empty and the dining area lights had been turned down low. "The staff would probably like us to leave, too, so they can close up."

Harry looked disappointed. "I suppose you're right." He made a move like he was about to get off his bar stool, then his face brightened and he said, "Maybe the chef has some pie back there. We could get a piece and take it back to my place and split it and talk to Rona. She might have some ideas."

Pete shook his head. "Another night. I'm tired from the drive." He didn't feel like engaging in their usual banter, but knew he'd been hard on Harry and forced out, "Besides, what would Eve say if she heard that her star workout pupil was eating pie just before going to sleep."

"You mean going to bed, don't you? I'm not sure Rona and I will go to sleep right away." He leered at Pete and gave him a wink.

"You *are* a tiger."

Harry grinned and said, "You know, I'm down another pound. Actually, a pound and a half. Those digital scales are a lot better for monitoring your progress than those old scales where you have to guess at what number the arrow is pointing to."

"After that sandwich, you've probably gained half a pound back."

"Yeah, but as I said, I might be working that off later." He winked again.

Pete slid off his barstool and said, "Come on lover boy. Time to go."

Harry got off his stool, too, but leaned against it and said, "You know, you really ought to talk to Eve and get her advice about what kind of a workout program would be right for you. The way people are coming after you all the time . . ."

"Let's not get on that again."

Harry said, "Still . . ."

"Let's go," Pete said, eyeing him. "You don't want to leave your entire game on the barroom floor, do you?"

"Touché. I'll tell you what. I'll find out when Eve is free and then the four of us can have drinks some night. You know, just to see whether you'd be comfortable working with her."

Pete rolled his eyes and said, "Whatever."

Maybe it was the conversation with Harry, but when Pete got home, his body was crying out for exercise. He flipped through his mail and found nothing of interest. Then he switched to a heavier coat and pulled a knit cap over his ears and headed out. He walked at a brisk pace south on M-22, and when he came to the junction with South Shore Drive, he veered left along the lake. A half-moon glittered on the water and he could hear the choppy waves slap against the shore as he walked east.

Pete felt good about pressuring Maureen Fesko into letting Julie return to school. When it came to jousting with Wayne Sable, or in his absence his sister, he was always determined to win. But driving back to the lake that afternoon, he had time to think and began to worry about Julie's safety going forward now that the stalker was using her as a pawn in the game against him. He had a plan and tomorrow he was determined to put it in place.

The best protection for Julie, though, would be to find the sonofabitch who was behind this. He had to keep putting pressure on Tessler to question the Seitz brothers and Kurt Romer and try to get warrants to search their places and vehicles. The knife-in-the-door incident might help with that. If necessary, he was going to march into Richter's office and demand that he do something. But he wasn't going to depend on that alone. It was time to amp up his own efforts.

His thoughts shifted back to how the stalker knew that Julie was at Meadowbrook School. He ticked off in his head the names of people who did know. Once he got past Wayne Sable and his crowd—Maureen, his attorney, whom he barely knew—he was down to a handful of friends. Harry McTigue, Rona Martin, his former law partner Angie DeMarco, the family law attorney in his old firm that he used. A few clients knew as well, but two who did were dead and it was inconceivable that any of the others had anything to do with the stalking incidents. That brought it back to the people on his suspect list. And if it was one of them, how did he get that information?

How the stalker had managed to get into Julie's dorm that night troubled him, too. He knew that the doors were locked at night and, as additional security, someone stood watch in the lobby. Maybe the security guard had let the person in, which made no sense in the circumstances. Or maybe the person had a key. That, too, seemed improbable, but not as improbable as the guard being in cahoots with the assailant. A stalker as resourceful as this one, who had found out that Pete had a daughter at the school, might have been clever enough to come up with a master key for the dorms.

He came to the public beach at Seventh Street and stopped and gazed out at the water. The raw spring wind out of the west had been at his back as he walked along the road, but now it whipped the side of his face. He turned up his collar and pulled the stocking cap lower and stood there hunched against the damp cold, thinking about his life.

What prompted him to give up the managing partner position at Sears & Whitney, something he'd strived for all of his life, and pursue cases that brought him nothing but trouble? He knew himself fairly well, but even he couldn't fully answer that question. For twenty years, the practice of law had anchored his life and then, *poof!*, it was gone. Maybe the change started when he had to deal with Doris's death. It was a question he'd wrestled with before.

Soul-searching wasn't going to do him *or* Julie any good at this point. Only action would do that. He'd stay out of law enforcement's way to the extent he could, but if their interests collided at some point, that was too damn bad.

SIXTEEN

Pete called Joe Tessler the next morning to tell him about the incident at Julie's school and promised to drop off the photographs he'd gotten from Nowitzki and a copy of the note. So Tessler wouldn't miss the point, he emphasized his conviction that the incident was related to the ones at the lake. He also asked Tessler to call John Nowitzki.

"Have you questioned the Seitz brothers and Kurt Romer yet?" Pete asked.

A pause at the other end, then Tessler said, "I'm planning to talk to Frank later this morning about Calvin and Randy. Romer is more of a problem. We know he's in the Thompsonville area, but I don't have an exact address."

"I know where Romer is. He's living with a woman named Bonni Calhoun."

Another pause, then, "Do you have this Bonni's address?"

"I'll get it to you tomorrow. I'll be over in a half-hour with the stuff Nowitzki gave me so you'll have the full picture when you talk to Frank. When you question Calvin and Randy, you should press them on alibis for the night the knife was stuck in my daughter's door as well as everything else. And don't forget about going for a search warrant. Or search warrants. We need to search Randy's Silverado for trace evidence, too."

"Okay, boss," Tessler said. He sounded like he regretted taking Pete's call.

Pete stopped at the sheriff's office and then ran some other errands. He called John Nowitzki early that afternoon.

"John, it's Pete Thorsen. Has Detective Tessler from our county sheriff's department called you?"

"Just got off the phone with him. Nice fellow, big city law enforcement experience. Seems very competent."

"A pretty good guy, too," Pete said. "Did the two of you decide anything?"

"Mainly we agreed to keep in close contact on the case. Not much specific beyond that. He did say he was hoping to question a couple of people up your way to see if they have alibis for the night of the incident involving your daughter."

"I know about that. Anything else?"

"No, not really."

"Okay, next point," Pete said. "I've been wondering how the guy who stuck the knife in Julie's door got into her dorm. Any thoughts?"

"I've been thinking about that, too. I questioned Bernie Tobin, the guy from campus security who was on duty in the dorm lobby that night. He told me that when the doors are locked, the building can only be accessed by a key card and that only students and members of the school administration have cards. There's also a switch on each lock that disables the mechanism so even someone with a key card can't just insert it and get in after 10:00 p.m. You can get out, of course, but not in. Tobin says he checked all of the doors twice that night and the disabling mechanisms were on."

"But someone inside the building could open one of the doors and let a person in."

"Yeah, I suppose." Nowitzki paused for a moment and then asked, "What's your point, Pete?"

"Nothing in particular, just thinking of the possibilities."

"Do you suspect Tobin of something?"

"I'm not saying that I suspect him, but I think we have to consider all of the possibilities until we know what happened. Did you check his background?"

"*We* didn't check, but I'm sure the school vetted him before they hired him."

"I'm a lawyer, not a detective. But when I was in the army, I drove a jeep for a major in the CID. One of the things I learned from him was to follow up on all points no matter how innocuous they might seem at the time. Then when you've completed your investigative work, sift and winnow everything you have. The truth will eventually come out."

"That's sound advice. I suppose I can ask the school for a copy of Tobin's employment application."

"I think you should. Discreetly of course."

"I'll warn you, sometimes we run into privacy issues unless we have a warrant signed by a judge."

Pete grunted disgustingly and said, "I've already bumped into the school's privacy policy. I don't think we need to talk about that anymore."

After he was off the phone with Nowitzki, Pete thought about Julie. If everything worked as he thought it would, she'd be back at school the following day. He dialed her cell phone number just to make sure she hadn't gotten back early, and when there was no answer, he called Adam Rose.

"Where are you these days Adam?"

"In the Big Easy. Remember that case I was handling when I talked to you the last time? I got hooked on New Orleans and moved down here. Lots of crime, plenty of clients. And if you're selective, they actually pay you. I have two guys working for me now."

"A regular conglomerate," Pete said.

Rose laughed. "So what's cooking up north?"

"I have someone after me." Pete summarized the story for him.

"And you think it might be someone from your past."

"Has to be. He knows a lot about me, where my daughter goes to school, everything."

"Umm," Rose murmured. "Sounds like an interesting case."

"Interesting isn't exactly a word that comes to my mind."

"I didn't mean it that way. How can I help you? I have a new client coming in to see me in a few minutes. Big bucks, hopefully."

"I'm worried about my daughter. Since you're not in the area any longer, can you recommend someone I could hire to watch over her until we find the guy who's been stalking me?"

"High end or low end?" Rose asked.

"Reliable and capable, first of all. And hopefully not *too* pricey. It's stakeout work essentially."

"Okay." Rose went silent for a couple of minutes and then gave him two names. They chatted for a while longer and said their goodbyes.

He dialed Nowitzki's number for the second time. "John, it's Pete Thorsen. Sorry to bother you again, but I'm worried about my daughter in case whoever is after me decides to take another run at her. Does your department provide security in this type of situation?"

"Not unless it's a major case and there are extenuating circumstances. With your daughter, I could tell our patrol guys on duty to swing past her dorm once or twice a night and look for someone who might be prowling around. We don't have the resources to do more than that."

"That's what I expected. Next question. If I hire someone on my own to watch the dorm, is there some way we can coordinate to make sure he isn't picked up as a suspicious person by one of your officers?"

"A licensed private investigator you mean?"

"Yes."

"What's his name?"

"I haven't hired one yet."

"When you do, have him stop by and see me. I'll introduce him to the others in the department and let them know what he'll be doing. I'll tell the campus police, too. That should cover the bases."

Pete called the first of the private investigators Adam Rose had recommended. He interviewed him over the phone and then did the same with the second investigator. He settled on the second, a no-nonsense woman named Rae Acton who'd been in the business for eighteen years and had once served as bodyguard for a former Detroit mayor. He patched John Nowitzki into the call and arranged for Acton to begin watching Julie's dorm effective Friday night.

His thoughts shifted to the Seitz brothers. He hoped that Tessler wasn't just selling him a bill of goods when he said he was trying get Richter's go-ahead to question them and go for search warrants. He intended to keep pressuring him. It was the wrong time to stop being a thorn in Tessler's side.

Pete checked two telephone directories that included the Thompsonville area and didn't find Bonni Calhoun listed in either. He decided to visit to The Nighthawk again to see if he could find someone, other than Bonni, who knew where she lived to take away Tessler's excuse on that front. If he happened to bump into Romer while he was there . . . well, that wouldn't be the worst thing.

He was about to lock up and get something to eat before he headed to Thompsonville when Harry called.

"I forgot to tell you when we were at the bar at Rona's, but you made the papers the other day," he said.

"Not your rag, I hope."

"The Traverse City Record-Eagle ran a feature story about alpaca farms in Michigan. How they're growing like mad, what their fleece is used for, that sort of thing. That place your girlfriends own — what's the name, Serendipity Meadows or something —"

"Heavenly Meadows," Pete corrected him.

"Right, Heavenly Meadows. Anyway, the article was a big spread with photos and everything. Two or three columns dealt with the killing of those two alpacas. The story also mentioned that a bag filled with the animals' blood was thrown against a local citizen's door along with a note."

"Were those words used in the story, local citizen?"

"It was slightly more specific. Let's see, Mr. Peter Thoraison of Frankfort. That's you, right?" Pete could hear Harry giggling in the background. "If you like, I can call the reporter and demand a correction of your name."

"No, that's okay," Pete said. He'd asked Harry to keep his name out of his pieces in *The Northern Sentinel*, which he'd done, but the facts had trickled out by word of mouth. The story in the *Record-Eagle* probably didn't make much difference because most people in the area already knew he was one of the victims. They just didn't know the entire story.

"I'll keep the paper and the next time you're in you can pick it up."

"For my scrapbook."

Harry must have picked up on his sarcasm because he said, "Understand, I wasn't making light of the incident or anything. I was just amused by the way they butchered your name."

"I understand, Mr. McTigski."

They both laughed.

"Do you want to grab a bite? We could talk about other things. Fishing, baseball, stuff like that."

"How about tomorrow night? I'm nursing something I probably picked up from you. I'm going to settle in by the fire and read a book."

SEVENTEEN

The Nighthawk was half-full when Pete walked in. George Strait wailed from the jukebox about moving with the good Lord's speed, carrying his woman's love with him, and Bonni Calhoun worked the bar in her trademark outfit. She swayed to the music and flirted with customers as she plunked down a bottle of beer here and served up a shot there.

Pete scanned the crowd and didn't see anyone who looked like Kurt Romer, taking into account that he could have changed in four years. He did see Irma at the end of the bar in her usual spot. He took a deep breath to steel himself and walked in her direction. She might be light on the beauty side of the scale, but she seemed to have a capacity for sucking up information. Two empty stools separated her from the closest customer.

He tapped her on the shoulder and said, "Is this stool taken young lady?"

Her face creased into a crooked smile when she saw him. She'd added a smudge of eyeliner since the afternoon he'd talked to her, but she was still a prime candidate for a makeover reality show. She swung off her stool and threw her arms around him. Their embrace drew incredulous stares from everyone nearby.

"Peter," she said, "I've been waiting for you to call and all of a sudden you just walk up." She kissed him on the cheek and whispered in his ear, "I like a man who's full of surprises."

Pete took the stool next to Irma. Bonni came down and said, "Welcome back. I guess." She shot Irma a hostile look. "Miller Lite?" she asked.

He nodded and turned back to Irma who was boring in like she hadn't talked to a breathing soul in six months. "I vacuumed my place and dusted and everything. I kind of hoped you'd take me up on my offer and come over some night. I even went out and got some of those Stouffer's dinners. Lasagna with meat sauce, both of them. You look like the kind of man who loves a good Italian meal. I got a bottle of wine from a friend a couple of years ago that I've been saving for a special occasion. We could have that, too."

"Sounds wonderful," Pete lied. "I'll let you know when I can make it." He hoped he could get her off the subject of romantic dinners and onto other things. Like Bonni Calhoun's address and whether she'd seen Kurt Romer recently.

"Make it real soon, okay? I've got some nice candles we can light, too."

He nodded, and so it wouldn't appear as if he just wanted to pump her for information, he asked her where her family was originally from. That was good for a half-hour of conversation as she laid out her family's genealogy on both sides going back several generations.

When he sensed an opening, he asked, "Remember that guy Kurt Romer we were talking about the last time I was in?"

"Sure, the man that slut Bonni is sleeping with."

"Does he come in often?"

She sniffed derisively. "Just about every night. I think he's got a drinking problem or something."

"How about this past Sunday night? Was he in then?"

"I'm sure he was," she said. "Why don't you ask me an easy question, like the last night he *wasn't* here."

"This is important, Irma. Do you have a specific recollection of seeing him in The Nighthawk on Sunday night?"

Irma seemed to go into deep thought. Then she said, "I'm sure he was. There aren't that many people here on Sunday nights and I think that's the night him and Bonni got into that fight. Kurt was talking to another woman and Bonni gets real jealous when he does that. She throws herself at every man who walks in the door, but Heaven save the country if Kurt talks to me or another woman."

She paused and thought some more. "I'm sure it was Sunday night they had the fight." She frowned and said, "Just a minute, it could have been Monday night." She took another gulp of her drink and banged her glass on the bar a couple of times to get Bonni's attention. Bonni rolled her eyes and poured a fresh drink and shoved it down the bar when she was five feet away, like she didn't want to come near Irma out of fear of contracting some dread disease.

"Bonni," Irma called. "What night was it that you and Kurt got into that fight?"

Bonni turned and walked down the bar closer to Irma. "Why are you talking about me, you old whore?" Her whisper sounded like the growl of a junk yard dog.

"No need to get all defensive about it," Irma said, playing the aggrieved party. "I just asked you a simple question. This gentleman wants to know if Kurt was here on Sunday night. I could care less myself."

"None of your business, both of you." Bonni walked back to the other end of the bar.

"Whew," Irma said, fanning her face with a hand. "Touchy, touchy."

They talked about other things. He was considering how to ask about where Bonni lived when Irma clutched his arm and whispered, "There he is. Maybe you can ask Kurt himself if he was here on Sunday night."

Pete looked down the bar and recognized Romer immediately. Tall, around Pete's height, lanky. He'd grown a trim circle beard and moustache with a soul patch under his lower lip and his dark hair looked shorter than Pete remembered.

Romer leaned across the bar and kissed Bonni on the lips. She whispered in his ear and he looked toward where Pete was sitting. Pete knew it was only a matter of time until they had a conversation.

He went back to his painful conversation with Irma while keeping an eye on Romer. Kurt talked to several people at the bar, then joined a couple sitting at one of the tables. Irma fought for Pete's attention by periodically nudging him in the ribs or raking his arm with her fingernails or asking him if he was listening.

She droned on about how she wound up back in northern Michigan after living in Memphis, Tennessee for seven years. He did his best to show interest, but saw Romer get up and head for the men's room. Pete's eyes flicked toward the men's room door every few seconds, but he didn't see him come out. A half-hour passed and Romer still hadn't reappeared.

He interrupted whatever Irma was babbling on about at the moment and asked, "Did you see Kurt leave?"

"Kurt don't leave until Bonni leaves," she said. "Now I was telling you about why I got divorced from my first husband."

Pete feigned interest again while continuing to watch for Romer. He was puzzled by his sudden disappearance. Romer clearly recognized him and he figured that at some point he'd come over to find out what Pete was doing at The Nighthawk.

"Do you know what that man was doing?" Irma asked, thumping Pete on the arm again to command his attention. Her voice became low and she said, "He was *cheating* on me."

"You're kidding."

She shook her head somberly. "Nope, I'm not. He claimed he was married to another woman at the same time he was married to me, and the fact that they was married meant that he really wasn't cheating on me. He was just trying to be a husband to both of us."

"A bigamist," Pete said.

Her brow furled and she said, "I guess he was one of those people they call plural men."

"Plural as in two or more wives?"

"Yes, that's it! I tell you, I've never been so shocked in my life. The man never told me a thing about it before I caught him."

"That's terrible," Pete said. He tried to shift the conversation and asked, "I wonder where Kurt Romer went to?"

Irma looked across the room and pointed to the table where he'd been sitting with the couple. "He must still be here. There's his beer."

"It's been sitting there for the past hour. I think he's gone."

"I could go over and ask one of those people at his table. They might know where he is."

"No, let's wait. He might come back."

"You and Kurt must have something important to talk about the way you seem to be so upset that he's not here anymore."

"No big deal. I'll catch him another time."

"Look, there goes that lady to the bathroom. I have to go, too, and I'll ask her about Kurt."

Before Pete could say anything, she was off at a gait he didn't know she possessed. Pete watched her go and shook his head. If friends knew he was hanging around a bar with the likes of Irma . . .

She returned at the same speed she'd departed and whispered breathlessly in his ear, "Kurt had to leave. No one knows why."

"Umm," Pete murmured, both disappointed and relieved at the same time.

"I knew we should have gone over and talked to him when he first came in. Then the two of you could have had that important conversation."

"Too late now, I guess. Say, you don't happen to know Bonni's address, do you?"

Irma got a hurt look on her face.

He patted her on the hand and said, "Don't worry. I just have to drop something off for Kurt. I'd prefer that Bonni not know."

Her face lit up. "This is kind of exciting," she said with a conspiratorial gleam in her eyes. "It's confidential, huh?"

He nodded.

"We could look in the telephone book. I bet they have her address."

Pete shook his head. "I've already looked."

"They have a telephone book here with everybody's name. I bet she's in there. C'mon."

She took him by the hand and led him through the crowd to the short hallway where the restrooms were located. He cringed when fifty pairs of eyes followed them. A pay telephone was mounted on the wall, but the phone book was missing from the chain that had once secured it.

"I can ask Bonni if she knows where the telephone book is."

"No, she might get suspicious."

"I know where the slut lives," she said slyly. "We could drive by and find out the address that way."

Irma's stock rose on Pete's scale. With Irma giving him directions, which included five wrong turns, Pete finally pulled up in front of the apartment building that Irma swore was the right one. He found Bonni's name stenciled next to one of the buzzers and wrote down the address.

Pete escorted Irma back into The Nighthawk and then called goodnight to Bonni and hoped that everyone saw him leave alone.

EIGHTEEN

P
ete was thinking about Romer and his sudden disappearance from The Nighthawk when Higgie Brown and Sunshine Warrick walked into his office for the second time. Their attire was less eye-catching than when they first came to see him.

"We were at the drug store," Higgie said, "and realized we hadn't thanked you for sending the beautiful basket of flowers in memory of Jane and Virgil. We forgot our manners when you were at Heavenly Meadows with that lady detective."

They accepted his invitation to sit.

"No thanks necessary," he said. "It was the least I could do after your loss."

Higgie and Sunshine's looked at each other with the sadness he'd come to expect on these occasions. "Thank you for being so caring," Sunshine managed to squeeze out.

"Amy isn't a detective, by the way," Pete said. "She just does forensic work for the sheriff's department part-time."

"She's very bright, though. We could tell from the way she speaks. She'll be a big help in solving the murders."

Pete was grateful Higgie hadn't said "a big help to *you*," although he suspected that might have been what she meant. "Has everything settled down?" he asked.

"Not really," Higgie said, shaking her head. "We can see from our other babies' eyes that they miss Jane and Virgil." Both women looked like tears were about to roll again.

Pete sat awkwardly behind his desk. His eyes flicked to the wall clock as they held each other's hands.

"Do you know if the sheriff's office has made any progress with their investigation?" Higgie asked.

"Maybe, but they haven't told me," he said evasively.

"Oh," she said, slumping. "We were hoping you might know something."

He shook his head sadly.

"Do you think Mrs. Ostrowski knows something?"

"Possible, I suppose. I haven't talked to her in a couple of days."

He wondered where the conversation was going and glanced at the clock again.

"We heard sounds in our barn two nights ago," Higgie said after a moment. "We called the sheriff's office, but they didn't have anyone they could send out until the next morning. The nice young man who did come out didn't find anything. All of our babies were still unharmed."

What Higgie had just said alarmed him. He suspected he knew the answer to the question he was about to ask, but asked anyway. "Do you keep a firearm in your house?"

Higgie gasped and Sunshine raised a hand to her mouth. "We don't believe in guns, Mr. Thorsen. We're pacifists."

He gently reminded them again to call him Pete. Then he moved on to something they'd discussed before. "We talked about this when I was at your farm the first time, but I really think you ought to consider locking the barn at night until they catch the man who . . . murdered Jane and Virgil. It probably won't keep him out if he's determined to get in, but at least it might deter him."

Both women shook their heads in unison. "That would affect our babies' psyches," Higgie said. "We can't lock them up and make them feel like prisoners."

As Pete hurried down Main Street to Rona's Bay Grille, he thought about Higgie and Sunshine and smiled to himself. They were living examples that the flower child mentality of decades earlier hadn't become entirely extinct.

He picked up his pace some more. Harry had arranged for his personal trainer, Eve Bayles, to join them for drinks, emphasizing again that the purpose was to give Pete an opportunity to decide whether he wanted to work with her. He could smell a fix-up attempt, though, and a romantic entanglement was the last thing he was interested in at the moment. He checked his watch and saw that he was a half-hour late because of Higgie and Sunshine's surprise visit.

Harry was waving both arms like a signal corpsman who hadn't yet mastered his craft when Pete walked into the restaurant. He said hello all around and took the open chair that was conveniently next to Eve. Her medium-length dark hair was down instead of pulled back like he'd seen it before. He didn't know what the hair style was called, but a wave swept forward and fell over her right eye, giving her an exotic look. She wore a long knit cardigan sweater that extended below her hips and complemented her peach-colored blouse.

"Sorry I'm late. Someone stopped at my office just as I was about to leave."

Harry shook his head. He looked at Eve and said, "I should warn you about Pete. He gives me grief if I'm two minutes late for some event. Then Mr. Consistency keeps the three of us waiting for an hour past the agreed time."

"Half hour," Pete corrected him, feeling sheepish.

Harry looked at his watch and appeared to be calculating. "Thirty-nine minutes if you don't count the minute it took him to walk across the room," he proclaimed to the ladies.

Rona rolled her eyes and Eve just smiled. Pete saw that they were both drinking white wine and ordered a glass of the same.

Harry apparently realized that he wasn't going to get much mileage out of pimping Pete for his tardy arrival and shifted gears. "I was just telling Eve that I'm down almost four pounds since I started working with her. To be more precise, three point eight pounds as of this morning." He grinned at Pete smugly.

"Now if I can just persuade him to lay off desserts," Eve said.

Harry glanced her way to see if she were serious and his eyes widened.

They chatted for a few minutes and then Eve asked Pete about his background. Never eager to talk about himself to someone he didn't know, he told her in condensed form how he'd grown up in northern Wisconsin, served a stint in the army, and gone on to a long legal career in Chicago, then moved north.

"A long and *prosperous* legal career," Harry added. "Now he's Mr. Viking. Shooting arrows with his ancient bow, wearing a helmet with funny little horns on it."

"I don't think you've ever seen me with a helmet," Pete corrected him. "You need to brush up on your historical knowledge, too. Viking helmets didn't have horns."

Harry's expression went blank for a moment. Then he said, "Baloney, every picture I've seen shows them with horns. Daguerreotypes, tintypes, those other old photographs. They all show Vikings with horns on their helmets. Statues too. Even the Vikings football team. Horns on every one of them."

"Look, Mr. Newspaper Editor, the Viking heyday was approximately the ninth through eleventh centuries. I don't think daguerreotypes and tintypes and those processes were invented until centuries later. Do you know how the horn thing got started? Some weak-kneed Scottish revisionists from later times had to rationalize why their forefathers didn't try harder to repel the Norsemen when they came to visit and came up with horns on their helmets to exaggerate their ferocity."

Harry didn't say anything, but it wasn't hard to visualize the wheels in his head grinding away, searching for a comeback.

Eve continued to smile and asked Pete, "So what were Viking helmets really like?"

"Most were cone-shaped and made of leather. Only the wealthiest Vikings could afford metal helmets." He looked at Harry. "And they were the same as the leather ones. No horns on either."

"I don't think you should debate Viking history with Pete, dear," Rona said, patting Harry's hand.

Pete sensed a weakness and took another shot, saying, "Harry's still mad about the old days. I explained to him one time that we were probably related and he's never gotten over it. It's a documented historical fact that Scottish women just couldn't resist those hunky Viking warriors."

Everyone laughed except Harry. He shot Pete a snarly look and continued to stew.

"How about you, Eve?" Rona asked, apparently searching for a way to create an armistice in the verbal sparring. "What's your background?"

"I can't claim to be descended from Vikings," Eve said, laughing and tossing her hair back from her eye. "I'm a New Jersey girl. Trenton." She went on to explain that she'd gone to Rutgers for two years, then dropped out and joined the army where she'd remained for five years. After she left the army, she said, she started to work in fitness clubs and eventually segued into personal training.

"That's a hot field these days," Pete said. "You've even gotten Harry to sign up."

"But not Mr. Viking," Harry fired back. "He couldn't take the pace." Harry was grinning again, seemingly confident his last shot had eaten into Pete's advantage from the last round.

They talked about other things and ordered a second round of drinks. "Are you two married?" Eve asked, looking at Rona and Harry.

"Not yet," Rona said. "And you?"

"Divorced. I was married to the king of the louse species for thirteen months."

"Thirteen," Harry said. "That's an unlucky number, you know."

"Not for me. It was the luckiest month of my life."

Harry said, "You're preaching to the choir at this table. We've all been divorced."

"Not Pete," Rona reminded him.

"Oh yeah, Pete is widowed."

Pete didn't say anything.

Eve looked at him and said, "If you don't have a hostile ex, who do you think messed up your cottage?"

Pete glanced at her. "I have no idea," he said. "Maybe some local delinquents. How did you hear about that?"

"The Traverse City newspaper. They ran an article on the alpaca farms that told about the two animals that were killed. The article mentioned the incident at your cottage."

Harry jumped into the conversation and said to Eve, "When Pete says local delinquents, he's not being entirely candid. He believes someone from his past could be responsible."

Eve looked at Pete with the brow of her visible eye cocked quizzically.

Pete shrugged and said, "The truth is, I don't *know* who did it. People kept asking me for possibilities, and I threw out some. But I have absolutely nothing to base it on."

"How about that night when someone set off your alarm system?" Harry persisted.

Eve looked interested.

Pete tried to control his irritation at his blabbermouth friend and said, "I talked to the alarm company and they did some trouble-shooting. They concluded that it might have been a malfunction due to low batteries. I replaced them and haven't have had any problems since."

"What —"

Pete cut him off with a question for Eve. "Harry's always after me to start working with a personal trainer like he does. What kind of program would you put me on if I were to sign up?"

"Let me turn your question around. How would you describe your condition?"

"He's—" Harry started to say.

Pete cut him off again. "Not great, not terrible. I run a few miles several times a week during good weather, go to the fitness center with Harry now and then."

"Let me put it another way," Eve said. "On a scale of one to ten, with one being the Pillsbury doughboy and ten being Arnold Schwarzenegger, how would you rate yourself?"

"About in the middle, I suppose."

From the look on his face, Harry was enjoying watching Pete squirm under Eve's questions.

"How about body fat?" she asked.

"Less than Harry's." He shot his friend a look.

"If you want to get in peak condition," Eve said, "we'd probably have to design a program for you over the next nine to twelve months." She went on to tell in general terms the workout regimen that would entail.

She looked at her watch and said, "I'm sorry, I have to go. I'm working at the animal shelter tonight."

She rose to leave and everyone else stood as well. After she thanked Harry for the drinks, she asked Pete for his business card. "A person never knows when she's going to need a good lawyer," she said.

When she was gone, the three of them sat down again. Pete hadn't been anxious to attend Harry's fix-up event, but had been pleasantly surprised.

"Harry," he said, thinking about his earlier comments again, "I wish you wouldn't talk about the incidents at my cottage or the one involving Julie in front of other people. I'm trying to keep things off the radar."

"The word has gotten around anyway," Harry protested. "You just heard Eve say she read about it in the *Record-Eagle*."

"I don't think the word has gotten around about the knife in Julie's dorm door."

"I didn't say anything about that."

"Only because I cut you off."

Harry looked chastened. "Okay," he said, "I won't say anything in the future now that I know you're so sensitive about it. I thought that with just us and Eve, what I said wouldn't go any farther than this table."

"Pete's right, dear," Rona said. "If one of us lets something slip to another person, and that person tells somebody else, pretty soon the news is all over town."

"Alright, already," Harry said. "I get the message. In the future, the only time I'll mention anything is if only the three of us are around and a cone of silence has dropped over our heads."

They sat quietly for a few moments and then Harry said, "Boy, Eve sure looks different when she's dolled up and not in her working clothes, huh?"

Rona looked at him, and in a tone that was suddenly as frosty as the polar icecap, said, "Most of us do."

NINETEEN

When Pete got home, he collected his mail and sorted through it inside his cottage. Sandwiched between flyers from travel agencies, new credit card applications and the monthly statement from AT&T was an envelope with the Indiana Women's Prison's return address. He stared at it in disbelief. After three years, she'd resurfaced.

Seeing the envelope added to the frustration he already felt. He wanted to stab it with his letter opener, rip it to shreds, burn it in his fireplace. Everything but read the letter inside with, he was sure, the same drivel that he'd seen many times before.

He mixed a weak vodka and tonic and looked at the envelope again. He shook his head and sliced it open. Like the letters he'd received from Robyn Fleming earlier, it had her prison number instead of a signature.

The news clipping enclosed with the letter was the article from the *Traverse City Record-Eagle* that both Harry and Eve had mentioned. In the margins, Robyn had written "Ha! Ha!" in several places and "Isn't that too bad!!" in another and "Justice?" in yet another. She'd underlined several sentences she seemed to have found particularly amusing.

The letter was brief with the same old theme:

Gee, Peter, what a shame. There must be someone else who hates your guts as much as I do. What did you do, violate your professional duty to him, too? Or was it some slimy act? I sincerely hope he didn't mess up that cute little house of yours too bad. I guess I shouldn't have said little. It's certainly bigger than my cell, wouldn't you say?

8673

Pete shook his head and tossed the letter on the table. *What the hell was wrong with that woman?* He threw a couple of birch logs in the fireplace and coaxed the flames to life, then settled into his favorite chair with his head back. Even the sound of the Eagles drifting from his Bose didn't improve his mood.

When Pete poked the nozzle into his Range Rover's tank at the Shell station the next morning, he was so preoccupied with everything from Robyn Fleming to how he could increase the pressure on Joe Tessler to intensify his investigation that he paid no attention to the black Silverado that had just pulled in on the other side of the divider. He finally looked up when he heard the pickup's door slam and saw a wiry man with a Detroit Tigers cap fish around in his wallet and slip a card into the pump's pay mechanism. Pete went back to his own filling chores, but looked up again when he heard knuckles rap against glass. The pickup's passenger door flew open and a man with a dirty yellow cap and a stringy red ponytail came bolting around the back.

The man in the Tiger's cap stepped over the low divider toward him. His eyes were shaded by the brim and he had a three-day stubble. He didn't say anything, just kept coming. Pete finished screwing the cap on his gas tank. The man leaned against the Range Rover's driver-side door and stared at him. Calvin Seitz stood on top of the divider, looking like he was about to explode but saying nothing, as though waiting for permission to speak.

"Well, well," Pete said, "it's the Seitz brothers."

Randy had an insolent smirk on his face. "We understand you've been complaining to the sheriff that Calvin and I have been visiting you after hours."

Pete stared at him. It was clear that Tessler had been out to question them.

"Accused us of doing a lot of naughty things, I understand," Randy continued. He was still smirking.

Pete still didn't say anything.

"Calvin and me," Randy said, "we like to watch television at night. It couldn't have been us. Right, Calvin?"

Calvin took his brother's remark as a signal that he was unshackled and screamed, "You asshole, you're lucky I don't put a load of buckshot in you!"

Randy blocked Calvin's path to Pete. "You need to be careful, Pete, my brother gets a little edgy when someone says untrue things about him."

Pete had been glancing around and didn't see any other vehicles at the gas pumps. He also knew it wasn't a winning hand to get into it with the Seitz brothers there. He took the keys from his pocket and said to Randy, "It's been nice talking to you fellows, but I'm done gassing up and have to leave. Now if you'll excuse me."

Randy didn't move away from the Range Rover's door. His hand flashed up and he flicked the keys away. They clattered to the asphalt on the other side of the divider.

"We haven't finished talking yet."

"*I've* finished," Pete said.

Randy ignored him and said, "If a man didn't know better, he might think you had a vendetta against the Seitz family."

"What are you talking about?"

"Last year, you tried to pin a murder on my brother. Then a few days ago you ran him off the road. Now you send the sheriff after us with all kinds of lies."

"I think you have your facts wrong."

"Are you calling me a liar, Pete?"

"I said you have your facts wrong. All I did was tell the sheriff what kind of weapon he hunts with. As for his accident, I think he's just a shitty driver."

"You friggin'—"

Randy held Calvin back again.

You're a lucky man, Pete. "If Calvin and I were nocturnal people . . ." His smirk got wider.

Pete stared at him a moment longer and then turned and retrieved his keys. He walked back toward his Range Rover and said to Randy who was still leaning against his vehicle's door, "Get out of my way, please."

"Did I say that we're finished?"

Pete's eyes met his again.

"Maybe you really do need a visit some night," Randy said. "You know, to give you some manners instructions."

"Is that what you were doing with your ex-girlfriend? Hanging around outside her apartment to teach her some manners?"

Randy's eyes hardened under the low brim of his cap.

"Do you know how we settle matters like this in Detroit?"

Pete ignored him and withdrew his cell phone from his pocket and started to punch in a number. "I think you should continue this conversation with the sheriff."

Randy flicked at the cell phone like he had the keys, but Pete was ready this time. He turned his body to protect it and nudged Randy away with his elbow. Calvin watched the whole scene unfold with his mouth open.

"Are you going to get out of my way or not?" Pete asked.

"Sleep tight, Thorsen." He gave Pete a shove and hopped over the divider and got in his pickup. Calvin followed him but turned and stabbed a finger in his direction and said, "Leave us alone, asshole, or you'll be sorry!"

As Pete watched the Silverado pull out of the station and head out of town, he was conscious that his undershirt was damp in spite of the cool weather. He'd bluffed his way through other situations in the past, but knew he was pushing his luck with the Seitz brothers.

TWENTY

Joe Tessler listened quietly while Pete told him about his confrontation with Randy and Calvin Seitz at the Shell station.

"I take it you've been out to question them," Pete said.

"Yesterday afternoon. I didn't get crap out of them. They covered for each other and swore they were together watching television on each of the nights in question. Their story is that they're both *Seinfeld* buffs and watched reruns non-stop on a late-night cable channel."

"Did you try to verify what they told you?"

"I did what I could. I checked and found that a channel has been running *Seinfeld* stuff for two weeks. Of course, I have no way to prove or disprove that they were actually watching the shows."

"Randy as much as said the same thing to me, but the way he was smirking, I think he viewed it as a joke."

Tessler was silent for a moment. Then, "I hope you weren't too confrontational with them."

"Confrontational? As I told you, I was gassing up and they crowded me and wouldn't let me leave. I hardly said a word."

"I understand, but even if they're not the ones who've been stalking you, you've got to watch out for those two loons."

"What am I supposed to do? Hide under my bed 24/7?"

"I'm just saying that you need to be careful."

"Getting back to when you questioned them," Pete said, "how do you judge their credibility?"

"You want the truth?"

"No, I want something you make up just to get me off your back."

Tessler was silent again, then said, "I think they're both pieces of lying scum. But with them supporting each other, I don't know how we can break their alibis."

"How did you get Frank to go along with the questioning?"

"It wasn't easy," Tessler said, sighing. "I showed him the picture of the dagger in your daughter's door and the latest note. I think he felt that he didn't have a choice. He told me to go ahead, but made me promise not to put in for overtime on any extra hours I spend on your case."

Pete shook his head. "About what I'd expect," he said disgustedly.

Tessler didn't say anything.

"Don't worry, I didn't expect you to comment," Pete said.

"Did Randy have any weapons on him that you could see?"

"Nothing obvious. But you met him. His prison stint and time on the street shows. I'd hate to meet the guy in a dark alley."

"Mmm," Tessler murmured. "Did he threaten you at the Shell station? If he did, that might give us a peg to hassle him some more."

"Does leaning against my door so I couldn't get in, knocking the car keys out of my hand, and trying to do the same with my cell phone count?"

"That sounds like it could be assault."

"I agree, but there was no one around who witnessed it."

"Except Calvin, right?

"Yes."

"And we know what he would say."

"I think we do."

"So I gather you're not making a formal complaint."

"No, but I thought you should know. Do you have something to write with? I want to give you Kurt Romer's address. I think you have to question him next."

Tessler took down the information. "I didn't ask before, but how did you find out he's living with this Bonni Calhoun woman?"

"A little birdie told me."

"A little birdie," Tessler repeated. "Was it a chickadee or the first robin of spring?"

"Does it really matter?" Pete suddenly felt snappish.

"I suppose not."

"Question. When you got Frank's okay to question the Seitz brothers, did you also get an okay for Romer?"

"I didn't. I felt I couldn't lay too much on him at once."

"Can you catch him today?"

"It'll have to be in a couple of days. He's in Lansing for a two-day conference."

Pete's lips tightened and he didn't say anything for a while. Then he floated something that had been on his mind. "I think we need to coordinate our activities a little more in order to be effective," he said.

"There's only one problem with that. I have a boss and it's not you."

"We've worked together in the past and it's turned pretty well," Pete argued. "Not just pretty well, but damn well."

"Those cases were different."

"I don't see how. If we catch the psycho who killed the alpacas and is after Julie and me, you'll make the department look good. By extension, that'll be good for Frank Richter. There's nothing Frank likes better than to look good in the eyes of the voters."

Tessler was quiet again and then said, "What are you proposing?"

"There are certain things that can only be done under the guise of law enforcement. You have access to all of the data bases, you can question suspects, you do forensics work, that sort of thing."

"And how about Pete Thorsen?"

"I'd do things you don't have time to do. Or might not want to do."

"Such as?"

"Occasionally taking a look at certain things without a warrant, for example."

Tessler was silent again. "You're not talking about anything illegal are you?"

"That's hard to answer in the abstract."

"If you are, I don't want to know about it. You ought to have enough sense not to do something like that, either."

"Sometimes you have to ignore a few niceties when a slimeball is stalking you and threatening to carve up your daughter. Besides, you can't tell me you've never cut corners in the course of your police work."

More silence. "You know what we've done," Tessler said. "Anything I should know about what Thorsen Investigations has been doing?"

Pete told him everything, including what he'd planned to do at Calvin Seitz's place before Randy entered the picture and how he'd snooped around The Nighthawk to find out what he could about Kurt Romer, including Bonni Calhoun's address. He also told him how Robyn Fleming had resurfaced with her hate-filled letters and about the security he'd hired for Julie. He got the feeling Tessler's head was spinning by the time they got off the phone.

❖ ❖ ❖

After checking in with Rae Acton again to assure himself that everything was set for that evening, Pete hurried up the street to the hotel where he'd agreed to meet Eve Bayles. She'd called that afternoon and invited him for drinks.

Eve was already there sitting on a bar stool and playing with her swizzle stick. Like the time they'd met at Rona's Bay Grille, her hair was down and her dark tresses swept over one eye. He slid onto the stool next to her and said, "I hope I'm on time today."

"You are. You're improving."

He saw that she was drinking a mixed drink of some kind so he ordered a vodka and tonic, light on the vodka. The hotel bar never seemed to have Thor's Hammer vodka so he settled for Absolut.

"No last minute visitors, huh?"

"Not today. Nonstop appointments during regular business hours, though."

She smiled and said, "It must be nice to be retired. How do you spend your time these days? Apart from tending to all of those people who show up without appointments, of course."

"I don't consider myself retired. I've just segued into a different phase of my life. I occasionally take on legal things that interest me. I write, fly fish when the weather permits, give Harry a hard time, things like that. It keeps me busy. How about you? You said you worked at various fitness centers. Any in big cities?"

"Of course. Matter of fact, my last stop was in your old stomping grounds."

"Chicago?"

She nodded. Pete was sitting on her right side so unless she turned her face toward him, all he saw was her dark hair.

"Where did you work in Chicago?"

"River North Spa & Fitness. I was there for three years."

"I heard that some of the rich and famous have migrated there from the East Bank Club."

"Along with a fair number of the East Bank Club's jerks."

"Jerks are like mice. They're everywhere. How did you find your way to Frankfort?"

"A guy I used to date has a vacation home near here. I liked the area, and when I was ready for a change, I headed north."

"What's his name? Maybe I know him."

"I'd rather not say. He's married and wives can be touchy about these things. It's in the past anyway."

Pete didn't press her. He was the same way. Once he put a relationship in his rearview mirror, he didn't look back. He switched subjects and asked, "Was Harry in today?"

"No," she said. "He called this morning and cancelled his appointment. Something to do with his newspaper."

"Don't let him slack off. He told me his goal is to be a Greek god in six months."

She turned to him and laughed and asked, "He said that?"

"In more colorful language, of course."

"Cute man."

Eve had been twisting her swizzle stick into various shapes as they talked. In the middle of a sentence, she reached across and took his swizzle stick from the bar. Her breast pressed against his arm and her leg lingered against his for a moment after she straightened up again. "I like to play with these things," she said, bending the straw into a configuration that resembled a crude trapezoid.

"Must be a Freudian thing," he said.

"Are you suggesting that my fixation with swizzle sticks has something to do with repressed sexual feelings?" She brushed her hair back so he could see both of her eyes and smiled seductively.

"Not at all. You seem like a perfectly adjusted woman."

"How about you? Do you have any fixations or fetishes I should know about?"

He stared at the bar and said, "It's kind of hard to talk about."

"Try me. I'm a good listener."

He looked up with her with the most sorrowful expression he could conjure up and said in a contrite whisper, "I'm addicted to oldies rock and roll music."

"No, tell me it isn't true!"

"It *is* true. I've tried to kick the habit, but I don't know, it seems hopeless." He looked at her again with a hangdog expression.

"Poor baby," Eve said, taking one of his hands in both of hers. "Tell Dr. Eve how it started and maybe we can come up with a cure."

"It was that terrible squad-room bunkmate I had in the army. He wanted to be a disc jockey specializing in classic rock and roll and he got me hooked, too."

"I'm sorry," Eve said after thinking about it, "you're too far gone. If you'd come to me earlier . . ."

They looked at each other sadly for a moment and then both laughed.

"Harry told me you liked the old stuff. I was wondering when you were going to come clean."

"Do you like oldies?" he asked.

Eve shook her head. "I don't *dislike* them, but I prefer real classical. Tchaikovsky in particular gets my blood tingling."

They talked about the Chicago Symphony Orchestra and their favorite conductors.

"Speaking of music," Pete said, "when are you going to get the stuff they play at the fitness center replaced with some Tchaikovsky?"

"Not soon," she said, sighing. "I've suggested it, but the manager thinks he was a Russian ax murderer."

They ordered another round of drinks. When Eve had a fresh swizzle stick to play with, she asked, "How's your investigation going?"

He looked at her with a quizzical smile. "Why do you ask that?"

"People tell me you have a reputation for investigating on your own when you think the sheriff isn't doing enough. With everything that's been happening, I was just wondering."

"If I have a *reputation*, as you say, it's because I've had a couple of clients where I've had to pin down facts in order to represent them properly. All of a sudden, some people view me as Dick Tracy."

"That must get irritating."

"I'm too even tempered to get irritated."

"Oh."

"Except when someone stops in my office and insists on hiring me to find an uncle who disappeared from the planet twenty-nine years ago."

She laughed. "Now *that's* a cold case."

"I guess."

"Somebody—I think it was Harry—told me you gave the sheriff's office a list of people who might have done those things to your house. Does the sheriff keep you informed about what's going on with their investigation?"

"It was hardly a list. Just the names of a couple of people I came up with when they continued to press me in order to develop leads. The last time I talked to the detective in the sheriff's office, they were thinking more and more that it might just be a couple of isolated incidents. Actually maybe only *one* incident. As I said at Rona's the night we had drinks, my house alarm could have malfunctioned because of low batteries."

"So what you're telling me is that the whole thing may be dead."

"I don't know if we can say that yet, but at least it doesn't seem to be as serious as it was the night the bag of blood was thrown again my door." He knew that wasn't true, but wanted to downplay the whole thing.

"Can you share with Eve who was on the list you gave the sheriff's office?"

"Are you sure you weren't with the FBI instead of the army?"

She laughed again. "Just the woman in me coming out. We like to know everything."

"To put your mind at ease, you weren't on it."

"Oh damn! So much for my *femme fatale* reputation."

Now it was his turn to laugh. "Maybe I should have said CIA rather than FBI. You have a certain mysterious look to you."

She turned her collar up and gave him a furtive glance.

"I'll tell you what. If you take me out some night and get me over-served, maybe I'll share a name or two with you."

"Will I have to sign a confidentially agreement?"

He held her hair back so he could see both eyes. "You might, depending on how things go."

She insisted on paying for the drinks since she'd invited him. Then she left for the animal shelter.

Walking back to his office, he reflected on how nice it had been to talk to someone other than Harry who he enjoyed being with. It was almost like his life was back to normal again.

When he got back to his office, there was a voicemail message from Joe Tessler saying he went to talk to the Seitz brothers again, ostensibly to ask some more questions, but also to signal he knew about their confrontation with him at the Shell station. A precautionary move he said.

TWENTY-ONE

Pete stalked around his office and every few minutes paused to look at the legal pad on his desk with the four names on it. Five with Randy Seitz added next to his brother's name. It was a jumble of lines and question marks and arrows and marginal notes.

He crossed off the words "search shack" by Calvin Seitz's name. It was a crazy idea from the get-go and fraught with risks. Doubly so now that he knew what Randy was like. He had to trust that Tessler would persuade the sheriff to request a search warrant. If Tessler wasn't successful, then he'd consider alternatives.

Major Baumann's philosophy of looking at everything even though you believed you knew the answer rattled around in his head as he stared at the names below the Seitz brothers. He put a check mark next to Romer's name because he didn't know what else he could do with him, and moved on to Gil Bartholome.

He jotted down what he knew about Bartholome. Right hand man of Alain Conti, now dead, who ran the counterfeit immigration document ring. Lived with Lynn Hawke, a woman Pete had also dated. Fled his Seattle base as soon as news of Lynn's death reached him. Showed up back in northern Michigan and got caught in the middle of a power struggle between Conti and another gang member. Last seen at the Days Inn where Pete had tracked him.

Pete rummaged through his desk and found Keegan Harris's business card. She was the Homeland Security agent who'd been in charge of the immigration case. He didn't part with her on the best of terms when the case was over, and wondered whether she'd mellowed with the passage of time.

What the hell, he thought, and dialed Keegan's direct number shown on her card. A man eventually answered. Pete explained who he was and said he'd worked on the Conti case with Special Agent Harris a couple of years earlier and needed to speak to her. That led to five minutes of haggling with the man and a second man who got on the line.

Several minutes later, a female voice said, "You're damn lucky you're not in prison, Thorsen."

That answered his question about whether she'd mellowed. "Why do you say that, Special Agent?"

"You know why. You tried to pass off a box of worthless paper as the counterfeit documents. We know you intended to keep the real documents and sell them."

"That's not true, Keegan. A detective with our local sheriff's office called to tell you where the real documents were."

"Sure," she said sarcastically, "after I scared the crap out of you on the phone."

"Come on."

She continued to bore in. "Some of our people wanted to prosecute you, you know."

Pete took a couple of deep breaths to calm himself down and said, "I didn't call to reopen old wounds, Keegan. I called to ask if you ever caught Gil Bartholome? He's the one who got away if you'll recall."

"You think I'm a moron? Of course I recall. If you'd brought us in when you should have instead of playing cowboy, we'd have Bartholome behind bars now."

"Oh for God's sake, you know what was going on. I was caught in the middle of things through no doing of my own. I risked my behind to help you bring that case to a successful conclusion. I'm lucky to be here talking to you."

"Well bully for you. Wouldn't it be nice if the rest of us were so lucky."

It was clear that he wasn't going to get anywhere with her. He said, "Goodbye, Keegan" and slammed the phone down. When he'd cooled off, he realized that while she hadn't told him whether Bartholome had been apprehended, which was the reason for his call, it was clear from her comments that he hadn't.

His thoughts shifted to where Bartholome could be hiding if he were back in northern Michigan. A hotel or motel almost surely would be out. Maybe he'd rented a place in the area under a different name. If he had, Pete was right back where he started because he had absolutely no idea where to begin looking or under what name.

He did know where Conti Vineyards was, though, and that was the other possibility. He'd heard that the couple who'd bought the vineyard after Conti was killed had gone bankrupt. If the place was vacant, maybe—and it was just a wild possibly—Bartholome was holed up there.

Pete found the old Conti Vineyards card with its trademark grape cluster logo and dialed the number. The telephone rang until a recorded message finally came on and said, "You've reached Peninsula Vineyards. We're temporarily closed. Please check back often because we hope to reopen soon."

He thought some more about the manor house at the vineyard. Bartholome almost certainly had been in the house when he came to see Conti. What better place to hide out than one that was shut down because of bankruptcy? He checked the time and saw that it was a little past 1:00 p.m. He had nothing else on for that afternoon and decided to take a drive.

Unpleasant memories came back as Pete drove north along West Traverse Bay and passed the place where Lynn Hawke's car had been run off the road into the jagged rocks two years earlier. His lips tightened as he thought about the day at the morgue.

He tried not to become distracted by memories as he passed through the brown countryside and rows of dormant grape vines that covered the gentle hills. He came to the sign with Peninsula Vineyards burned into the wood. A chain stretched across the entrance to the winding drive that was lined with aspen trees, and a Coldwell Banker Schmidt Realtors sign announced that the property was for sale. Bart Ford and Alison Siles were shown as the brokers to contact.

Pete trained his Bushnell PermaFocus binoculars on the buildings on the crest of the hill and saw no vehicles or other signs that anyone was there. He drove on, looking for a secluded place to park his Range Rover.

A quarter-mile up the road, he came to a sway-backed barn with a gaping hole in the roof and assorted other dilapidated farm buildings. Confident that the place was abandoned, he turned in the dead-grass-clogged driveway. After fifty feet, he swung right and parked behind a large weeping willow. He locked his Range Rover and hoped he wouldn't have a problem getting out of the soggy area when he was ready to leave.

Pete crossed the road and walked on a diagonal toward the vineyard buildings on the hill. As he made his way through rows of brown grape vines, he paused periodically to scan the buildings. Still no signs of life. He circled around the manor house and tasting room building and saw that all of the windows were shuttered. There were no vehicles parked behind the buildings.

The gargoyle fountain in the courtyard plaza was still shut down for the winter, but he saw tire marks on the cobblestones. Most likely they'd been made by realtors who were showing the property to prospective buyers, but he had no way of knowing for sure. He inspected the area leading into the garage and saw no tire marks or signs that they'd been swept away. The garage had no windows.

He circled the manor house again and tried to see in between the blinds and window jambs. In the back, he thought he saw a light on inside the house but he couldn't be sure. He went to an adjacent window and tried to get a better look, but his view was completely blocked by something. He went back to the first window and looked in again. He saw the same light. He was tempted to break a window pane and reach in and move the blind to one side so he could get a better view, but his temptation lasted for only a fraction of a second. He peered in again and still saw the light.

TWENTY-TWO

"Coldwell Banker Schmidt Realtors," a woman answered.

"Could I speak to either Bart Ford or Alison Siles, please?"

"Who should I say is calling?"

"Pete Thorsen. I understand the old Conti Vineyards is for sale. I'm interested and would like to talk to one of them about it."

"One moment, sir."

Two minutes later, a man's voice said, "Mr. Thorsen, this is Bart Ford. I have my colleague, Alison Siles, with me and we have you on the speaker phone. We understand you're interested in the Peninsula Vineyards property."

"Yes, I was at the vineyard a couple of years ago when it was owned by Alain Conti. I thought it was the premier winery in the area. I just found out it's for sale and thought I'd inquire."

"A lot has happened in the past two years," Ford said. "Mr. Conti passed on and the couple who bought the vineyard from his estate got over-extended and had to file for bankruptcy. We're in the process of identifying potential buyers for the property. As you said, it really is the premier vineyard on the Leelanau Peninsula."

"Hypothetically, if I'm interested, what kind of complications would I run into given that the present owner is in bankruptcy?" He knew the answer to that, but wanted to sound like an interested buyer.

"That wouldn't be a problem," Siles said. "If your offer is the one accepted, the deal would be presented to the bankruptcy court judge. If he approves it, you'd be home free."

"No chance I'd become liable for any of the bankrupt party's debts?"

"None. We've done this many times."

"When can I see the property?" Pete asked.

"I should tell you up front that the asking price is $11.4 million," Ford said.

"I thought it might be in that range," Pete said, trying to sound casual. He could see Ford and Siles smiling at each other at the other end of the line, mentally calculating the commission they'd earn on the deal.

"Can you wait two weeks?" Ford asked. "Another party has an option on the property that precludes us from showing it to other potential buyers during the option period."

"An option, huh? I'll have to check with the other members of my group and see what they want to do. We have another vineyard we're also considering."

"Where's the other vineyard?" Siles asked.

"In the area. I don't want to say more than that."

"In the same price range?" she persisted.

"Sorry, I don't think it would be prudent of me to get into details."

Silence, then, "Vineyards are very hot properties these days. There are a limited number of them and a lot of interested buyers."

"Why don't we do this," Pete said. "Put me on your list. If the option holder declines to exercise for some reason, I'd appreciate it if you'd call me right away." He gave them his office number and cell phone number.

"We will," Ford said, "and if the property should open up before the option period ends, we'll call you immediately."

"I'd appreciate that."

When Pete was off the telephone with the Coldwell Banker people, he called Joe Tessler to explore an alternative for getting into the manor house. Tessler called back an hour later.

"Remember our conversation about how there are some things you can do that I can't and vice versa?"

"Of course," Tessler said. His voice sounded wary.

"I gave you a list of four names I thought could be the stalker. One of them is Gil Bartholome."

"Pete, I know that. What's your point? I only have a few minutes."

"Bartholome worked for Alain Conti if you'll recall. He's been on the lam since Conti and Sandy Sandoval shot each other. No one knows where he is, right? It occurred to me that he could be hiding out in the old Conti place." Pete told him about how Conti Vineyards had been sold, but the buyer had gone into bankruptcy and the vineyard was now vacant.

Silence, then, "You're suggesting that I search the Conti place for Bartholome if I follow what you're saying."

"Right."

Tessler didn't say anything for a few moments. Then, "I don't know, Pete. I've already pushed Frank to let me question several people on your suspect list and I'm working on him to go for search warrants. If I tell him I want to search yet another place . . ."

"I think it's worth a try, don't you?"

"Do you have anything more tangible than your suspicion that Bartholome might be there?"

"No, but I've arrived at the suspicion by putting together facts that we both know are true."

"Here's the reality. Even if I got it past Frank, I doubt the judge would buy it unless we gave him something more. He can be pretty prickly sometimes when it comes to search warrants."

"Maybe we can come up with something."

Another pause, "Uh uh, I'm not going there."

"I'm not talking about manufacturing evidence. Just shaping how we present our case."

"Have you thought about talking to Special Agent Harris as an alternative? Bartholome is a fugitive in a federal case. She shouldn't have any trouble getting a warrant."

"I've already talked to her. She as much as wished me dead."

"You irritated the hell out of her in that immigration case, you know. Maybe if you apologize to her—"

"Screw apologies."

"Pete—"

"I have to go. My daughter is calling on the other line."

"Hi, Dad." Julie sounded melancholy. Depressed even.

"Hi, Sweetie," he said, doing his best to sound more cheerful than he felt. "Anything new at school?"

"Not really."

"In a bit of a rut, huh?"

"Wayne and Aunt Maureen just left."

"It was nice of them to visit," he said, keeping his true feelings to himself.

"Not really."

"Why do you say that?"

"I was feeling good until they came. But I had to spend all my time with them and all they wanted to talk about is the knife thing. Now I'm depressed again."

Pete wanted to cut loose with a string of expletives, but kept calm and said, "Sometimes it's best to talk about ugly things as a way of getting past them. Otherwise, they linger in your subconscious and fester."

"Now you sound like that weird Dr. Speidel."

"I hope not."

"One thing I've learned from you, Dad, is to put unpleasant things behind you and look to the future. Control what you can control and don't keep angsting about the past. If angsting is a word."

"These things can take time. Besides, it won't happen again."

"How do you know it won't happen?"

"I just know. Trust me."

"Wayne and the bitch told me it *could* happen again."

"It won't. And you shouldn't call your aunt a bitch."

"She *is* a bitch. Do you know what she tried to do, Dad? She tried to drag me back to Chicago to see that shrink of hers again."

"You didn't go, obviously."

"I screamed and said if they tried to make me go, I was going to call campus security and say they were trying to kidnap me."

Pete smiled. He and her mother had raised a fighter.

"They also keep saying nasty things about you. They told me you're bad for me and said I'd realize that when I spend more time with Wayne again. He's my *real* father," she said sarcastically.

Pete seethed as Julie spoke. He was hardly surprised to hear that Wayne Sable and his sister had bad-mouthed him, but it still angered him.

"Would you come down and stay with me for a few days, Dad? You could use my bed and I could sleep on the floor. I know sleeping on the floor is hard for you older people."

Julie's request tugged at his emotions. One side of him wanted to be with her and comfort her, but the other side felt like the best thing he could do for both of them was to devote his time to finding the stalker. Either way, he knew he couldn't delay telling her the whole story any longer.

It was almost cleansing to let it all pour out. He told her how the knife incident appeared related to what had been happening to him at the lake and that the sheriff's department and the Bloomfield Hills police were coordinating their investigations. He said she had nothing to worry about because he'd hired Rae Acton to watch her dorm, emphasizing that this was just a precaution since he was the real target.

Julie was silent for a long time. Finally she said, "Why didn't you tell me this sooner, Dad?"

"Because I didn't want to worry you. I thought we had everything in hand."

"Obviously you didn't!" she said, her voice rising. "I think this is the first time you haven't been truthful with me."

"Julie—"

"You people are all the same! I'm almost seventeen, for God's sake! I'm not a baby anymore!"

"I tried to explain—"

"You're just as bad as Wayne and the bitch!" The sound of the receiver slamming the cradle rang in his ears.

Pete sat in his office and just stared at the phone. One minute he felt unburdened by telling her the truth, and the next he was under attack for not telling her sooner. He considered calling her back, but decided to give her time to settle down and regroup.

His telephone rang and his morale picked up again when he saw it was Julie. "I'm sorry for yelling at you, Dad. I'm just so . . . confused about everything."

"I know, Sweetie. You don't have to apologize. I should have told you what was going on sooner."

"No, I was wrong. And the fact you hired that person to watch my dorm . . . Now I feel terrible. You're trying to protect me. Have you hired someone to protect your cottage, too?"

"No, but I have my alarm system, remember?" He didn't want to tell her that those systems were essentially worthless based on what he'd learned from Amy Ostrowski.

"Oh yeah, I forgot." Then, "That thing about the alpacas makes me *so* mad. When Sarah was at the lake with me that time, we went to the alpaca farm south of town. They're such sweet animals. Who would do a thing like that, Dad?"

"I don't know, but we're going to catch him, that much I promise you. Tomorrow I'm going to drive down to school so I can introduce you to Rae Acton and we can talk about this some more. And Julie, please don't worry about anything. Rae is a former bodyguard for a Detroit mayor and will be outside your dorm all night to make sure nothing happens."

When they were off the phone, Pete's thoughts returned to the Conti house. He was down to his third option.

He called Rae Acton to ask her to join them for lunch the following day and then meet with him alone that afternoon.

TWENTY-THREE

J ulie met him in the dorm lobby and they hugged and she clung to him for a long time.

"I have study hall at 1:00 p.m.," she said, "but I've arranged an excused absence so we can have lunch off campus."

They piled into the Range Rover, and with Julie driving, headed for Lazzaro's in downtown Bloomfield Hills. She'd gotten her driver's license less than a year earlier and being behind the wheel was still the pinnacle of excitement for her.

Acton walked into the restaurant ten minutes after they did. She looked exactly like Pete had pictured her over the telephone. Five-five, stocky, dirty blonde hair that looked like she cut it herself, a blue leather bomber jacket over black pants and a turtle neck, very little makeup. Pete introduced her to Julie.

After they'd settled in, Julie continued to stare at Acton wide-eyed and finally blurted out, "Are you really a detective?"

"Private, honey." She looked like it wasn't the first time she'd gotten that question.

Julie asked hesitantly, "Do you — what's that expression — carry?"

"Wouldn't leave the house without it," Acton said, continuing to look amused.

Julie hadn't satisfied her curiosity about the first female detective, private or otherwise, she'd met. "Where do you keep it?" she asked sheepishly.

"Julie . . ."

"That's okay," Acton said to Pete, "let's get this out of the way." She glanced around to make sure no one was watching, then opened her jacket to display a small semi-automatic in a modified shoulder holster. "When you have my waist, honey, you don't have to worry about the bulge your firearm makes."

Julie's eyes were glued to the gun. "That isn't very big," she finally said.

"Believe me, the few bad guys I've had to pull it on thought it was *very* big."

"Have you ever shot anyone?" Julie asked.

"Haven't had to."

"Then how do you know you could if you had to?" Julie asked with a tinge of doubt in her voice.

"Look at my eyes, Honey. Do I look like the kind of girl who kids around?"

Julie stared at her awe-struck and shook her head.

"Alright, young lady," Pete said, "enough of the interrogation. Now do you feel comfortable knowing that Rae is around?"

"Yes, that awful man won't *dare* come near our dorm now."

They ate lunch and chatted. Then Pete told Acton that he'd see her in an hour and drove Julie back to school. She hugged him and thanked him for coming down and told him about seven times how much better she felt with Rae watching over her. Then she raced into the dorm and disappeared. Pete watched her go with a lump in his throat.

Rae Acton's office was in Clawson, closer in to Detroit, over a pizza parlor. The pleasant aroma from the ovens shadowed him up the narrow staircase to the second floor. Maybe Acton's choice of office locations had something to do with her expansive waistline.

Pete knocked on the door with "Acton & Yuba" stenciled on the pebbled glass. He pushed it open when he heard a gruff voice call, "Door's open." Rae Acton was sitting on one side of a partner's desk writing in a spiral notebook. The other side had an empty chair and overflowed with paper. Acton saw who it was and waved toward the only side chair in the office. "Take a load off, hon. I'll be with you in a jiff."

Acton snapped her notebook shut and swiveled her chair around to face him. "That daughter of yours is a real sweetheart."

Pete nodded and smiled.

"I'm planning to keep watching her dorm until you call me off."

"I want to be sure she's not in any danger before you stop."

"It's your dime, hon. I can always use the cash."

"I have something else I want to talk to you about." He proceeded to give her more detail about the stalking incidents than he had before, including the two at the lake, and told her about the names on his suspect list. He said that one of them, Gil Bartholome, might be holed up in the vacant manor house at the vineyard once owned by Alain Conti.

"When you were there, you thought you saw a light on inside, huh?"

"Yes, and there were car or truck tracks in the courtyard, but I couldn't tell whether they'd been made by the real estate people or someone else."

"Namely, this guy Bartholome."

"The thought crossed my mind."

"Did you look in the garage to see whether there were any vehicles in there?"

Pete shook his head. "No windows. Plus any tracks in or out of the garage might have been swept away."

"What exactly would you like me to do?"

"Help me get a look inside the house."

She looked at him impassively. "I thought that's where you might be headed." She tapped her pencil on the desk for a few moments, then looked at him again and said, "I could get my ticket pulled for breaking into someone's house, you know."

"If you're caught."

"You always have to assume you *might* be caught."

"I'm a lawyer, Rae. What do you think might happen to me if we were to get caught?"

"I don't know anything about your professional rules, but I suspect you might get your ticket pulled, too."

"I might. But I have to know whether Bartholome is around or if I can scratch him off my list and focus on other suspects. You met my daughter. I think you can understand how I feel."

She tapped her pencil on the desk some more, then looked at her watch. "I have to call my partner about a business matter that involves confidential client information," she said. "It'll take ten or fifteen minutes. Rather than have you stand in the hall, could I ask you to go downstairs and pick up two pieces of pepperoni for me? I need an afternoon pick-me-up." She dug around in her purse for money.

"Put that away. The pizza is on me."

As he walked out, she called, "Get something for yourself, too."

Pete took his time negotiating the bare concrete stairs again. The pizzeria was empty except for a young guy maybe twenty-five or thirty years old kneading dough into crusts for the evening trade. "What can I do you for?" Pizza Guy asked. "If you want special order, it'll be a half-hour, forty minutes."

"I want two slices of pepperoni for a friend," he said, looking at the pizzas in the warming oven.

Pizza Guy's freckled face crinkled into a Howdy Doody grin. "Your friend wouldn't be Rae Acton, would it?"

"How did you guess?"

"She comes down for her pizza fix every afternoon around this time. Two slices of pepperoni. Has to be fresh made since noon, nothing left over from the previous day. I just took one out of the oven."

"You know your customers."

He chuckled. "After four years, you begin to catch on."

"I still have ten minutes to kill. Take your time."

Pete sat in one of the two booths and watched Pizza Guy work the dough. He gave it a few extra minutes and walked back to the counter.

"Two pieces of fresh pepperoni, coming right up," Pizza Guy said. He removed the pizza from the warmer, rolled his slicer, and put two generous pieces in a Styrofoam box.

Pete paid him, left a healthy tip, and climbed the stairs to the second floor again. Acton was off the telephone and said as he walked in, "I could smell the pizza coming up the steps." She opened the box, inhaled the aroma, and began to munch on a slice like she hadn't had anything to eat since the previous day.

"I talked to Adam," she mumbled between bites. "He assured me that you aren't trying to set me up." She opened a desk drawer and pulled out a handful of paper napkins and mopped the tomato paste off her lips.

"You called Adam Rose about me?"

"I'm a careful lady, Pete. That's why I'm still in business."

Pete just stared at her.

"Accepting a stakeout assignment for you is one thing," Acton said. "Breaking into someone's house is a whole different animal."

"I'm glad I passed muster," he said caustically.

Rae shrugged and took another bite of pizza.

Pete got over his momentary pique and laid out the former Conti house for her as he remembered it. He told her about the alarm system and how he'd set off the metal detector in the foyer in the middle of the day.

"Do you know if the alarm system also has a silent feature that connects to the security company or directly to the police?"

"I don't know, but we should assume that it probably does. I also don't know if the people who bought the vineyard from Conti's estate kept the alarm system, but again, we need to assume they did."

"And whether the alarm system is operative even though the house is vacant," Acton said.

Pete nodded. When Rae didn't say anything, he drew on his meager knowledge of alarm systems from his conversation with Amy Ostrowski and said, "I understand there are devices that can suppress alarms or create false alarms."

"I think that's right."

"Do you know how they work?"

"I know a little."

Pete smiled and said, "So you've done this before."

"I didn't say that. I said I know a little about the devices."

As Pete drove north on I-75, he felt like he'd had a successful day for a change. Most importantly, he was back in Julie's good graces and had calmed her fears. He'd also arranged for someone who was competent at what she did to accompany him back to the old Conti house to determine whether Bartholome was hiding out there. They'd set the operation for the following night. Acton's partner, Xavier Yuba, would handle the stakeout duties at Julie's dorm while she was gone.

Pete pulled into his driveway after 10:00 p.m. feeling drained. He went to the mailbox and got his mail and tossed it on the kitchen table. He ate a container of yogurt and then went through what had become a nightly ritual of checking the doors and windows to make sure they were locked and setting his house alarm. As he'd learned more about residential alarm systems, he wondered what use they were.

Before going up to bed, he flipped through the mail and saw another letter from Robyn Fleming. He grimaced and threw it back on the table with disgust. He walked up the stairs wondering if she'd put a new spin on her usual vitriol or whether it was the same-old, same-old.

TWENTY-FOUR

As Pete guided Rae Acton on the best route to the former Conti Vineyards, they went over their plan again and she asked him some questions he couldn't answer. She looked as calm as if she were headed to bingo night at the American Legion hall. He, on the other hand, tried to control the butterflies flitting around in his stomach and hoped he didn't look as nervous as he felt.

The latest letter from Robyn merely repackaged her familiar grievances based on her distorted view of what had happened. It tore him up to think that a woman he once counted among his close friends now viewed him as an arch-fiend to be vilified whenever possible. When this was over, maybe he'd make another trip to the prison and try once again to convince her that he wasn't the one who led to her arrest.

He must have looked distracted because Acton glanced his way and said, "Having second thoughts about this venture, hon?"

"Just thinking about something else," he said. They passed through Suttons Bay and he told her where to turn off M-22 to get to the vineyard.

Acton stopped when they got to the entrance. The buildings on the hill looked eerie in the moonlight. "That's it, huh?" Acton said.

Pete nodded.

According to plan, Acton continued past the vineyard entrance and parked behind the same willow at the abandoned farm Pete had used as cover before. Acton shouldered her backpack and they started toward the manor house. The moon provided enough light to see and let them avoid using flashlights that someone driving past might notice.

When they got within a hundred feet of the house, Acton stopped by a tree and slid the backpack off. She pulled out a pair of night vision goggles and slipped them on. Then she took another device out of the pack that looked like it had a miniature touch pad. She punched in a number and waited. She repeated the process several times. Fifteen minutes later, she said to Pete in a low voice, "The system was armed. I'm pretty sure I disabled it, but be prepared to haul tail if I'm wrong."

They moved to the house and worked their way around the perimeter. Pete squinted in the narrow gap between the shade and window frame where he saw a light the last time he was there. It was still on. Acton peered in and saw the light, too.

When they got back to the front door, Acton fished in her backpack again and withdrew two pairs of latex gloves and handed one pair to Pete. Then she took out a small case and unzipped it to reveal a collection of long, thin instruments. Burglar tools, he thought, smiling. He could never have done this by himself.

Acton probed in the lock with one of the instruments, listening for the tumblers to move, then tried another instrument. Pete glanced toward the road every minute or so as she worked. After what seemed like an eternity, Acton nodded at him.

She reached under her jacket and pulled out her Colt Challenger. Then she slowly opened the door which moved silently on its hinges. The house was dark inside except for a light at the end of the hall. That must be what they'd seen through the window. Acton closed the door and whispered, "Let's check the garage first. No flashlights. Put your hand on my shoulder."

He followed Acton like she were a guide dog. They passed through what he thought was the foyer where he'd set off the alarm earlier. Not a sound this time. Either the metal detector was off or Acton had disabled it along with the rest of the system. He did his version of the penguin walk so he wouldn't step on the backs of her feet, and had constant visions that Gil Bartholome was about to pop up behind him and blow a hole in his back.

Acton turned right and stopped. He kept a hand on her shoulder and felt her lean forward. Lights suddenly came on and the brilliance blinded him. His heart thumped and he raised an arm to shield his eyes. He looked behind them, panicked, but then realized what had happened. It wasn't Bartholome. The lights had come on automatically when Acton opened the door to the garage. It was empty.

Acton backed up and eased the door closed again. The lights faded. "Upstairs?" she whispered.

He nodded.

"We should do it in five minutes max and then split," she said. "Follow me again because I have the weapon."

She squeezed past him and he put his hand on her shoulder again. They used the stairs instead of taking the elevator Conti had installed because of his failing health, and following her instructions, he switched from her shoulder and grabbed the bottom of her jacket. He scrambled to keep up with her and banged his knee on one of the marble steps when he slipped. What if Bartholome *was* here and had a gun? That would be bad news whether he shot at them or Acton got her shot in first.

They reached the second floor and Pete placed his hand on Acton's shoulder again and penguin-walked behind her. His heart thumped again and he wondered if his misstep on the stairs made as much noise as he imagined it did.

When they came to a bedroom door, Acton reached in and clicked on the light and jumped into the doorway in a crouch. Her Colt swept the room. Empty. She turned the light off and moved to the next door and did the same thing. That room was empty as well. They checked the other three bedrooms and found all of them empty. There were no signs that someone had been staying in any of the rooms.

"Satisfied?" Acton whispered.

Pete had been thinking about the basement, and when they got back to the first floor, he said, "Can we check the basement?"

He could feel her eyes on him in the dark. "Follow me. But two more minutes and then we have to get out of here."

Without waiting for him to say more, she said, "Hand on the shoulder. Let's hurry."

They found the stairwell to the basement. Pete followed her down the steps with one hand on her shoulder and the other on the handrail. When they reached the bottom, Acton paused to listen, then snapped the light on and jumped forward with her weapon in the ready position again. They made their way around the basement and looked in several smaller rooms and found nothing.

"No one here, Pete," she said in a hoarse whisper. "Time to exit."

Pete followed her back up the steps. He'd thought about suggesting that they check the tasting house, too, but the chances of Bartholome hiding out there were remote at best. Besides, if he were to suggest it, he'd probably have to do it alone because it was clear that Acton felt that they'd accomplished their mission.

They made sure all of the lights in the house were out, then eased out the front door. Acton tested the handle to make sure the door was locked. As they walked hurriedly away, Acton held out her hand and whispered, "Gloves." He stripped them off and she jammed both pairs in her backpack.

They retraced their route through the grapevines toward Acton's car. When they were halfway down the gentle hill, a vehicle with its headlights on bright pulled into the vineyard entrance and stopped in front of the chain. They crouched behind some dormant grape vines. The driver got out of his vehicle and fussed with the lock that secured the chain, then got back in and continued up the drive.

The vehicle's lights illuminated the buildings as it approached the top of the hill. The driver maneuvered around the closed-down fountain and through the parking area. He flashed his spotlight on the buildings and around the vineyard. Then he headed back toward the highway and his spotlight probed the grapevines again.

They watched as the man re-hooked the chain and drove off. Pete expelled air. Thankfully, it was just a private security service and not someone responding to an alarm at the property.

"Timing is everything," Acton said, still looking relaxed. "Things might have gotten hairy if we'd still been in the house and that guard saw lights inside go on and off. Or if his spotlight had picked us up on the hill."

They walked through the brush along the road, then cut over to the abandoned farm driveway where Acton's car was parked. Acton tossed her backpack in the rear of her SUV and pulled the protective cover closed. She fired up the engine, but before she turned on her headlights said to Pete, smiling, "Are you sure you don't want to go back for another look?"

"Not tonight, ma'am."

"Adam will enjoy this story." She looked at him with a smile still tugging at her lips.

Pete was quiet on the way back to the lake. He'd let himself get pumped up over the prospect that Bartholome might be holed up in the manor house, and now that he knew that wasn't the case, he felt a little deflated. Like he'd felt some other times recently.

It was after midnight when Acton pulled in his driveway and parked with her motor running and the headlights on.

"What's my tab to date?" Pete asked her. "I want you to continue the stakeouts, but let's settle up through tonight."

Acton clicked on the overhead light and went through the math and showed him a number. "That includes double my usual rate for tonight. Combat zone pay I call it."

Pete gulped when he saw the total and was writing out a check when Acton said, "What's that on the side of your vehicle?"

He hadn't paid any attention when they drove in, but now he looked at his Range Rover and saw something that resembled words. He handed Acton the check, then got out and shined his flashlight beam on the side of his Range Rover.

TWENTY-FIVE

P*ete Thorsen a/k/a Asshole* had been scratched into the paint in double-line letters six-inches high. He went around to the driver's side and saw a similar message in even more graphic language. The note tucked under his wiper blade read, *Just so people know what you are Pete. If they had any doubt.* Like the other notes, it was printed in oversized letters.

Acton had been following him around the vehicle. "Maybe you should be looking closer to home," she said.

Pete stared at the ground and didn't speak for a long time. "Goddamn it!" he suddenly screamed into the night. He kicked at the gravel and sent a shower of pebbles into the air. Some of them pinged against metal. He kicked again. And then again, trying to purge the anger and frustration he felt.

Acton didn't flinch at his outburst. She gave him a few moments and said, "Are you going to call the sheriff?"

Pete continued to stare at the ground.

"Anything I can do to help?" she asked, clearly beginning to feel uncomfortable with his silence.

"Not now, Rae," he muttered, finally focusing on her words. "Just continue to watch Julie's dorm as we agreed."

"I think I'll hit the road then. I'm sorry about your vehicle."

Pete looked at her and said, "If you want to stay overnight and drive down in the morning, you're welcome to use Julie's bedroom."

"Thanks, but I think I'll go tonight. My internal clock is so used to night stakeouts that I'm wide awake. Daytime is when I get sleepy."

"Okay, drive safely. And thanks for tonight."

When she was gone, Pete walked around his Range Rover again and saw another obscene message on the hatchback that he hadn't noticed before.

He kicked at the gravel again.

Joe Tessler recorded the words scratched into the Range Rover's paint in his notebook and shook his head. "What is this, the third incident?"

"Fourth."

Tessler appeared to count. "That's right, four with the one involving your daughter."

Pete's anger had dissipated and now he felt drained and unfocused.

"I'm going to get Frank out for a first-hand look at this," Tessler said. "Then I'm going to put the screws on him to go for a warrant to search Calvin Seitz's shack. And his pickup, too. I keep thinking about the blood. Killing a couple of alpacas is messy business and we might find trace evidence in his vehicle from the bag."

"Don't forget Randy's truck."

"That too. Then I'll take a drive over to Thompsonville to question Kurt Romer."

All things he'd been harping on for days, Pete thought, but he didn't say anything.

Tessler looked at the Range Rover again. "What's your plan for the vehicle?" he asked. "Are you going to have it repainted or what?"

Pete laughed disgustedly. "Maybe I'll burn it. With Calvin Seitz inside."

Tessler's eyes flicked his way. After a few moments, he said, "I'm going to take some photographs. Can I use your camera again?"

"You *have* my camera, Joe. Remember?"

Tessler got a blank look on his face, and then a light went on and he said, "I didn't give it back, did I?"

The sheriff arrived an hour later with a sour look on his face, like he resented being called to Pete's cottage for the second time in ten days, and handed Pete's camera to Tessler without looking his way. He walked around the Range Rover and looked at the words scratched into the paint.

"What proof do you have that this is connected to the blood thing?" he asked Tessler.

"This is the fourth incident. All of them have been targeted at Mr. Thorsen. Same M.O. in each case. An event of some kind, usually on Mr. Thorsen's property, and a note. There's a pattern. The notes also seem to have come from the same printer using oversized letters."

"Where's the note the perp left this time?"

Tessler retrieved it from his vehicle and showed the sheriff.

"This was left under the wiper blade?"

Tessler nodded.

Richter glanced at the note again, then toward Pete who'd been standing quietly while the sheriff and his detective talked. "This guy must really be pissed at you. So far, he hasn't tried to physically attack you though, right?"

Pete glared at him. "I'm still alive if that's what you mean."

"A man can only sustain his anger so long," Richter said. "Maybe this is the last of it."

"It's not the last of it," Pete muttered.

Tessler said, "When I was with the Chicago PD, we had a case something like this. The perp toyed with this woman for a month, did all kinds of crazy things to get into her head, and then killed her. The police psychologist said the perp got his jollies as much from the preliminaries as he did from the actual killing."

"Do we have any evidence something like that might happen here?" Richter asked.

"Evidence!" Pete said, raising his voice. "For crissakes, do you know what's been happening?"

"We think someone is stalking Mr. Thorsen and his daughter," Tessler said, trying to ease the tension.

Richter looked at Pete. "If you're sure of that, you should give us a name."

Tessler jumped in again and said, "He did, Frank. He gave me a list of possibilities." He seemed to be trying to walk the line between not sounding too eager to take Pete's side and setting the record straight.

"Is old Calvin Seitz one of them?" Richter said. "I already gave you permission to question him."

"He is and I did question him. He denies having anything to do with it. Claims he was with his brother on the nights in question."

"Calvin has lived in this area for twenty years," Richter said. "I can't believe he's the one we should be looking for. He's a character, is all."

"His brother is more than a character."

Richter looked at Tessler with raised eyebrows. "I don't know the brother. Have you met him?"

Tessler nodded. "I questioned him when I questioned Calvin. He has a long record. Drug convictions. In the joint a couple of years for carving a guy up with a knife. Domestic violence charges involving his girlfriend, including for lurking outside her building day and night."

"Drugs huh?" Richter said. "Do you think that's why he's up here?"

"Possible, but I haven't seen anything so far to tie him to the problems we've been having," Tessler said. "He claims he's visiting his brother and I can't prove or disprove his story."

Richter looked at Pete and said, "You've got your own problems with Calvin from what Deputy Varga tells me. I understand he's considering filing a complaint against you for running him off the road."

Pete scoffed. "That's a bunch of bull. It's part of his vendetta against me. Joe knows the story. When you were investigating the Thomas

Edinger murder last year, I mentioned that Seitz hunts with a smooth-bore and Joe questioned him. He's been after me ever since. That's why I put him at the top of my suspect list. The guy's a psycho."

"Just because he's a little eccentric doesn't make him a psycho."

"A *little* eccentric? He's certifiably nuts. And dangerous with his brother around. The two of them assaulted me the other day at a gas station right in the middle of town."

"I haven't heard anything about an assault."

"It happened, trust me."

Tessler shifted around nervously. It was obvious that he hadn't said anything to Richter about the incident at the Shell station.

The sheriff walked around Pete's Range Rover again and inspected the damage. He looked Tessler's way and said, "Keep me posted. We need to sort this out."

Tessler came back that afternoon to return Pete's camera.

"We must have softened Frank up this morning. Just before I left to come over here again, I asked him if he had any objection to me questioning Kurt Romer to make sure we were on the same page. He acted like he'd ordered me to do it a month ago. He also wanted to know where the request was for a warrant to search Calvin's shack and the Seitz brothers' vehicles."

Pete grunted derisively. "I suppose I should be grateful. I'm not dead yet."

A smile tugged at the corners of Tessler's mouth. "You had some help. Earlier, the two ladies from Heavenly Meadows were in our office working on Frank like a couple of buzz saws. They were crying and holding his feet to the fire for answers about what he was doing to find the killer of their alpacas. I swear, I've never seen Frank look so uncomfortable in all the years I've known him."

Pete had to smile in spite of everything. He let Tessler savor the moment and then said, "Do you know what else you can do?"

"Is it legal?"

"Yes. You contact the prison in Indianapolis where Robyn Fleming is locked up and find out if they keep a visitors log. I'd like to know who's been visiting her."

Tessler's eyes narrowed as he studied Pete. "You suspect she might be pulling the strings from inside the prison the way she did when she hired the guy from Traverse City to sabotage her old boyfriend's hang glide wing, right?"

"I don't know what to believe anymore. I'm just covering all the possibilities."

"Okay, I'll see if I can find out. The only one on your list that we haven't talked about is that Bartholome guy."

"Forget him for now. I'm convinced that he's not in the area." He knew better than to tell Tessler what he and Acton had done the previous night and he had no idea where else to look for him.

Tessler put his spiral notepad and pen in his pocket and said, "I'm finally beginning to think we're making some progress with Frank on board and everything."

"We'll see," Pete said wearily.

"Question — and don't get me wrong, I'll try to get a list of Robyn's visitors and plan to question Kurt Romer — but why do you want to do these things if you're sure the Seitz brothers are behind this?"

"I told you, I'm being thorough."

"Okay."

"Do you think there's anything else we can do with Calvin and Randy?" Pete asked.

"Such as?"

"Maybe stake them out at night to see if they make another move?"

Tessler shook his head for about thirty seconds. "I don't think there's a chance in hell of that. With our budget cut-backs, we have barely enough staff to maintain one deputy on duty through the night."

When Tessler was gone, Pete looked at his Range Rover again. He grimaced and wandered down to the strip of sand in front of his cottage and sat on a fallen birch and thought. He tossed pebbles into the quiet water and watched the concentric circles spread and gradually fade.

The notes didn't sound like something crazy Calvin Seitz would write, but he couldn't say the same for brother Randy. Or for Kurt Romer.

TWENTY-SIX

Pete was thinking about what he was going to do for dinner when the telephone rang.

"Pete, it's Eve. I know this is a *very* late invitation, but I need to get out of the house for a couple of hours. I remember you saying that The Manitou is one of your favorite restaurants. If you're free, can I invite you for dinner?"

"You must be telepathic because I was just thinking my choice of food tonight was going to be between Lean Cuisine's Swedish meatballs or its turkey medallions with dressing."

"Does that mean yes?"

They agreed to meet at the restaurant at 7:00 p.m.

As Pete was showering, all he could think about was his Range Rover with the obscene words scratched into the sides and how he would keep Eve from seeing them.

He arrived at The Manitou early. Normally, he parked along M-22, but tonight he pulled into the small lot adjacent to the low-slung building that was protected on three sides by trees and bushes. He found a spot at the very end, as far from the restaurant as possible, so only the driver's side of his Range Rover was exposed. With the dim light in the lot, the chances of someone seeing the vehicle in its sorry state were slim. That's what he hoped anyway.

He checked in with the hostess and waited in the small seating area for Eve to arrive. The familiar black bear glared down at him with its beady eyes, and in the central dining room straight ahead, the walls were adorned with trophy fish and antlers and artifacts like a pair of old-time snowshoes. In the bar area to the right, a miniature pontoon airplane hung over the booth that he and Harry McTigue frequently occupied when they dined there.

As he waited for Eve, he flipped through an issue of *Field & Stream*, a publication he hadn't read in two decades. It contained articles about hunting whitetail deer with a smoothbore, which seemed apropos given how much Calvin Seitz was on his mind these days, and running a trap line for muskrats. He was looking at a glossy four-page spread of photographs taken at a Ducks Unlimited dinner in Manhattan, that mecca of outdoor activity, when Eve walked in.

A spark coursed through his body. Her raven-colored hair was down again and she wore black pants that caressed her curves and a blood-red blouse under her short leather jacket. A silk scarf knotted around her neck gave her a flamboyant look.

"Been waiting long?"

"Hours and hours," he said with a straight face.

She gave him a knowing smile and a little nudge and they followed the hostess to their table. They had their choice of where to sit because the restaurant was at most half full.

Eve looked tense, but there were no signs that she'd seen his Range Rover. She took her jacket off and hung it on the back of her chair and tossed her hair away from the eye it usually concealed. Even in this day and age, Pete thought, women still seemed uncomfortable calling a man for dinner after treating him to drinks only a short time before. He did his best to put her at ease.

"And your day was?"

"Busy," she said, breathing out and flipping her hair again. "I have two new clients. Personal trainer doesn't quite describe my role with them. Personal slave would be a better term."

"Demanding, huh."

She shook her head and looked exasperated. "When they aren't in the fitness center, they call me on my cell about the weight they're scheduled to lift in their next session, whether they should go completely glutin-free in their diets, what I think of Nike versus Adidas shoes, and blah, blah, blah. It never ends."

"All weighty questions."

"Would you pick out some wine for us while I unwind?"

"Happy to. There's some great Pinot Noir on the card that was bottled before glutin-free ever entered our vocabulary."

She smiled.

The waiter brought the wine and opened it and gave him a splash to taste.

"As good as ever?" she asked.

"I think so." He smiled and clinked her glass and said, "To clients everywhere. Life would be great if you could separate their money from the hassle."

"Do you put your Chicago clients in that category?"

"I was lucky," he said. "I had great clients." He told her about the evolution of his practice with Sears & Whitney from associate to partner to managing partner. He also told her about deal-making, which was a major part of what he did, and some of the clients he represented, particularly those in Europe and from other countries. He told stories about his frequent trips abroad to tend relationships or work on transactions.

"And you gave all of that up to move up here to the sticks?"

"The locals would prefer you say God's country. But that's right, I gave it up because I wanted to do something else with the rest of my life.

Sounds like I'm not much different than you." He didn't say anything about the death of his wife and the other things that factored into his decision.

"Where did you live when you were in Chicago?" he asked, changing the subject.

"North side. Wrigleyville, that area."

"If you lived in Wrigleyville, you must be a Cubs fan."

The one eye he could see was cloaked in horror. "Baseball? I hate baseball. It's like watching two tortoises race."

"What sport do you like then?"

"Boxing."

"You're kidding. I've never met a woman who likes boxing."

"You have now. It's fast, has a skill-set that's similar to the martial arts."

"Have you ever boxed?"

"No, but I've thought about trying it."

"If you do, maybe I could be your manager. We'd make you as famous as Muhammad Ali's daughter."

"Laila," she said. "I might be a shade below her in ability, but I bet I could hold my own."

"Harry tells me you're a black belt, too."

"Now who's checking other people out?"

"That's the way we men are. We like to know everything."

They both laughed at the familiarity of what he'd said.

"What degree are you?"

"Third."

"My late wife was a first degree."

"How about you? Are you into the martial arts?"

"Of course. I hold a green belt. Some people don't know what that is. I tell them it's the skill level just below defenseless."

They laughed again.

They got their orders in and moved on to other subjects. She seemed endlessly fascinated with his rural upbringing and wanted to know what it was like to put up hay for the winter and create silage and milk cows.

His stories about squirting milk at barn cats during his milking chores amused her.

The waitress came with their food and interrupted further conversation about his youth. He had The Trawler like he did much of the time when he went to The Manitou and she had the Nutty Trout. Eve didn't look anything like Lynn Hawke, but she had the same coy habit of occasionally leaning over to sample his sea scallops or shrimp.

"What did you do in the army?" Pete asked.

"If I tell you, I'll have to kill you, you know that don't you?" she said with a feigned gleam in the one eye he could see.

He chuckled and said, "I'll take my chances."

She leaned forward and whispered "Human intelligence" while looking around furtively.

He thought back to his days in the army and said, "That's where they collect the dope on enemy forces, isn't it?"

"That's what they say and it's supposed to be oh so covert. Do you know what my job was? I read newspaper articles all day about how many tanks the Cuban army reportedly had and how many troops comprise a platoon in the Polish infantry."

"You must be multi-lingual."

"Hardly. One section of our group translated foreign newspapers and periodicals into English and the rest of us read the translated articles and summarized them."

"Specialization," Pete said, chuckling again.

Eve rolled her visible eye. "Do you know what my most interesting army assignment was? I was stationed at Fort Lee in Virginia for a year and finagled my way into becoming a judge for the Best Warrior Competition."

"No kidding."

"I convinced the colonel in charge of the competition that a woman should be on their judging team. I think he had something in mind other than my judging skills when he agreed to add me, though. How about you? I understand you were a sleuth when you were in the army."

"Flunky would be a better term." He told her how he'd volunteered for temporary duty driving a major in the CID around Germany and how the temporary assignment continued to get extended until it was time for him to rotate back to the States.

"Well you have Harry convinced you were a sleuth."

He shook his head and laughed. "In case you haven't discovered it yet, you can only believe about ten percent of what Harry tells you." He also knew it would be useless to lecture his friend about talking about him. Much as it irritated him at times, he knew it was his way of building him up, especially to women.

"With your training as a sleuth, I'm surprised you haven't been able to find the person who's been stalking you."

He remembered their conversation at the hotel bar and said, "So that's why you invited me to dinner. You're planning to get me over-served so I'll tell you who's on my suspect list."

"If that's what it takes." Their wine was gone so she flagged the waitress down and ordered two more glasses of Pinot Noir. "Do you want to take a sip before you tell me?"

"Boy," he said, "you should have stayed in the military and requested duty at Gitmo interrogating prisoners."

"Are you impressed?"

"Particularly with your persistence. All right, I'll give you a couple of names if you promise to keep this conversation quiet." He told her about Kurt Romer and the Seitz brothers and what their motives might be for stalking him.

"Both logical suspects. Do you want my opinion?"

"Sure." He took another sip of his wine.

"I lean toward Romer. He sounds like what a friend of mine used to call a 'scary dude.' Plus it seems like he might have a crafty side. Calvin Seitz sounds like a crazy who lets it all hang out. I don't know about the brother. He doesn't have the same motivation as Calvin and Mr. Romer, but you never know."

"Pretty much my analysis, but I'm not ready to cross anyone off yet." He told about his confrontations with the Seitz brothers.

She shook her head. "You *are* a cowboy. Car chases, rumbles with guys at the gas pump. I never would have expected it from just looking at you."

"I may look like Clark Kent, but under this oxford shirt I've got blue Spandex with a big 'S' on the chest."

"Anyone else on your list, Clark?"

"No one worth mentioning."

"I thought you said your old mentor in the CID taught you to be thorough and gather all of the possibilities and then sift and winnow them down."

"The sifting and winnowing part is my term. It's from the motto inscribed on the front of the flagship building on the campus of my alma mater."

"But that's what Major What's-His-Name meant isn't it?"

"It is."

"Knowing that, you're saying there aren't *any* other suspects in the back of your mind?"

"Maybe a name or two, but they're so far-fetched that they aren't worth mentioning."

"Such as? If you want me to help you analyze this, I have to know what you know, Mr. Sleuth."

Pete was becoming tired of fending off Eve's questions. He wanted to find out more about her and instead she was prying details out of him that he preferred not to get into. "Okay," he said, "last name. Gil Bartholome." He told her how Bartholome fit into the picture and what his motive might be.

"It sounds like he might be an even stronger suspect than that Romer guy."

"Except that we've pretty much established that he's not in the area. He's of Mexican descent and the detective in the sheriff's office thinks he might be hiding out down there."

"It would be pretty hard for him to do the things that have been happening to you if he's in Mexico."

"Harry's perceptiveness must have rubbed off on you. Anyway, I'm thinking more and more like the sheriff's department and wondering if the dirty tricks have run their course. Both Romer and the Seitz brothers know they're being watched and nothing has happened for a while." He purposely didn't get into the latest incidents at Julie's school or his defaced Range Rover.

"Then your life will settle down again, huh?"

"Back to a ho-hum existence," he agreed.

She reached across the table and put her hand on his. "It's been a rough period, hasn't it?"

He shrugged and turned his hand over so he could hold hers. It was warm and soft, not like the hand of a third-degree black belt who could shut his lights off with a solid kick to the head.

"I have an idea," he said. "If you follow me home, I bet I can scrounge up some premium Pinot Noir for us to sip. Then I'll regale you with a few of the oldies you've heard so many lies about from Harry. Does that sound like a plan?"

"It sounds like a *wonderful* plan, but I'm going to have to pass for tonight. You know those slaveholders I told you about earlier? One of them is coming to the fitness center at 7:00 a.m. tomorrow for one of our sessions. If I greet him with a fat head, he'll trade me in for a younger slave."

Pete tried to conceal his disappointment and said, "Just a thought. We'll do it some other time." As he spoke, he remembered his defaced Range Rover and wondered how he would have explained the graphics on the sides if she'd accepted his invitation.

Eve snatched the check as soon as the waitress placed it on the table between them and insisted on paying because it was her invitation. Pete walked her to her car which thankfully was parked on M-22 and not in the restaurant's lot. She clicked the door opener and turned to face him and say goodnight. No one else was around so he moved close and kissed her on the mouth. She kissed him back and pressed her body against his. Their tongues probed each other's mouths. A car was approaching and Eve stepped back and held each of his hands in hers. When the car had passed, she kissed him again and murmured, "Call me."

She slipped into her black Ford Escape, fired up the engine, and picked up speed as she headed south on M-22.

Pete watched her go and began planning their next date.

TWENTY-SEVEN

Pete had just gotten back from Traverse City after dropping off his Range Rover at the body shop when his office telephone rang. It was Kyle Cummings from his old law firm in Chicago. Cummings was the partner who handled the family law issues for him when his wife, Doris, died.

"Have you checked your e-mail today?" Cummings asked.

"Not yet. I had to do something this morning and just got in my office."

"I'll hold while you read the one from me. Your friend Wayne Sable has just filed a motion asking Judge Rosenberg to modify his order and revoke your visitation rights with Julie."

"Just a minute, Kyle," Pete said. He pulled up the e-mail and scanned the attachments. He got a sickening feeling in his stomach.

"I've glanced at everything," he muttered. "I think I've got the gist."

"You may recall that after Doris died," Cummings said, "custody of Julie was awarded to Wayne Sable as her biological father. You were granted liberal visitation rights because while you never adopted her, she lived under your roof from the time she was a very small girl and actually—"

"Kyle, I know all of that. What I'm looking at is the grounds Sable's lawyer is alleging as the basis of his motion. They're saying I lead a reckless lifestyle and it's endangering Julie's physical well-being and psychological health." Front and center as support for the motion was the knife incident at Julie's school.

"They've also attached an affidavit from some psychiatrist who claims he examined Julie and concluded that she's suffering—and I'm interpreting here—substantial mental trauma as a result of finding the knife in her door."

"Is Angie in the office?" Pete asked, referring to his former partner Angie DeMarco who had handled the litigation aspects of the original custody case. He waited while Cummings checked.

Cummings returned to the line and said, "Her secretary said she's in court. She's expected back around noon our time. I—"

Pete cut him off again and said, "I'd appreciate it if you and Angie would call me back as soon as she returns from court. My impression is that the motion is bullshit, but we need to come up with a response."

When he was off the phone, he printed out the documents that Sable's lawyer had filed with the court and read them more carefully. Besides the knife incident, the documents listed three other incidents that Pete had been involved in as examples of his so-called reckless lifestyle: The shooting incident in the Colonel's office where Pete had been an innocent bystander, another shooting incident involving rivals in a counterfeit immigration document ring where Pete was also caught in the middle, and the time Pete was trapped in a basement and barely escaped with his life. Julie wasn't involved in any of those incidents, and in fact Pete had deliberately kept the details from her, but they were asserted to buttress the knife incident and show a pattern.

He read the psychiatrist's affidavit. It was filled with jargon, but as Kyle Cummings had said, essentially concluded that Julie had been badly traumatized by the knife incident. Dr. Speidel said that in his professional opinion, Julie needed psychiatric care on an ongoing basis to adjust to what had happened and recover her mental health.

A second affidavit from Maureen Fesko recounted what happened at her house following the incident when Pete showed up unannounced and pressured her into allowing Julie to return to school in spite of Dr. Speidel's advice. The affidavit painted Pete in the worst light possible, saying among other things that Pete forced his way into the house, was abusive to her, and refused to leave even though he was repeatedly asked to do so. No mention was made of competing facts such as that Julie was ecstatic to see him and that she had told him she was being held in Maureen's house against her will and wanted to return to school.

Pete reread the documents and seethed as he focused on the omissions and distortions in them. As a lawyer, he knew that was typical of court pleadings and affidavits. A competent lawyer, if she were ethical, didn't misstate anything, but packaged the facts and legal arguments in a way that would best support her client's case. He'd seen it dozens of times, but that didn't take away the sting when his own actions were at issue.

He glanced at the wall clock and grimaced when he saw that it was only 11:35 a.m. Chicago time. He had morphed into a fighting mood and wanted to get on with it. At the same time, even the possibility of losing his right to see Julie left him with a bottomless pit in his stomach.

He considered calling Julie because he knew she was still on her lunch break. He picked up the receiver, thought about it some more, and put it down again. If Julie knew about Sable's motion to modify the judge's order to revoke his visitation privileges, he reasoned, she would have called him by now.

Then he began to worry because he hadn't spoken to her in two days. Maybe she'd suffered a relapse of the mental trauma that enabled Maureen to get her away from school in the first place. He'd been fairly certain that she would side with him if she knew about the motion, but uncertainty crept into his mind and ate away at him. Maybe Sable, whom she called "Wayne," and his sister had convinced her that for her own good, she needed to stay away from Pete. His anxiety built as he waited.

Julie *couldn't* know about the motion, he told himself again. After fourteen years, he couldn't believe that she'd turn on him. If he talked to Julie now, before receiving Angie's counsel, he'd be deceitful if he didn't mention the motion. Dragging Julie into a fight between himself and Sable was the last thing he wanted to do. He'd already done enough to hurt her, albeit inadvertently, and didn't want to do anything else.

He fussed around his office, feeling restless, eager to develop a plan of action. The telephone finally rang. He snatched the receiver from its cradle and took a deep breath before he answered. He prided himself on being calm whatever the situation and didn't want to sound panicked.

"Pete, it's Angie and Kyle."

"Thanks for calling back. Busy morning in court?" He tried to sound casual.

"Sitting around waiting for my case to be called. I see we have a new problem with your friend Wayne." His telephone conversations with Angie typically began with ten minutes of good-natured banter and ribbing, but she apparently recognized that this wasn't the time for that. He was grateful.

"Have you read the pleadings and affidavits?" Pete asked.

"Yes. The only thing that surprised me was the recent knife-in-the door incident. And what's in the two affidavits."

"Let me bring you up to date." He told her about the stalking incidents and his call to the school when he was unable to reach Julie. That lead to his trip to Bloomfield Hills, he said, and ultimately to Lincolnshire.

"You were in the Chicago area and didn't call me?"

"I thought about it, but I wouldn't have been good company. But back to my problem, what do we do?"

"We better decide fast because this motion is up before Judge Rosenberg in the morning."

Pete shuffled though the papers until he came to the notice of motion and looked at the date. *Crap* he muttered under his breath. He'd been so fixated on the substance that he missed the date.

"Can you call the judge and get an extension?" he asked.

"I think I'll have to try to work it out with Larry what's-his-name first. How much time do we need?"

"A week?"

"That might be tough. When I talk to him, what do you suggest I say?"

"Tell him that if he doesn't drop this bullshit motion, I'm going to move to reopen the entire custody case."

Cummings chimed in and said, "The custody issue was fully litigated a few years ago when your wife died."

"Things have changed since then."

"How?"

"At the original hearing, Sable got some schlock MD to swear he was on the wagon. He's called me at least twice since then when he was so drunk he could hardly speak. Julie told me he drinks a lot, too."

Angie interrupted the conversation and said, "Let me call Larry and try to get this thing kicked over for as long as I can. I'll call you back as soon as I reach him."

While he was waiting, Pete found his calendars for the past few years and paged through them looking for his notes. He was wrong; he'd recorded *three* instances when Sable sounded over-the-top drunk. The worst was a few years earlier when he returned calls Pete had made to him to inform him that Julie was spending a week at his cottage on the lake. He sounded nearly incoherent on that occasion.

He looked up Sable's address in Wilmette and dialed Hal Nilsen, a private detective he knew in Chicago. Nilsen was forever hounding him for business by playing on their common Norwegian-American heritage.

"Hal, Pete Thorsen."

"As I live and breathe, it's Mr. Viking. What can I do you for, partner?"

Pete explained the background of the dispute with Wayne Sable, including that he'd once represented to the court that he was on the wagon and had joined Alcoholics Anonymous and straightened out his life.

"So what you're looking for is evidence that he's a liar."

"That's putting it in street terms." Pete told him about the instances when he'd called him obviously inebriated.

"When do you need this by?"

"The court hearing is presently set for tomorrow morning. We're trying to get it bumped forward, but we'll have to see."

"It would be better if you could get it bumped, because even for you, Mr. Viking, I don't know what I'd be able to do by the morning."

"I need whatever you're able to dig up and just as fast as possible. I'm willing to pay double your normal rate. Are you doing anything tonight you can't get out of?"

"I've been following this guy trying to get shots of him banging another woman that the wife's lawyer can use in her divorce case against him. We used to say get Polaroids but everything is digital now. Five straight nights and I'm scheduled to tail him again tonight."

"Okay, I guess I'll have to get someone else. I need something by the morning just in case."

A pause at the other end of the line, then, "Double my normal rate, huh?"

"Double."

"Maybe I can skip a night following Mr. Hot Skivies. What kind of evidence are you looking for?"

"Anything and everything to show that Sable is drinking again. Or is back to his old ways with the ladies."

He gave him Sable's address and asked that he call him on his cell phone first thing in the morning. He'd barely hung up with Nilsen when Angie called back.

"I talked to Larry. What a jerk. He wasn't going to agree to *any* extension. I told him that if that was the case, I was going in to see Judge Rosenberg. I threatened to tell the judge that Sable's camp refused to agree to an extension even though one of the parties lives out-of-state and has to travel to Chicago for the hearing."

"How did you end up?"

"He agreed to two days."

"That gives us a little time."

"Are you coming down in the morning?"

"Tonight. I'll be in your office at 8:30 a.m."

TWENTY-EIGHT

Memories returned as Pete entered the lobby of the building that had been his second home for twenty years. He'd been back several times since he withdrew as a partner in Sears & Whitney and always had the same feeling of no longer belonging. He put a clamp on his emotions and punched the elevator button for his old law firm's main floor.

He waited for Angie in the reception area. Some of the art had changed and the seating had been upgraded, but otherwise things looked pretty much the same. Elegant but understated. He was glad that current management had continued the look he felt was important for a successful but unpretentious business law firm.

Angie's heels beat a rhythmic *Click! Click! Click!* as she crossed the marble tile. She wore her trademark tailored navy suit—her court rags as she liked to say—and her dark curls framed a face that had mesmerized many an opponent over the years. She had succeeded Pete as managing partner of the firm four years earlier, and the last time he saw her, he had the feeling that she'd finally become comfortable with the mantle of power.

She gave him a hug and said, "Gibsons will be happy to see us tonight. It'll be like old times."

"If we're not working."

She nodded and repeated his words, "If we're not working."

He followed her to what had once been his office. She'd redecorated and he recognized nothing except the splendid view of Millennium Park. The furnishings were now a careful blend of femininity and authority.

They spent fifteen minutes covering firm gossip. Then Pete said, "I want to say something before Kyle arrives. I don't want to be unkind to the man, but he doesn't have the fire in his belly for this kind of fight. I know he regards himself as the expert in all matters involving the family, but I'd appreciate it if you led the charge on this motion."

Angie frowned and said, "I seem to remember that you're the one who brought him into the firm."

"I did and I'd do it again. Every business law firm needs a lawyer who can look at a chart and figure out how much child support an executive should provide based on his income and then paper the agreement. But this is war and I need your toughness. This motion is a must-win for me, Angie."

"Understand. Do you have a plan?"

"Let's wait until Cummings gets here so I don't have to go over everything twice."

When Cummings arrived, they moved to a nearby conference room and Pete refreshed their memories about his conflict with Wayne Sable. "Sable hates me because I've been a good father to Julie since I married his ex-wife Doris. His sister Maureen hates me even more, mostly because that's just her personality, but also because she thinks I stole her niece from her. Remember how she clapped when Judge Rosenberg awarded custody to Wayne merely because he was the biological father?"

"The judge admonished her for that," Cummings said.

"He admonished her, but my point is that Maureen couldn't contain her glee."

"Now that you've had time to think about it, do you still want to re-raise the custody issue?" Angie asked. "Or are you satisfied to beat back Wayne's motion to revoke your visitation rights?"

"Both. The way I see it, if I only challenge Sable's motion, I'm giving him a free shot at me. I want to raise the stakes by putting the custody issue back on the table."

"I don't know," Cummings interjected, shaking his head. "Judge Rosenberg might say that he's already decided custody."

"He's already decided visitation rights, too," Pete said. "Things have changed since he made his decision. That's the point I was making on the phone."

Cummings didn't look convinced. "If we do what you're proposing, isn't there a risk that the judge will regard it as tit-for-tat because Wayne is challenging your visitation privileges?"

Pete stared at Cummings for a few moments and said, "Whose side are you on, Kyle?"

Cummings looked uneasy and muttered, "Yours, obviously."

"You don't sound like it."

Cummings fidgeted with his pen. "All I'm saying is that the judge may not *want* to reopen the issue of custody."

"We have to make a strong enough case that he *will* want to reopen it. If you remember, Sable swore he was off booze, but I have contemporaneous notes of telephone conversations I've had with him since then when he was so drunk he probably couldn't have walked across the room. His sobriety was a pivotal issue in granting custody. He wasn't telling the truth. Later this morning, I expect to have more proof of that."

Cummings kept shaking his head like a bobble-head doll and said, "Remember, I have to appear before Judge —"

Pete cut him off and said, "Angie, how do you see it?"

She shrugged and said, "You know me. What's the use of having a sword if you don't use it?"

"Okay," Pete said, "then, let's get to work and see what kind of case we can make on paper."

Angie began to rough out a motion asking the court to reopen the custody question while Pete worked on a draft affidavit detailing his knowledge of Sable's personal conduct since the original hearing. As they worked, Angie occasionally asked Pete about an issue of fact or Pete asked her something. Otherwise the room was quiet as Angie tapped on her laptop or Pete tore a page from his legal pad and started fresh.

Cummings sat with a sullen expression and drummed his pencil on the table. Finally he said, "We could shortcut this entire process if we brought Julie in to testify. If she's as attached to you as you say she is, she'll tell the judge that she wants to continue to see you. A child's preferences, if she's old enough to make an informed decision, is given a lot of weight in these cases. Maybe Judge Rosenberg will split the baby by cutting down your visitation rights, but still allow you to see her. It'd be win-win for both sides. Both parties would walk away unhappy which is the essence of compromise."

Pete seethed as he listened to Cummings. The part of his speech where he said "as you say she is" particularly irritated him. He had all he could do to resist the temptation to grab him by the collar and throw him out of the conference room. He stared at him again and said in a low voice that had no equivocation in it, "I don't want to involve Julie in this unless it's absolutely necessary. Understand?"

Cummings didn't say anything.

Pete looked Angie's way and asked, "When you talked to Larry Helms, did he say anything about bringing Julie in to testify?"

"He wouldn't say either way," Angie said, "but I got the impression they weren't going to bring her in. You can expect to see your friend, Maureen, though. Helms was gloating about the unflattering things she's going to say about you and how that will further damage you in the judge's eyes."

"They're not bringing Julie in because they're afraid of what she will say. They know she'll side with me."

STALKED

Cummings kept staring at the table. He shook his head again, signifying that he thought his suggestion was the best tactical move.

Pete saw Cummings and said, "I'm not going to bring Julie in and that's final, Kyle. If it looks like things are going badly at the hearing, we can always reconsider and offer to let the judge talk to her in chambers or on the telephone before he rules on the motions. But that will be a last resort. I'm not going to have her be a ping pong ball between Sable and me."

Cummings continued to sulk. Finally he said to Angie, "I have some things I have to do this morning. I'm going back to my office. If you need me to look at drafts, give me a shout."

When he was gone, Pete looked at Angie and said, "Weak-kneed sonofabitch."

Angie frowned and replied, "You're being too hard on him, Pete. He was just trying to be helpful."

Pete scoffed and said, "If I need someone to show me how to tie a white rag to a stick and walk into court and surrender my daughter, I'll hire the guy at the corner newsstand."

"That's harsh."

Pete shot her a look and went back to working on his affidavit. He tried to block out everything that had been happening to him lately and concentrate on his work. At times, it seemed like the only ally he could count on when things got tough was the woman sitting across from him.

An hour later, Angie's secretary poked her head in the conference room and said, "Mr. Thorsen, were you expecting a Mr. Halvor Nilson?"

"I was, Brenda. Show him in, please."

Nilsen looked like he'd just crawled out a crypt. Suit rumpled, nondescript tie askew, hair mussed, bags under his eyes, fleshy face flushed. Pete introduced him to Angie.

"Find anything?" Pete asked.

Nilsen's face broke into a weary grin and he said, "I think you're going to like this." He withdrew a stack of photographs from his briefcase and dropped them on the table.

Pete was in his room at the Fairmont Hotel getting ready for dinner when his cell phone burred. It was Joe Tessler.

"I've been trying to call you all afternoon. Are you out of town?"

"I had to make a trip to Chicago to take care of something. I've been in meetings and had my cell turned off. What's up?"

"I think your information about Kurt Romer may be off. I went to Thompsonville today to question him. He wasn't at the address you gave me."

"Maybe he was out."

"I don't think so. I talked to the lady in the apartment, the babe named Bonni you mentioned. She made a big deal out of having no 'e' in her name and told me she never heard of Romer."

"She's lying. She's been living with him for the past month. I also saw the two of them in a bar just a few nights ago and they didn't act like they were exactly strangers."

"I don't know, that's what she told me. She left for work about 3:00 p.m. I hung around and watched her apartment for two hours after that just in case she wasn't leveling with me about Romer. No sign of him or anyone else."

"This doesn't make sense."

"I'm just telling you what I found. I can't question him if I can't find him."

TWENTY-NINE

Pete sat in the Daley Center courtroom with Angie DeMarco and White Flag Cummings. Halvor Nilsen and Rae Acton were in the spectator section waiting to be called as witnesses. Across the aisle, Larry Helms huddled with Wayne Sable and his sister, Maureen Fesko. A woman Pete didn't know—another lawyer from Helm's firm presumably—also was involved in the conversation. Fesko periodically looked their way with lasers firing from both pupils.

Pete ignored her. The two motions had been consolidated by the judge for purposes of the hearing. On paper, at least, he felt they'd made a persuasive case. Nilsen had come up with some good ammunition against Sable that they'd worked into their memorandum in support of their motion.

Promptly at the appointed hour, the bailiff announced Judge Rosenberg who took his seat on the bench and asked everyone to be seated. The motions regarding custody of Julie and visitation rights were the third and last matter on Rosenberg's calendar for that day. Pete and his team sat impatiently while the judge heard the first two matters—both disputes over child support—and listened while the lawyers haggled over details such as what should or should not be included in the fathers' net income.

The clerk called their case at 10:30 a.m. and both sides stood. Judge Rosenberg looked at them over the glasses perched on the tip of his nose. "Let me say something before we begin. I remember this case very well from a few years ago. It was an unusual case. A man who bore no blood relationship to the young lady who was the subject of the proceeding was asking the court to grant sole custody to him, and another man who happened to be the biological father but had seen very little of the girl since she was two years old was fighting to deny the first man visitation rights even though the girl had lived with the first man and his wife, the girl's mother who is now deceased, for ten years and the girl called him 'dad.'

"I thought we arrived at a sensible resolution of the dispute. And most importantly, one that was in the best interests of the child. Now some years later, the case is before me again. I read both motions and the supporting papers last night and have to say I felt like I was in the middle of a cat fight. *He* did this. Yeah, but *he* did that. And so on and so on."

"Your Honor—" Helms started to say.

"Please sit down counsel," the judge said. "I'm not finished. Even though I'd much prefer that the two sides work this out between them like grown-ups, I'm going to hear the motions and make a decision based on what's presented to me. I hope to get through this today so we're not sitting here listening to this tit-for-tat *ad nauseam*. With that in mind, I'm going to take a dim view of a lot of frivolous objections and other lawyer grandstanding.

"I see both sides have brought witnesses to testify in support of their respective positions. Mr. Helms, you're going to go first since your motion was filed first. When you've finished with a witness, Ms. DeMarco will cross-examine. Then we'll reverse the process for Ms. DeMarco's motion. Only if one of you makes a truly persuasive case will I permit a witness to be called back for re-direct. When all of the testimony is in, I'll render my decision. That might not be exactly how the great jurist Learned Hand would have handled it, but it's how Solomon Rosenberg plans to proceed. Any questions?"

Neither side had any.

"Mr. Helms, you're up."

Helms called Maureen Fesko as his first witness and took her through a series of questions designed to elicit testimony about how she'd been contacted about the incident by the school because Wayne Sable was out of the country; how she picked up Julie and took her back to her home in Lincolnshire, Illinois; how she took her to see Dr. Speidel, a Chicago-area psychiatrist; and how Pete came to her house and threatened her if she didn't take Julie back to her boarding school.

After nearly an hour of testimony, which had Judge Rosenberg checking his watch, Helms turned her over to Angie for cross-examination.

"When you got to the school and found out what had happened, did you call Mr. Thorsen to tell him?"

"No, why should I?"

"I think you just heard Judge Rosenberg's summary," Angie said. "Julie lived under Mr. Thorsen's roof since she was two years old, she calls him 'Dad,' he provides most of her support including school expenses, he has liberal visitation rights."

"My brother, Wayne Sable, is Julie's father and has legal custody of her. He's the one I contacted."

"So you never contacted Mr. Thorsen."

"I just *said* I didn't."

Angie gave her a long stare and then moved on and asked, "Why do you think Mr. Thorsen came to your home in Lincolnshire?"

"I don't know. Maybe Dr. Speidel could get inside his twisted mind and tell you. Oh, and that man," she said, jabbing a finger at Pete, "doesn't pay Julie's expenses. They're paid from a trust her mother set up for her before she died."

"Really," Angie said, looking at her with a quizzical expression. "How much money is in the trust?"

"How should I know? I'm not the trustee."

"How do you know that her expenses are all paid from the trust then?"

"You bitch!" Maureen shrieked. "They're paid from the trust! My brother told me!"

Judge Rosenberg banged his gavel and pointed to Larry Helms and said, "One more outburst or foul word from her—about *anything*—and I'm going to have her removed from the courtroom and bar all of her testimony from this proceeding. Do I make myself clear?"

Angie pretended to shuffle some papers and glanced sideways at Pete and winked. She turned to Fesko again and said, "I don't think you answered my question, Ms. Fesko. Why do you think Mr. Thorsen came to your house?"

"I already answered," she said sullenly.

"You don't know?" Angie asked.

She looked like she was ready to explode again, but controlled herself and said, "No."

"That's interesting. Mr. Thorsen claims he called you earlier to ask about Julie and you hung up on him."

"I hung up on him because I didn't think my niece should be around him. I feared for her safety."

Angie stared at her for a few moments and smiled. "Let me rephrase my question. How did Julie react when the man she calls 'Dad' came to see her?"

"He's not her . . . !" she started to shriek again and then caught herself and modulated her voice. "I wasn't watching," she said. "I was so disgusted I couldn't stand to be in the same room with that man. I went to the kitchen."

"Really, Ms. Fesko? Mr. Thorsen will testify later that Julie was ecstatic to see him and that he had to *ask* you to leave the room so he could talk to her alone."

"Objection, Judge," Larry Helms said timidly, as if he were fearful the judge would hurl his gavel at him.

Judge Rosenberg raised a hand and said, "Sustained. Ask questions, Ms. DeMarco. Don't summarize what this witness or that witness will say later in the hearing." He looked at Helms over his glasses and said, "But don't make leaping to your feet a habit, Mr. Helms."

Angie said she had no further questions for Fesko. Helms seemed relieved and called Dr. Spiegel. Helms asked a series of repetitive questions designed to elicit testimony from the psychiatrist that Julie had been severely traumatized by the knife incident. Angie grilled him hard about his professional credentials and the opinions he expressed. Speidel, like this was the opportunity of a lifetime to spout his theories about the human psyche, pointed to the learned articles he'd written and pleaded patient confidentiality on just about everything of consequence to the case. While Dr. Speidel droned on, the judge alternated between looking at his watch and whispering to his clerk and cleaning his glasses with a handkerchief.

As his last witness, Helms called Wayne Sable. Sable was dressed in a dark blue blazer over a striped shirt with a pink tie. His dark hair was slicked back and he sported an even tan.

Helms took him through his personal background, his marriage to Doris, the birth of their only child, Julie, and the highlights of the first couple of years of her life. Sable told about a birthday party for Julie at Chuck E. Cheese's, trips to the zoo, and walks around their suburban neighborhood pushing her stroller while the family's toy poodle trotted blissfully behind.

Sable also claimed the divorce from Doris was the saddest day of his life, and looking like he was ready to shed tears, admitted that his immaturity was a major cause of the breakup of their marriage. He told how hard it had been to see his daughter only intermittently, but that he was delighted she'd grown into the fine young woman she was today.

Helms asked him how long he'd known Pete.

"Gosh, a long time. Before he married Doris."

"Were you at their wedding?

"No," he said, laughing. "I don't think we were *that* close."

"What did Mr. Thorsen do when you first met him?"

"He was a partner in a big Chicago law firm. At least it sounded big to me." He laughed again.

"And later he became managing partner of that firm, which is named Sears & Whitney, right?"

"That's what I'm told."

"But that changed when his wife, Doris, died, did it not?"

"Yes."

"I understand that he resigned as managing partner some years ago and moved to a small cabin in northern Michigan, is that also correct?"

"Yes. I know that because Mr. Thorsen and I had telephone conversations on occasion when I was worried about Julie and wondered where she was. Once when I called looking for her, she was at that cabin of his."

"Had this visit been cleared with you in advance? You had sole legal custody of her after all."

"No, unfortunately it hadn't been."

Helms glanced knowingly at Pete, then continued. "Julie is at a private boarding school near Detroit, is that right?"

"Yes, Meadowbrook School."

"We heard a little about that earlier from Ms. Fesko. The expenses of that school are paid from a trust established by Doris specifically for that purpose, is that also right?"

"That's what I'm told. I'm not the trustee."

"Who is?"

"Mr. Thorsen."

"I see," Helms said, looking at Pete again.

"You said Mr. Thorsen has changed since he resigned as managing partner of Sears & Whitney."

"Yes."

"What do you base that on?"

"What people have told me."

Angie rose to her feet and said, "Judge, I know what you said about not wanting a lot of lawyerly objections, but what Mr. Helms asked calls for the purest kind of hearsay I can imagine."

Judge Rosenberg nodded and said to Helms, "Sustained. Rephrase, counsel."

Helms said, "Do you know of any specific examples that indicate Mr. Thorsen has changed in recent years?"

Sable was nodding his head as his lawyer spoke. "The most recent example is what happened to my daughter at her school. I wasn't there personally because I was in Italy, but I've read the police report which describes the incident in great detail. The police concluded that the incident occurred because someone is after Mr. Thorsen and was using Julie as a pawn."

"Is this the report?"

Sable looked at the document and said, "Yes."

Helms handed a copy of the report to both the judge and Angie DeMarco. Attached to the report as an exhibit was a glossy photograph that showed a wicked-looking switchblade pinning the note to Julie's door.

Helms theatrically looked around the courtroom, like he was playing to a jury, and didn't say anything for a few moments. Then he said, "Do you know of any other incidents similar to this one involving Mr. Thorsen and Julie?"

"Yes sir, I do."

"Would you tell us about them?"

THIRTY

Pete's mind had been drifting back and forth between Sable's testimony and the telephone call he'd received from Tessler about Kurt Romer, but when he heard Sable's comment, his attention was riveted on him again.

"About two years ago," Sable said, "Julie was the victim of another incident at her school. She'd been at the library with a friend one night and they were walking back to their dorm when they noticed two men behind them. They immediately became apprehensive because as you know, rape is a big problem at schools and universities these days. They walked faster and the two men did the same. They started to run and Julie became so panicked that she dropped her cell phone. She never did recover it, by the way. The girls made it to the dorm ahead of the two men and the security guard on duty in the lobby immediately called the campus police who in turn called the Bloomfield Hills police."

"What happened when the police arrived?" Helms asked.

"They searched the area, but didn't find anyone. They were sufficiently concerned about the incident, though, that they stationed an officer in the dorm lobby to watch for possible intruders. I guess they later concluded that the incident might have arisen from something Mr. Thorsen was involved in, just like the knife incident. I shudder to think about what might have happened if the girls hadn't managed to reach their dorm ahead of the two thugs who were chasing them."

Sable's testimony caught Pete by surprise. The incident had occurred two years ago, just as Sable said, but since he never heard anything from him, he assumed that he didn't even know about it.

Helms continued and asked, "How do you know that what happened that night was tied to something Mr. Thorsen was involved in?"

"It's right in the police report. You don't have to take my word for it."

"Is this the police report you were referring to?"

Sable looked at the report Helms showed him and said, "Yes."

Helms gave copies of the report to the judge and to Angie, then made a show of glancing at Pete again in an obvious manner. He turned back to Sable and asked, "What concerns do these incidents raise in your mind, Mr. Sable?"

"My first concern, obviously, is for Julie's safety. Rapists chasing her across campus, a menacing switchblade stuck in her door at 1:00 in the morning with a threatening note. These aren't things a parent can take lightly. Going forward, I'm *very* concerned that if Julie continues to be associated with Mr. Thorsen, more of these incidents will occur. I can't tell you how much that frightens me."

Helms glanced at Pete yet another time and said, "I know what you mean, Mr. Sable. I have young children of my own and the concerns you just expressed for your child's safety are ones I live with every day. This is a dangerous world and we have to do everything we can to protect our children."

He shuffled his notes, then said, "Have you thought about the consequences if this court were to revoke Mr. Thorsen's visitation rights?"

"Yes, I've agonized over that and know it would be very unfortunate. However, balancing those consequences against a child's safety and well-being, there's really no choice, is there?"

Pete seethed as Sable's well-rehearsed testimony continued to drag on. Finally Helms finished with him and Judge Rosenberg recessed the hearing until 2:00 p.m.

"I'd completely forgotten about that earlier campus incident until Sable mentioned it," Angie said.

They were seated in the building's cafeteria. Pete and Angie nibbled on dry turkey sandwiches and shared a bag of kettle chips. Rae Acton and Hal Nilsen swapped private detective war stories while they wolfed down the cafeteria's flagship dish of meatloaf smothered in gravy. White Flag Cummings picked at the limp lettuce in his salad.

"I didn't think about it either," Pete said, "until Sable's testimony made it sound like the crime of the century. That was a case where I represented Mrs. Brimley in what I thought was a routine financial matter until I discovered her dead husband had taken out a juice loan from the mob. A thousand or ten thousand other lawyers could have been caught up in the same thing."

"Do you think Julie told Sable about the incident?"

"Possible, but I doubt it. Julie herself laughed about it later. She didn't know what was behind it and I've never told her. I straightened things out with the mob boss and was confident there'd be no recurrence of what had happened that night."

Angie said, "How would Sable know about it then?"

Cummings muttered from the end of the table, "If Julie were here, we could ask her."

Both Pete and Angie stared at him for a moment. Pete said, "It doesn't do any good to speculate about it. We have to find a way to reverse the tide. I feel wave after wave hitting us."

"It always seems that way when you listen to the other side put on its case," Angie said. "Remember, it's our turn next."

Pete's cell phone burred. It was Joe Tessler.

"I wanted to let you know what I found out from the prison," he said. "Getting information about an inmate's visitors wasn't as easy as I thought it would be."

"Joe, I've got to be somewhere in fifteen minutes and I can't be late. Just give me a quick summary."

"It seems like your friend Robyn Fleming isn't exactly the social maven of the Indiana Women's Prison. She's had exactly five visitors in the years she's been inside. The subject's mother, who I understand is now dead, visited her twice. Same for her sister who visited with the mother once and another time alone. The solo visit was a little more than a year ago. The third visitor was a Mr. Walter Rifenberrick—"

"I know Rifenberrick," Pete interjected. "Or I should say I know *of* him. We never met personally. He was Robyn's former business partner. When did he visit?"

"Shortly after Robyn was incarcerated. A couple of months after that."

"And the other two?"

"The fourth visitor, a man named Sage Johnson, visited not long after Rifenberrick was there. The last, an Ashton Feeney, visited six months ago. I don't know anything about Johnson or Feeney."

Pete didn't recall hearing their names before, either. "That's it?" he asked.

"That's it unless the visitor logs are incomplete or they're holding something back from me."

"Who did you speak with to get the information?"

"I was getting nowhere on the telephone so I drove down to the prison. That's where I am now."

"Frank let you do that?"

"He doesn't know. This is my day off."

"I owe you, Joe."

"Make a note of that and put it somewhere where you won't misplace it. 'I Peter Thorsen hereby acknowledge that I owe Detective Joseph Tessler one giant favor.' You don't have to have it notarized or anything. Signature only will be sufficient. I trust you."

Pete laughed.

"One more thing before you go," Tessler said. "I just talked to Frank. The judge won't sign the search warrants for the Seitz brothers unless we justify the warrants with more evidence."

"You're kidding."

"I knew you wouldn't be happy."

Pete saw the other members of his team standing and said, "I have to run. I should be back in the morning. Let's talk about it then."

THIRTY-ONE

"You have a great tan, Mr. Sable," Angie said. "You didn't get that in Chicago at this time of the year."

"I was in Italy for three weeks. I think I said that this morning."

"Lovely. Alone or with a friend?"

"Friend."

"What's his name? Or her name?"

Sable looked at Larry Helms who nodded. "Her," he said. "Patty Gill."

"Is she your girlfriend?"

"Five and a half years," he said proudly with a smile tugging at the corners of his mouth.

"Get to your substantive questions, Ms. DeMarco," Judge Rosenberg said. "This isn't a Match.com commercial or a travelogue. The clock is ticking."

"I was just easing into things again after lunch," Angie said.

"Well you've eased. Now put the pedal down."

Pete knew what Angie was doing in her disarming way and resisted the impulse to grin.

"Yes, Your Honor," she said.

"Mr. Sable, before we broke for lunch, you testified that Mr. Thorsen has changed in recent years and gave the court two examples of the consequences of that change. Do you have other examples?"

Sable's eyes flicked toward Helms. "None I know of offhand. There may be some."

"But you don't know of any, right?"

"Not offhand as I just said."

"Would you like us to give you some time to think about it so you can give me a yes or no answer to my question?"

"Your Honor," Helms said, "Mr. Sable can't be expected to know about the full universe of things Mr. Thorsen has been involved in."

"Mr. Sable is your witness," Judge Rosenberg said. "He's expected to testify about things of which he has personal knowledge, not what other people may know or not know. Ms. DeMarco asked him a straightforward question and I'd like to hear his answer."

Sable shifted around in his chair and said, "The two incidents I testified about are the only ones I know about."

"Thank you," Angie said. "Let's take your second example first. I'm reading from the police report your attorney introduced into evidence earlier. It says that Julie and another girl named Mikki 'claimed they were followed by two men when they left the library and were en route to their dormitory.' They weren't able to describe the men with specificity other than to say they had dark clothes and 'looked creepy.' The word 'allegedly' is used in six different places in the report.

"Neither the Bloomfield Hills police nor the campus security staff were able to identify any suspicious men lurking around campus. Nothing in the record indicates that either Julie or Mikki suffered any emotional trauma from the incident that required counseling or psychiatric care. That doesn't sound very traumatic, does it Mr. Sable?"

"As I said earlier, rape cases on school campuses are a big issue these days. You can't deny that."

"I'm not denying it. But there's nothing in the report to indicate that rape was a threat in the incident you cited. There's also nothing that ties the incident to Mr. Thorsen in any way."

"Pete Thorsen is specifically mentioned in the report," Sable said in a disgusted tone. His manner suggested that Angie was the dumbest lawyer to come down the pike in his lifetime.

"Let's see what the report actually says." Angie found the right place and read, 'If the incident in fact occurred, it might have had something to do with a case Mr. Thorsen had or was working on.' Note the words, '*if* the incident in fact occurred' and 'it *might* . . . .'Those aren't statements of fact. They're mere conjecture."

"As I read the report, Thorsen was involved in some way."

"Okay, Mr. Sable." Angie made little effort to conceal her disgust.

"Your Honor," Helms said, "Mr. Sable isn't a lawyer. He can't be expected to parse words the way a lawyer would."

"I think everyone understands that, counsel," the judge said caustically. "But the report says what it says."

"Now Mr. Sable, I have one more question about the second incident you cited. What did you do after you heard about it?"

"What do you mean?"

"There I go with my imprecise language again. I'll rephrase. Did you call or otherwise contact Mr. Thorsen to ask him about it?"

Sable's eyes flicked toward Helms again, as though looking for support. "I didn't call him. I thought, what's the use?"

"Let me get this straight. You have legal custody of Julie and profess to be so concerned about her safety, but you didn't bother to pick up the telephone and call Mr. Thorsen to ask him about this terrible incident?"

"I just told you, I thought it would be a futile gesture."

"I see." Angie shuffled her papers, which Pete knew was a ploy to allow time for the judge to digest the point.

"Now to back up a bit, Mr. Sable, since your divorce from Doris, how much child support have you provided for Julie?"

Sable shifted in his chair again and said, "I don't have an exact number."

"Take a guess. Five thousand dollars a year? Ten thousand? More?"

"I told you, I don't remember exactly."

"Let me refresh your memory," Angie said. "This form filed with the divorce court, which you signed, shows zero on the line for child support." She furled her brow. "Am I reading this right?" She gave Sable the form and pointed to a line.

Sable glanced at the form and looked away.

"I think I must be reading this right because in an affidavit attached to the form and signed by you—that's your signature isn't it?—you stated that you were unable to pay child support because you were unemployed and had no income. Is your memory coming back, Mr. Sable?"

"Whatever you say," Sable muttered.

"For a man with no income, you seem to live pretty well. Nice clothes, a big house in Wilmette, fancy trips to Italy with your girlfriend."

"I inherited money from my mother when she died."

"I see. When did she die?"

Sable appeared to think. "Seven years ago," he said.

"Thank you. When you came into your inheritance, did you contact your ex-wife, who I believe was still living at the time, and offer to pay child support for Julie going forward?"

Sable said "no" so quietly that his answer could hardly be heard five feet away.

"Was that a 'no' Mr. Sable?"

He glared at her and nodded.

"How about Julie's college fund? How much did you contribute to that fund?"

"I didn't know she *had* a college fund," he said flippantly.

"Well, if you didn't know she had a college fund, I guess you didn't make any payments to it, did you?"

"That's right," he said quietly.

"How about Julie's expenses at Meadowbrook School? Private college prep schools are expensive. Close to forty thousand a year with expenses I'm told. How much would you say you've contributed toward those expenses each year?"

"Those expenses are paid by the trust my ex-wife Doris established for Julie," Sable said in a cocksure voice that was normal again in its resonance. "My sister told you that earlier."

"The trust must have substantial resources to pay for four years of tuition and expenses at Meadowbrook, Mr. Sable. Your sister didn't know how much was in the trust fund. Maybe you know."

"How would I know? I'm not the trustee."

"So you don't *really* know whether Julie's tuition, room and board, and her other expenses at Meadowbrook have been paid by the trust or by someone else? By Mr. Thorsen, for example?"

"No," Sable said.

Angie nodded her head for fully a half minute and then said. "Let's see if I can sum up for the court. You haven't paid *any* child support for Julie, you haven't made *any* deposits into her college fund, you haven't paid *any* of her expenses at Meadowbrook. Is that right, Mr. Sable?"

Sable just glared at her.

"Answer out loud for the record, please."

"Yes," Sable muttered.

"Is that a 'yes' to my summary that you haven't paid anything?"

"Yes," he replied in a voice that was even weaker than before.

"Looking at it objectively, Mr. Sable, I would have to say it doesn't seem like you've been very generous toward a young lady you profess to have such love and concern for. When I put Mr. Thorsen on the stand later in this proceeding, maybe he'll have some idea of where the money to pay for everything has been coming from."

Angie wrapped up her questioning of Sable and then called Rae Acton as her first witness. After stating her private investigator credentials, Acton testified that just before Julie returned to school from Maureen Fesko's house, Pete had engaged her to watch Julie's dorm at night.

She said her surveillance activities had been conducted in coordination with the Bloomfield Hills police and campus security. In response to Angie's questions, she also told the court how much she was charging Pete for her services and that Pete asked her to continue watching the dorm even though nothing had happened so far. Helms asked Acton some perfunctory questions and then sat down.

Next, Angie submitted for the record the affidavit Wayne Sable had given in the original custody proceeding in which he'd represented, among other things, that he no longer drank alcohol and in fact was attending AA meetings on a regular basis. She then called Halvor Nilsen as her next witness. Nilsen stated his name and address, that he was a private investigator licensed by the State of Illinois, and that he'd formerly been a detective with the Chicago Police Department for seventeen years.

"Mr. Nilsen, on Tuesday night of this week, what were you doing?"

"I had a stakeout going of a house in Wilmette, Illinois owned or occupied by one Wayne Sable." He gave the address of the house.

"And what came to your attention during the course of the stakeout?"

"Several things. When I arrived, I observed Mr. Sable's recycling bin positioned in plain sight next to his detached garage adjacent to the alley."

"Is this the photograph you took of the recycling bin?"

Nilsen looked at it and said, "Yes ma'am. The bin was outside the garage as I just said."

Angie then showed him some additional photographs. "Did you also take these photographs?"

Nilsen looked at the photographs. "Yes," he said, "these are close-ups of the contents of the bin."

Angie handed sets of the photographs to Judge Rosenberg and to Larry Helms. Helms immediately leaped to his feet and said, "Objection, these photographs could have been taken anywhere at any time!"

"Mr. Helms, I've given both sides considerable leeway in this proceeding," Rosenberg said, "and I'll point out that Ms. DeMarco rarely objected when your witnesses were testifying. Are you going to follow her lead or object every time you see or hear something from her witnesses you don't like?"

Helms sat down again with a scowl on his face.

Angie tendered Nilsen's affidavit attesting that he'd taken the photographs on the night in question, in a specified location, at a specified time, and so on.

"And you found an empty Jack Daniels whiskey bottle in Mr. Sable's recycling bin and a large number of empty beer cans or bottles, right?

"Right. Seven empty Coors beer cans and nine empty Budweiser beer bottles."

"Over what period of time did these liquor and beer containers accumulate?"

Helms was on his feet again. "Your Honor, this is entirely inappropriate. There's no evidence the containers came from Mr. Sable's house or that the contents were consumed by Mr. Sable. The bottles and cans could have been dumped in Mr. Sable's bin by someone else."

Judge Rosenberg sighed audibly and said, "Mr. Helms, don't you think I'm smart enough to take all of that into consideration? This doesn't go to questions of your client's legal liability. It pertains to his character and much of the testimony you've introduced goes to the same issue. I've got to say, though, that my impression is that Mr. Nilsen has been pretty careful from an evidentiary standpoint."

Helms took his seat again with a sour look on his face.

"To answer your question, Ms. DeMarco, I checked with the Village of Wilmette and established that recycling on Mr. Sable's street is collected on Monday of each week. Therefore, the contents of the bin must have accumulated over a period of a day or two."

"What else did you discover that night?"

"After I inspected the recycling bin, I positioned my vehicle so I had an unobstructed view of Mr. Sable's street and could observe his house. Approximately 9:00 p.m., I observed a black Mercedes-Benz S Class pull up to the curb on the adjacent block. I observed this woman walk up the street toward me. She continued until she came to Mr. Sable's sidewalk, then she turned in and knocked on his door. A man I believe to be Mr. Sable let her in.

"While I was waiting to see if the subject woman would leave again, I walked down the street to her vehicle and made a note of the license plate number. I observed the subject woman leave Mr. Sable's house at approximately 3:30 a.m., more than six hours after she had arrived. She walked to her vehicle and drove off. The next day, I checked with the DMV and discovered that the vehicle is registered to a Mrs. Constance Koch."

"Not Ms. Gill, Mr. Sable's girlfriend?"

"No, ma'am. A Mrs. Constance Koch like I just said."

"Is this the photograph you took of the woman you're referring to?"

Nilsen looked at the photograph and said, "Yes."

Angie handed copies of the photograph to the judge and Larry Helms. "What did you do the following day besides checking with the DMV?"

Nilsen told how he staked out Sable's house again and saw another woman, who he identified as Mrs. Terri Taylor based on her automobile registration, enter Sable's house about 8:30 p.m. and leave at approximately 2:45 a.m. Angie introduced another photograph into evidence.

"It seems like Mr. Sable leads a very active social life," Angie said.

"Objection!" Helms squawked. "Counsel is implying that there's something improper with Mr. Sable having guests."

"Sustained," Judge Rosenberg said with an expression that suggested he was amused. "Stick to the facts, Ms. DeMarco."

Nilsen then told of encountering a man who'd been in the same AA group as Wayne Sable. Angie introduced into evidence the letter the man had given Nilsen stating that Sable had stopped attending AA meetings shortly after the date he'd been awarded custody of Julie. Sable's Italian tan faded a couple of shades.

Pete took the stand last but it was essentially mop-up duty. He testified that on three occasions, giving dates, he'd had telephone conversations with Sable during which Sable had continually slurred his words, suggesting that he had been drinking. He also testified that the reason he was named in the police report for the "second" incident was because when he talked to the police after he heard what happened, he mentioned that it *might* have been connected to one of his cases.

Finally, he testified that the balance in Julie's trust at the time Doris died was approximately $37,000 and tendered a bank statement at the end of the previous month showing that the current balance was $12,937.46. He showed the outlays he'd made for Julie's expenses over the years, including those at Meadowbrook School and her trip to Paris the previous summer to study art. Helms tried to trip him up on the details of the knife-in-the-door incident, but he stuck to the truth as he knew it and nothing material came out of that questioning.

Judge Rosenberg said, "Both sides have certainly done their jobs digging up dirt on the other. Going through the other guy's garbage, selectively reading police reports. I can understand why neither side wanted to bring Julie in to testify although it would have been useful to me in deciding what to do. I'm going to take the matter under advisement for a couple of weeks so I can digest everything I've heard. I need to let it all simmer in my mind and see if I can come up with a resolution that's befitting of my first name," obviously referring to Solomon.

"I'd like to say one final thing before we break up, though. Mr. Thorsen, it's obvious that you care deeply for the young woman you call your daughter. But it's equally obvious that some of the things you've become involved in precipitated this dispute. I'll look on it unfavorably if you don't do everything in your power to make sure Julie is protected until law enforcement gets to the bottom of the knife-in-the-door incident. As someone said earlier today, the child's interests are paramount in these cases and that's what must happen here."

THIRTY-TWO

I t was past midnight when Pete got back to the lake, and after a few hours of trying to sleep, he gave up and came downstairs. He put on a Patsy Cline CD and sat with a blanket wrapped around him and replayed the entire court hearing in his mind. He tried to divine which way Judge Rosenberg was leaning by dissecting his every comment. Whenever Pete's cottage creaked or groaned, he was instantly alert and listened intensely for signs that someone might be outside.

The morning light gradually filtered in despite the drawn shades. His head throbbed from lack of sleep and he was tempted to continue to sit there, hoping he'd eventually nod off. He forced himself to get out of the chair and opened the blinds on one window. The water was glassy, and at the east end of the lake, the sun was just crawling above the horizon into a sky that was so pale blue it was almost milky.

He popped a couple of aspirin and stood in the shower with the dial turned as far to red as he could stand. By the time he got downstairs again, the milky sky had morphed to gray clouds and April dreariness enveloped the area. He headed for town.

STALKED

Like most days during the off-season when the tourist crowds weren't around, the vehicular traffic on Main Street was light and Pete was able to park directly in front of the building that housed his small office. He exited the Ford Taurus he'd rented while his Range Rover was being repaired and made a mental note to call to the body shop to find out if it was ready.

When he unlocked the outer door and opened it, the sight struck him like a load of cinder blocks had fallen on his head. His office was a shambles of upended chairs, papers strewn everywhere, files torn apart, the framed photographs on his credenza gone, file cabinet drawers open, paintings ripped from the walls.

After he recovered from the initial shock, he stepped inside cautiously and saw photographs of various sizes, many of them yellowed by age, pinned to the walls like a makeshift gallery. A dark "X" was smeared across each of them. The words *Welcome home Pete* had been painted on his window looking out over the bay.

Pete backed away again and leaned against the wall of his waiting room. He put his head back and closed his eyes. He felt the will to fight drain from his body.

"Pete? Are you okay?"

The voice sounded like it came from far away. He opened his eyes and saw Brenda, the real estate woman from next door. She stood in his open door with a ring of keys in her hand, staring at him.

She stepped inside and stopped. "My God! What happened to your office?" She moved forward again, as if to get a better look.

He still hadn't spoken, but the realization of what she was about to do suddenly hit him and he said sharply, "Don't go in there!"

She stopped abruptly as though she'd slammed into an invisible wall. She turned her head slowly and looked at him, like she was afraid any sudden move would set him off again. "What happened?" she asked for the second time.

"Brenda, I don't *know* what happened? I just got here."

"Have you called the police?"

"For crissakes, I told you! I just got here!"

She backed away and held her arms up like she feared he was going to attack her. "Just asking," she said in a meek voice.

"I know," Pete muttered. Slowly his feelings of despair were replaced by anger. He wanted to lash out, to throw things. He took a deep breath and let it out. Then he took another.

"I'll be next door if you need me," Brenda said as backed out the door. She seemed afraid to be in the same room with him.

He stood there a while longer and then pulled out his cell phone and dialed Joe Tessler's number.

"Joe, it's Pete Thorsen. Someone trashed my office while I was in Chicago. Can you stop by?"

Silence for a few moments, then, "Is this related to the other incidents?"

"I don't know for crissakes! Probably! Why does everyone keep asking me these goddamn questions?"

Tessler was silent again.

"Sorry," Pete muttered after a few moments.

"No problem, counselor. There's nothing wrong with venting. I'll be right over."

"You better bring your photographer and a fingerprint person, too. If your boss will approve it."

Pete was sitting in his Taurus with his head back when he heard Tessler's Acura coming up the street. The detective made a U-turn and parked behind him.

He met Tessler at the front door. Tessler squeezed past him and peered into his office. "Mother of Jesus," he muttered under his breath. He looked back at Pete and asked, "Did this happen last night?"

"Last night or the previous night. I was in Chicago."

Amy Ostrowski walked in with her camera dangling from a strap around her neck. She looked at the office, shook her head several times, and said, "I'm going to shoot my pictures before the techs gets here." She went to her car to put on a pair of plastic booties and then began taking photographs. Brenda had heard the activity from next door and came over again to watch.

Pete apologized to her for his behavior. She kept repeating over and over what a terrible thing it was. He listened to her politely, and as soon as he could disengage without scaring the wits out of her again, he joined Tessler in his Acura and answered as many of his questions as he could. During a lull, Tessler said, "Frank oughta be here any minute."

Pete looked at him with a sour expression and asked caustically, "What's he going to do, ask where my body is?"

Richter made the same U-turn as Tessler had made and parked behind the lengthening train of vehicles in front of Pete's office building. He nodded to Pete and Tessler and went inside and surveyed the damage like everyone else had done. Amy was still photographing the scene.

When Richter came outside again, he said to Pete in an uncharacteristically civil tone, "Sorry about your office. It's a real mess."

Pete nodded in appreciation.

"Joe, you need to elevate this to the top of your agenda," Richter said. "Mr. Thorsen's right. This doesn't look like it's going to stop."

Pete looked at him like a different man had suddenly inhabited the sheriff's body.

"Have you ordered a tech?" Richter asked Tessler.

Tessler nodded. "Should be here any minute."

With that, Richter got in his SUV and drove off down the street.

"Let's get back in my car," Tessler said. "I'm freezing my buns out here."

Tessler revved up the engine and the heat began to flow. "It'll be interesting to see if the techs find any prints. The scene in your office is different than the other ones. There's a lot more he could have touched in there."

"They won't find anything," Pete said dejectedly. "Whoever this is, he's smart enough not to leave behind anything that would tip his identity."

"I'm not saying that he *did*. But we can hope."

"When I was in Chicago, Angie DeMarco had an idea. She suggested I make a list of everyone I know of who's aware that Julie is at Meadowbrook School. That might tell us something."

Tessler thought about it for a few moments. "Makes sense."

An unmarked van pulled up behind the other vehicles. A man and a woman got out.

"Our techs," Tessler said. "They sent two."

Pete stayed in the car and started on his list while Tessler briefed the techs and took them inside where they huddled with Amy Ostrowski. Tessler got back in the car and said, "They're going to dust everything for prints. Then they're going to try to figure out how the perp got in and scour the place for other evidence. They're probably going to be in there for most of the day."

"Big inconvenience," Pete said sarcastically. "Now where am I going to take my nap?"

Tessler's eyes flicked his way. "We've got some things to talk about. Romer. Robyn's guests. What we can do to spiff up that search warrant request."

Pete had his head back resting on the headrest and nodded.

"Tell you what," Tessler said, "if you're hungry, let's get a couple of sandwiches and go to our conference room on the bluff so we can talk some more."

Pete hadn't eaten anything yet that day, and while he wasn't hungry, he knew he'd probably feel better if he had something. He nodded again and they walked down the street to Ebba's Bakery.

The previous summer, Ebba had installed a number system to establish order among customers during the height of the season. The light on the monitor near the ceiling was on and Pete tore off a tag from the machine just in case she was already following the new system. While they waited their turn, he studied one of the plastic-encased menus, feeling unfocused and wondering whether he should have something other than his usual breakfast sandwich. Someone tapped him on his shoulder.

"You eat at all the finest places," Eve Bayles said. She had a gray North Face parka over her usual black workout clothes and her hair was up.

He smiled when he saw her. "I could say the same about you. I think this is the first time I've seen you in here."

"I spread myself around." She smiled back at him.

Tessler was standing by the glass case sizing up the doughnuts and assorted pastries and occasionally glancing their way. Pete took Eve over to introduce them.

"Eve, this is Joe Tessler from the county sheriff's office. He's a detective and formerly a Chicagoan just like us."

She looked at Tessler with a twinkle in her eyes and said, "A detective. What has Mr. Thorsen done to draw the attention of the sheriff's office?"

"It's not what *he's* done. It's what someone has done *to* him. Someone trashed his office last night or the night before. We're waiting for the evidence technicians to work up the scene."

Eve eyes widened. "Trashed? You're kidding."

"I wish I was," Pete said despondently.

"Is your office up the street? I saw all of the cars and wondered what was going on."

Eve got her food and waited until Pete and Tessler got theirs. They walked out together and Eve said, "I have to get back to the fitness center, but do you mind if I have a quick peek?"

"Why not?" Pete said. "Everyone else has."

Eve walked in and peered through the door of Pete's office where the evidence technicians were at work. She put a hand to her mouth and said, "My God." She stared at the shambles, seemingly transfixed, then turned away and asked Pete, "What's that stuff smeared on the photos and your window?"

"I'm sure these people will tell me after they're finished. It looks like more blood to me."

"Like the bag that was thrown against your house?"

He nodded.

She shook her head and looked horrified. She reached down and took his hand, trying not to be too obvious about it, and looked at him sympathetically. "I'm so sorry. Is there anything I can do?"

"Thanks, I'll get it cleaned up," Pete said.

Eve squeezed his hand and whispered, "I have to run. I'll call you tonight."

When she was gone, Tessler said, "Looks like you've got something going there, counselor."

Pete shrugged. "I've only seen her a few times," he said.

The overlook was vacant except for a silver Ford F-150 pickup. Tessler parked as far away from it as possible and kept eyeing it suspiciously. "I wonder what he's doing here?" he grumbled. "July I could understand, but this time of the year?"

"He's infringing on hallowed ground," Pete said in a hollow attempt at humor. "Why don't you flash your shield and tell him to move on?"

Tessler shot another look toward the pickup and unwrapped his sandwich and took a bite. The sun poked through the clouds and brightened the water. A stiff breeze kicked up waves that splattered against the base of the lighthouse and cascaded back to the lake's surface, leaving a frothy coat.

Tessler's cell phone burred.

"You're kidding," he said. "Another one?"

Tessler listened some more and said, "Can you tell when it occurred?

He said "Uh huh," then "Uh huh" again. "String some tape around the site and don't let anyone near it until we get Amy or someone out to examine the scene."

Tessler hit the disconnect button and looked at Pete. "They found another dead alpaca. That's probably where the substance smeared around your office came from."

Pete's lips tightened, but he didn't say anything.

"This guy's a real psycho," Tessler said.

The clouds knit together again and the lake turned gray and forbidding. Like it was an omen. The waves continued to pound the lighthouse.

"We better talk," Tessler said. "I want to get out to that alpaca farm and look at the site."

"You told me on the phone that Robyn has had five visitors. Two were her mother and sister. The third was Walter Rifenberrick, who I know about. The others — Sage Johnson and Ashton Feeney — I don't have the foggiest idea who they are."

Tessler nodded. "Let me ask you something," he said. "When I first asked you to come up with the names of possible suspects, you had Robyn Fleming listed at the bottom. Did you have a reason for that?"

"Yeah, like I told you, she's in prison and confined to a wheelchair to boot."

"But now you seemed to have changed your mind."

"We've been getting nowhere with the others," Pete said. "Plus she's the only one on my short list that knows Julie is at Meadowbrook School. That I know of anyway."

"That's something. It's a connection the other people don't have."

"The notes sound like something Robyn would write, too," Pete said. "I just can't figure out how she'd orchestrate all of this from prison."

"We talked about this before, remember. She knew one guy who was willing to sabotage her ex-boyfriend's hang gliding equipment for a price. Maybe she knows other people."

Pete nodded.

"So where does that leave us?" Tessler asked.

"I'm going to see what I can find out about Romer. Then I'm going to check on Rifenberrick and the other two non-family visitors to the prison."

"I know I sound preachy, but don't do anything to get yourself in trouble. Romer, at least, sounds like a real hard ass."

"I won't. And you've got to do something about your search warrant request and see if you can get the judge to reconsider. With another alpaca just killed, it's possible that the Seitz brothers haven't completely cleaned up the vehicle they used if it was them."

"The judge is eighty-one years old and sometimes he can get a burr up his behind about civil liberties. If I'd been there instead of just Frank, I might have been able to talk him into it."

"I think that has to be a priority," Pete said. "Just because we're looking at other possibilities doesn't mean we should forget about the Seitz brothers."

"Anything else, boss?"

Pete smiled for the second time that day. "As a matter of fact, yes. Robyn's partner in crime, who's still in prison himself, is from Traverse City. I suggest you get in touch with your contacts in the police department there and find out everything you can about the guy and people he associated with. Maybe we can find a lead that traces back to Robyn."

"Sort of like the division of labor you mentioned a while back."

"Exactly."

Tessler shot him a look and with a deadpan expression said, "When all of this is over, I'm going to talk to Frank about making you an unpaid consultant to our department."

"Yeah," Pete said dryly, "he'd like the unpaid part."

THIRTY-THREE

Pete passed on going to Heavenly Meadow with Tessler to see where the latest alpaca had been slaughtered and instead made a trip home and killed time by shooting arrows and walking on the beach. He returned to his office just as the techs were finishing their work. They told him he was free to start cleaning up.

He stared at the mess around him. It was like being in a horror chamber. The message scrawled on his plate glass window mocked him in the same way the earlier notes had. The blood had run down the glass before it dried and gave the words a macabre look, like they'd been written in some grotesque script. It was also obvious that whoever had written it knew he was gone. He found it unsettling that someone knew his every movement.

The defaced family photographs were disturbing as well. They were everywhere. Tacked to the walls. Scattered around the floor with frames twisted and glass broken. Without exception, they had a bloody "X" smeared across them.

He picked up the framed photographs of Julie and Doris and scraped at the dry alpaca blood with a fingernail and removed pieces of broken glass so he could see their faces. A shard of glass pierced his skin and a finger began to drip blood. He wiped it on his jeans and laid the mangled photographs on his credenza since the frames would no longer stand upright.

Many of the photographs tacked to the wall were irreplaceable. The grainy, yellowed photograph of the ship that had carried some of his ancestors from Norway. A staged photograph of the relatives who'd gathered at his family's farm for one of their infrequent reunions. A photograph of his father, Lars Thorsen, in combat attire and holding his M1 rifle aloft after the victorious American troops entered Palermo, Italy during World War II.

He stared at the one of his father and uncomfortable memories came back. He'd often thought that the moment in Palermo might have been the highlight of his father's life because after he returned home from the war, he resumed his former place at the bottom of the social and economic totem pole. Pete never understood the bitterness that festered within him and how he seemed to make little effort to raise himself up. Pete's determination to be different fueled his personal drive and competitive streak.

He began to put the family photographs in a shoe box so he wouldn't have to see them in their defaced state when he came in in the morning. When he had time, he'd look for a photo restoration firm. He found a bottle of Windex in his closet and began to work on his window. The blood came loose in flakes, and when he saw it in the daylight, he was sure the glass would be a mass of smudges.

Pete was listening to a Roy Orbison CD on his Bose music system when the telephone rang.

"I'm sorry to leave so quickly today," Eve said, "but one of my slave-owners was coming to the fitness center for a session and knew I couldn't be late."

"Hey," he said, making an effort to sound buoyant, "slave-owners have to be served. Besides, there wasn't much you could have done if you'd hung around except join in a hand-wringing session."

"Still . . ."

"If you're really concerned about my state of mind, maybe you'll have dinner with me tomorrow night. That might give my morale a boost."

"What did you have in mind, Mr. Thorsen?"

"I have to be in Traverse City late in the day. Maybe we could meet someplace on my way back."

"Like a McDonald's?"

"McDonald's would be good. Another possibility is La Becasse."

"Near Glen Lake."

"You've been there before with that old boyfriend you were telling me about."

She laughed. "No, but I heard it has great food."

"That sounds like an acceptance."

"It is, but with a condition. You have to let me cook dinner for you at my place on another night."

"That's like buying one dinner and getting one free. How could I pass on a deal like that?"

They agreed to meet at La Becasse at 7:00 p.m. That gave him a cushion in case the body shop was overly optimistic about when his Range Rover would be ready.

After he was off the phone with Eve, he checked in with Julie, saying nothing about his office, then logged on his computer and found the website for Rifenberrick Antiques. His screen showed a smiling Walter Rifenberrick talking to a customer in the tony shop. That would be the earlier part of tomorrow's chores.

He unfolded the sheet of paper with the list of people who knew that Julie was at Meadowbrook School and added three names to it. The first was Charlie Cox, his neighbor during the summer months, who still harbored ill feelings toward him over an incident a couple of years earlier when Pete over-imbibed one night and played music so loud that it woke up half the county in the wee hours, notably including Charlie. But it would take ten alligators nipping at his privates to get Charlie out of Florida at this time of the year.

Bud Stephanopoulis, his one-on-one basketball buddy, was the second name, but it was inconceivable that it was him, either, for reasons that included he wintered in Costa Rica and hadn't been in the area since October. The last name he'd added was Millie Tate who ran a small resort over on the Brule River. He saw her twice a year when he fished the legendary trout stream. She was definitely out. But he wanted the list to be complete.

In all, he had seventeen names on his expanded list, and when he eliminated various individuals for what he thought were sound reasons, he kept coming back to Robyn Fleming. He seriously doubted that the others on his short list of suspects even knew he had a stepdaughter, much less where she went to school. He could be wrong, though. Whoever was stalking him clearly knew a lot about him and he suspected it wasn't by accident.

Playing the percentages, Pete knew he had to dig deeper into how Robyn Fleming might be pulling the strings from prison to get back at him for her crazy belief that he'd betrayed her. The starting point would be her former business partner, Walter Rifenberrick.

THIRTY-FOUR

When Pete walked into Rifenberrick Antiques, the only people there were Walter Rifenberrick, whom he recognized from the shop's website, and a young woman sitting across from him at a cluttered writing table sipping coffee. Rifenberrick looked like he was in his late fifties with longish silver hair slicked back. With his tweed sport coat over a black turtle neck and pressed blue jeans, he looked like the quintessential urbane antiques dealer.

Pete introduced himself and gave Rifenberrick one of his cards. He waited while Rifenberrick studied the card, then said, "You might remember me. I used to represent your former business partner, Robyn Fleming."

A look of recognition passed over his face. He said, "Of course."

"I'd like to talk to you about Robyn if you have time."

Rifenberrick studied him for a moment, then said hesitantly, "What about? She's in prison, as I'm sure you know. Nothing that had to do with our shop or me, thank goodness."

"Yes I know," Pete said. "I'm just looking for information."

Rifenberrick looked at him with a trace of suspicion. "What kind of information?"

"It involves Robyn's activities since she went to prison. I understand you've been down to see her."

Rifenberrick fidgeted with his pen. "Only once."

"That's what I'd like to talk to you about."

"If it involves legal things, maybe I should have my lawyer present."

"It's not really legal and has nothing to do with your business. I'm just looking for information, like I said."

Pete waited for Rifenberrick to say something and could tell that the wheels in his head were grinding.

"Information is a vague word, Mr. Thorsen. Could you be more specific?"

"Is there somewhere we could talk in private?"

"You can speak freely in front of Melissa. My wife and I don't keep secrets from each other."

Pete tried not to show surprise. Melissa looked like she was half Rifenberrick's age.

"I understand," Pete said, "but I'd still feel more comfortable if we could speak alone."

More wheels grinding, then, "Maybe I should call my lawyer and see if he can come over."

"Why would you want to do that?" Pete persisted. "Our conversation wouldn't involve your business in any way, as I just said. I really don't think you need a lawyer."

"Still . . ."

Pete tried not to show his impatience. Rifenberrick looked nervous about speaking with him alone so he relented. "Okay," he said, "call your lawyer and see if he's available. But I have to warn you, I think you'd be better off having the conversation with me instead of being dragged into the police investigation."

Rifenberrick's urbane exterior seemed to melt and his eyes widened. "Police investigation?"

"That's what I said."

Rifenberrick looked confused. Finally he blurted out anxiously, "Now I'm going to call Dennis for sure." He hurried toward the back of the shop.

Pete made small talk with Melissa while he waited for Rifenberrick to return. In five minutes, he was back and sat down again with a worried expression on his face.

"Dennis said he's in the middle of drafting some important papers for a limited liability company, but he's putting that aside to come right over. Fortunately, his office is just down the block."

Rifenberrick fidgeted while they waited for his lawyer to arrive. Fifteen minutes later, a gaunt owlish-looking man with a receding hairline and round tortoise shell glasses burst into the shop. He seemed out of breath and fumbled with the buttons of his black rain coat and looked around for someplace to hang it. Melissa took the coat from him. The man straightened his narrow dark tie and squinted at Pete through thick lenses as he walked up to where he was sitting with Rifenberrick.

"Mr. Thorsen," he said, "Dennis Sheets." He extended a hand that was small-boned and clammy. "I'm Mr. Rifenberrick's attorney. And also the attorney for Rifenberrick Antiques."

"Thanks for coming over, Dennis. I really appreciate it." Pete gave him one of his business cards. "Where can we talk in private?" he asked Rifenberrick.

Rifenberrick led them to an office in the back of the shop that was cluttered with antiques magazines and other trade publications.

"Can I get anyone coffee before we begin?" Rifenberrick asked.

Pete asked for his with sweetener on the side. Sheets gave detailed instructions about how he'd like his coffee, saying that he'd prefer skim milk to artificial creamer and specifying the brand of sweetener he'd like.

While Rifenberrick was away on his coffee run, Sheets cleared his throat and said to Pete, "I understand this is a criminal matter, Mr. Thorsen."

Pete thought about that for a moment and said, "Indirectly, possibly."

Sheets squinted through his thick lenses again and said, "I might have to instruct my client not to answer if you ask something that could be incriminating. You realize that, don't you?"

Pete smiled disarmingly. "I don't think you have to worry about that."

Rifenberrick returned with the coffee.

"I'm sure both of you are busy," Pete said, "so I'll get right to the point. Dennis, at one time I represented Robyn Fleming, Walter's business partner."

"*Former* business partner," Rifenberrick corrected him.

"Sorry, former business partner. Several years ago, Robyn was arrested and charged with a variety of offenses, including conspiracy to commit murder. She was found guilty in a jury trial and sentenced to twenty-eight years in a maximum security women's prison in Indianapolis. I didn't defend her in the case so I don't know every detail, but the essence of what happened is as I just described. After she was incarcerated—"

"Excuse me Mr. Thorsen," Rifenberrick said, "I didn't know Robyn had another attorney. I thought *you* represented her."

"Only in civil law matters such as her business arrangement with you. I don't handle criminal cases. That's a whole different field."

"I handle both civil and criminal law matters," Sheets volunteered with a hint of professional pride in his voice.

"Okay, but I don't," Pete said, not being entirely truthful in view of some of the things he'd been involved in in recent years. "I recommended a criminal lawyer in Chicago when Robyn told me she might need one. He represented her at trial. Getting back to what I started to say, after Robyn went to prison, I started to get hate letters from her essentially accusing me of having turned her in, which is completely false. The police got onto her because the man she hired to sabotage her former boyfriend's hang glide wing fingered her when he was trying to cut a deal for himself."

Pete gave them copies of two of the earlier letters he'd received from Robyn. Sheets stood behind Rifenberrick and peered over his shoulder so he could read the letters at the same time as his client. Rifenberrick read part of one letter and then turned his head and gazed into space. Sheets' eyes widened as he read both letters all the way through.

When Sheets finished reading, Pete said, "The letters stopped coming about three years ago and I thought that was the end of it. Then a few weeks ago, bad things started to happen to my family and me." He summarized the incidents for them. "The hate letters from Robyn started coming again shortly after that first incident. She said she found out about it from an article that appeared in the Traverse City newspaper, but I'm not sure I believe her." He gave them copies of two of the recent letters from Robyn.

Rifenberrick glanced at the letters and averted his eyes again. Sheets read them word-for-word just as he had the first two. When he was finished, he looked at Pete and said, "She says you violated your sacred duty as a lawyer and divulged confidential conversations you had with her."

"Dennis, were you listening when I told you how Robyn happened to get arrested? Nothing she says in any of those letters is true."

Sheets looked back and forth between Pete and Rifenberrick a couple of times, as if uncertain of what to do, and then said in as commanding a voice as he could muster, "I need to speak with my client, Mr. Thorsen."

Pete looked at him impatiently and said, "Okay. Do you want me to wait outside?"

"I believe that would be most convenient for everyone, sir."

Pete walked out and closed the door behind him and went over to where Melissa was sitting at the writing table and began to kibitz with her again. Every thirty seconds, her gaze flicked toward a customer who'd entered the shop and was examining some antique silver pieces. In due course, Dennis Sheets poked his head out of Rifenberrick's office and said, "We're ready for you, sir."

Pete sat down again and took a sip of his cold coffee.

"Mr. Thorsen, we have two questions. Or rather, one statement of position and one question. As I said earlier, I might have to instruct my client not to answer if something you ask might incriminate him in some way. The other thing, the question, is why aren't the police investigating this matter instead of you?"

"The police *are* investigating. I'm just helping the detective who's handling the case because the sheriff's office is thinly-staffed. He knows I'm here."

"What's the name of this detective?" Sheets asked, squinting at Pete suspiciously.

"Joe Tessler. I have his telephone number right here in case you want to talk to him. He's the lead detective in the office." He didn't tell Sheets that he was the *only* detective in the office.

Sheets and Rifenberrick looked at each other again. Sheets said, "We need to confer again if you don't mind."

Pete wanted to wring Sheets' scrawny neck, but compliantly went out to keep Melissa company again. She was still keeping an eye on the customer who was hanging around the antique silver table.

Sheets called Pete back for the second time and asked whether Pete had proof of his authority to participate in the investigation. Pete's temperature was edging toward red.

He said evenly, "Nothing in writing. But you can call Detective Tessler and speak to him directly. He'll confirm that he knows I'm up here."

Sheets and Rifenberrick exchanged quizzical looks again and Sheets said, "Would you mind calling him? In our presence, of course, so we can hear everything and be sure you aren't coaching him."

For once Pete was glad he'd been open with Tessler about what he was going to do. Tessler answered on the second ring. "Joe, I'm in Harbor Springs meeting with Walter Rifenberrick and his attorney, Dennis Sheets. They want to ask you some questions about my authority to inquire about Robyn Fleming."

He passed the phone to Sheets. The attorney cleared his throat twice and then introduced himself again and repeated the purpose of their call. Sheets listened for a while and said, "Uh huh." He listened some more and said, "Uh huh" again. Pete couldn't hear the entire conversation, but he heard enough to know that Tessler was giving Sheets a choice between talking to Pete or having him, Tessler, come to Harbor Springs with some deputies to talk to them under more formal circumstances. Tessler didn't get into the fact that he had no jurisdiction in the county where Rifenberrick resided.

Sheets ended the call and hung up. "The detective confirms that you have authority," he said, nodding at Pete. He turned to his client and said, "I'm satisfied if you are, Mr. Rifenberrick." Rifenberrick looked confused but nodded as well.

Pete said, "Walter, can you tell me about the conversation you had with Robyn when you visited her in prison?"

Pete could see Rifenberrick nervously open and close the fingers of one hand. He chewed on the inside of his lip and finally said, "You can imagine how shocked I was when I heard about Robyn. She'd been my business partner for years and was a personal friend as well. Then she was convicted of murder and sent to prison." He shook his head and stared into space with a disbelieving expression as he appeared to relive the experience.

"It was so tragic," he continued. "I thought about it for several weeks. You hate to talk business at a time like that because you feel so bad on a human level. But at the same time, I knew I had to raise the issue."

"Is that what you talked about then? Buying her out?"

"I tried," Rifenberrick said, sighing. "After commiserating with Robyn about her situation, I tried to shift to the business end of things, you know? It wasn't easy. I was a basket case and could barely hold back my tears. But Robyn didn't seem emotional at all. She had this strange look in her eyes and kept repeating that you'd betrayed her and were the one responsible for her being sent to prison. I couldn't get her to focus on anything related to business. I have to tell you," he said, "it was *surreal*." He kept shaking his head. "That's the only word I can think of to describe it. *Surreal*."

"How did you leave it with her?"

"My visiting time was up. I left a sheet of paper for her with one of the guards detailing the way I'd calculated the purchase price for her interest in Rifenberrick & Fleming. I even added ten percent to the price because I felt so terrible about what had happened to her."

"Did you go down to see her again?"

"No. I sent Sage in the hopes he'd have better luck since he wasn't as close to her as I was. He told me she signed the papers without even reading them. But I guess it was the same as when I went down. All she was interested in doing was to rant about you."

"I assume Sage is Sage Johnson."

Rifenberrick's eyebrows raised. "Do you know him?"

"Only by reputation," Pete lied. "Getting back to Robyn, and realizing what you said about your conversation with her, at any time did she ask you to do anything for her?"

"Objection!" Sheets said in a screechy voice, punctuating the word by thrusting his finger in the air.

Pete stared at him incredulously. "Dennis, this isn't a court of law. We're just talking about the conversation."

"You asked your question in a way that could incriminate Mr. Rifenberrick."

"Excuse me? If I asked whether Robyn wanted Walter to do something *and* he said 'yes' *and* he told me what she wanted him to do *and* then he told me he did it and it constituted a criminal offense, it conceivably might incriminate him. But that's not what I asked. I just asked whether she *wanted* him to do something, like contact someone or give someone a message."

Sheets looked like he was trying to figure out how to respond to Pete's comment.

"It's okay, Dennis," Rifenberrick said. "I don't have anything to hide. No, Mr. Thorsen, Robyn didn't ask me to contact anyone for her or to deliver a message to anyone."

"Nothing," Pete said.

"Absolutely not. As I said, I couldn't get her to focus on anything."

"How about Sage Johnson?"

Rifenberrick shook his head. "I'm sure she didn't ask him to do anything either. He would have told me if she had."

"Is Johnson's office close to here? I'd like to ask him directly about his conversation with Robyn."

"With all respect, Mr. Thorsen," Sheets said, "you can't just show up without an appointment and expect to talk to half the people in town. I came right over because Mr. Rifenberrick is such a valued client. Mr. Johnson may be very busy right now."

"I'm busy, too, Dennis. Busy fighting off a psycho who's been sticking switchblades in my daughter's door, trashing my office, and doing all manner of other things. I have a suspicion that Robyn Fleming may be pulling the strings from prison. I intend to find out whether I'm right with or without your cooperation." Pete's eyes burned into Sheets.

Sheets squirmed under his gaze and adjusted his tie. "I suppose we can call and find out if Mr. Johnson is available," he mumbled.

Pete continued to glare at him.

"Mr. Rifenberrick, do you have any objection to me calling Sage?" Sheets asked.

Rifenberrick looked like he'd been blindsided by a double decker bus and shook his head meekly.

THIRTY-FIVE

When Sage Johnson arrived, Pete took him through the same questions that he'd asked Walter Rifenberrick. Like Rifenberrick, Johnson denied that Robyn had asked him to contact or communicate with anyone on the outside, with one exception.

"She asked me to deliver a letter to you, Mr. Thorsen, but I declined. I know a little about prison procedures on account of a client I once had who'd been convicted of embezzlement. I knew I'd have to disclose the letter when I left the prison or violate the rules. And if I did disclose it, the prison authorities almost certainly would have opened the letter. Either way, I didn't want to get involved."

"Robyn didn't ask you orally to give someone on the outside a message?"

"I know what you're asking Pete and, no, she didn't."

Pete liked Sage Johnson. He seemed like a straight-shooter who'd been around the block. Unlike Dennis Sheets who flinched when his own shadow crossed his path, or Walter Rifenberrick who had an urbane exterior but was a bowl of mush inside.

"How much did you pay Robyn Fleming for her interest in the antiques business?" Pete asked.

"I don't know that we should—"

Sage Johnson cut Sheets off and said, "Walter, I don't see any problem with telling him, but it's up to you."

"You can tell him," Rifenberrick said in a weary voice.

"Forty-eight thou and change," Johnson said.

"Did you send her a check?"

Johnson chuckled. "The only currency that's worth anything inside the joint is cigarettes and drugs. Robyn doesn't use either. We transferred the money to an account we'd been using to deposit other funds that were due her."

"Do you remember the bank?"

Johnson dug around in his file and pulled out a piece of paper with a business card stapled to it and handed it to him.

"Are these numbers the transfer information?" Pete asked.

Johnson nodded.

"Do you know if Robyn has drawn on the funds?"

"I have no idea. We initiated the transfer and received confirmation that the funds had been received by the bank and posted to her account. That satisfied our obligation as far as I was concerned."

Pete stared at the paper for a minute, thinking, and then grabbed the telephone on Rifenberrick's desk and dialed the number on the card. "Mr. Humphries, please," he said when someone answered.

"Who shall I say is calling?"

"Walter Rifenberrick."

Three sets of eyes widened and then Dennis Sheets blurted out, "You can't—"

Pete held up a hand to silence him and waited for Humphries to come on the line.

"You can't pretend you're Mr. Rifenberrick to try to get information," Sheets protested in a hoarse whisper.

Pete cupped a hand over the mouthpiece and said, "I just want to find out whether Robyn has drawn on the funds you transferred."

"But—"

"Mr. Humphries, this is Walter Rifenberrick of Rifenberrick Antiques in Harbor Springs. A few years ago, we transferred some funds to a Robyn Fleming who has an account with your bank." He gave him the date, the amount, and Robyn's account number.

Sheets flapped his arms and hissed like an irritated snake. "I demand that you immediately cease impersonating Mr. Rifenberrick!"

After a pause at the other end of the line, Humphries asked, "What are those voices I hear in the background?"

"I'm sorry for that, sir," Pete said. "There are two customers right outside my door and they're arguing over an antique table."

"I see," Humphries said. "And what is it you'd like from us, Mr. Rifenberrick? I've pulled up the funds transfer information on my computer. That's a very old transaction."

"I'd like to know whether the funds have been drawn on after they were deposited to Ms. Fleming's account."

"This is highly inappropriate," Sheets complained again. His voice had risen two more octaves.

Pete jabbed his forefinger at him angrily and held the finger to his lips in the universal request for silence.

"It sounds like those customers are still fighting," Humphries said. "Getting back to your question, I'm afraid you've asked for confidential information that only the customer can access."

"All I want is a 'yes' or 'no' answer to my question. I'm not asking for confidential information."

"Mr. Thorsen," Sheets pleaded again. He was near tears.

Pete glared at him and turned his back to muffle his voice.

"I'm sorry, Mr. Rifenberrick," Humphries said.

"Okay," Pete said, sighing. "I guess I'll have to tell the sheriff that you won't disclose whether the funds I transferred have been drawn upon.

It's up to him, but I suspect he'll make you a formal part of his investigation to get the information."

Silence, then, "What kind of investigation are you talking about?"

"Robyn Fleming is in prison and is suspected of paying people on the outside to perform criminal acts on her behalf. The funds may be coming from an account at your bank."

"That sounds serious."

"It is." Pete sensed possible give in Humphries' position and remained silent until he spoke again.

Humphries finally said, "I can't give you details, but I will tell you that the account has been inactive since you transferred the funds to our bank."

"I interpret that to mean there haven't been any transfers out."

"I can't argue with that," Humphries said.

Pete concluded that was all he was going to get out of Humphries and thanked him. He hung up and turned to face Rifenberrick and the others. "Sorry for that, but I had to know whether Robyn Fleming has been using any of the funds you transferred to her. Humphries' Caller ID likely showed Rifenberrick Antiques as the calling party and I thought it might needlessly complicate things if I gave my own name."

"I could have told you that Ms. Fleming would *never* do what you're suggesting," Sheets said. "Mr. Rifenberrick has known her personally for a long time and I know her, too. You didn't have to impersonate my client and strong-arm a banker to get that information."

"Dennis, I've known Robyn for a long time as well, but she was convicted of attempted murder and other crimes. She might have been a good person at one time, but she isn't one now."

Rifenberrick stared at the floor. He looked ashen and continued to have a dazed expression on his face. Everyone else was silent.

Pete said, "I have one last question and then I'll get out of your hair. Do any of you know a man named Ashton Feeney?"

Rifenberrick looked at the others. They all shook their heads in unison.

"No one?" Pete asked. "The name doesn't ring a bell with any of you?"

Three heads shook again.

THIRTY-SIX

P ete made it to La Becasse by 7:00 p.m. He parked his freshly repainted Range Rover near the front of the quaint building and saw Eve's black Escape parked a few cars over. He pushed through the heavy velvet curtain that served as the restaurant's second front door and saw her at a table near a window. She was staring intently at a swizzle stick she'd bent into a geometric shape.

She jumped when he walked up to the table and squeezed her hand and gave her a peck on the cheek. He sat down and looked at her drink and said, "Sorry to deprive you of an extra swizzle stick, but I think I'm going to have a glass of Pinot Grigio."

Eve feigned a pout. "What will I play with?"

"If you get desperate, I'll get you a supply from the bartender."

"So, how were the bright lights of Traverse City?" she asked.

"Same as usual. I had a bunch of things to do. I hardly noticed."

"One of those things wasn't buying a fresh supply of oldies, was it?"

"Now why would you ask that?" he said, smiling.

"Harry tells me your favorite music store is in Traverse City."

Pete shook his head. "Did he tell you what brand of diapers my mother used on me when I was an infant, too?"

"I already knew that. You can always tell a Pampers guy."

"But you can't tell him much, right? Actually, McGee's is my *only* music store. That I'll willingly go into anyway. I do most of my shopping on late-night cable infomercials."

"Does McGee's carry classical?"

"Some. I might be able to get you a discount if you've persuaded the fitness center manager to switch tunes."

Eve rolled her eyes.

"Speaking of the fitness center, what's the story with the towel guy?"

She appeared to think for a moment and then said, "You mean Lyle?"

"I don't know his name. But every time I'm in there with Harry, he stares daggers at us whenever we talk to you."

Eve smiled coyly and said, "Maybe he's your stalker. Jealously can be a powerful motive, you know."

Pete didn't say anything.

She apparently picked up on his reaction. "Sorry, that was meant as a quip," she said. "I wasn't making light of the things that have been happening to you."

"I know," he said, patting her hand. "Let's talk about more pleasant things."

They talked about fitness programs and the progress Harry was making under Eve's tutelage. He listened to her vent about her demanding clients again.

They got their orders in. Eve had the Duck Duo and he had the Lake Michigan Whitefish. While they were waiting for their food, Eve excused herself and left for the ladies room.

As he waited for her to come back, his mind returned to the subject he'd been determined to put aside for the night. Harbor Springs had been another dead end, with everyone he'd talked to at the antiques shop denying that Robyn had asked him to pass word to anyone on the outside and the banker saying, in essence, that she hadn't drawn on the funds in her account. He needed to locate Ashton Feeney and hear what he had to say.

Kurt Romer's disappearance puzzled him, too. He'd seen the guy in The Nighthawk with his own eyes. The only explanation he could think of was that Bonni had had a parting of ways with him and decided that she didn't want to become involved when Tessler showed up at her apartment and announced that he was with the county sheriff's office.

"You look deep in thought," Eve said as she rejoined him at the table. "You weren't fantasizing about some other woman, were you?"

He returned to the moment and pushed his sense of humor to the fore. He looked at her with a serious expression and said, "I've always believed that honesty is the bedrock of every good relationship, so while you were in the restroom, I decided that I *had* to come clean. I've been seeing three other ladies, too, and just can't give any of them up yet. But you're number one with me, so I'm giving you your choice of date nights. Then I'll work out a schedule with the others."

"Well," Eve said with false huffiness, "after hearing that, I think I'll just go back to Lyle."

Pete stared at her blankly.

"You know, the hunky towel boy."

Pete slapped his forehead and shook his head. "I *knew* something was going on there. I could sense it."

They laughed.

Their dinners arrived. Pete tested his whitefish and after he'd savored it for a moment, he said, "Almost on a par with The Manitou."

Eve pilfered a piece from his plate and nodded approvingly.

They compared restaurants in the area and talked about the atmosphere in each. Eve named her three favorites, placing The Manitou at the top.

"Harry's going to be disappointed that you didn't include his girlfriend's restaurant on your list."

"I've never eaten at the Bay Grille," Eve confessed. "The only time I've been there was the night we had drinks."

"I've hardly been there myself," he said with a straight face. "Fifty or sixty times at most. Since Rona stole the chef away from a place in Petoskey, the food has been terrific. We should go some night."

Eve had her mouth full of duck and could only nod.

"Do you have any brothers or sisters?" Pete asked during a lull in the conversation.

"One of each."

"Where are they?"

"Still back east. I'm the only one who had the gumption to get out of Jersey."

"How about parents?"

"Both dead. Yours?"

"My mother died a few years ago. My father is in a facility in Wisconsin with terminal Alzheimer's."

She shuddered and said, "Terrible disease."

Eve, who'd been nursing her mixed drink, ordered a glass of Pinot Grigio.

"Is Bayles your family name or your married name?" Pete asked.

"Family. I changed it back after Mr. Louse and I got divorced."

"What was your name while you were married?"

"Oh I don't know. Smith or Jones or something like that. Isn't everyone named Smith or Jones sometime in their life? Sort of an immutable law of nature."

They were weighing the dessert possibilities when Eve peered over her card and said, "Does the fact you always order fish for dinner have something to do with your love of fly-fishing?"

Pete smiled. "Or maybe avoiding cholesterol?"

"Fly-fishing a wonderful sport. My dad taught me to cast when I was growing up. Or at least he tried to. It's an otherworldly experience to be on a nice stream with buds in your ears listening to Tchaikovsky and watching your favorite fly drift under an overhanging tree where you just *know* a lunker trout is lurking."

"I've never thought of New Jersey as trout fishing country."

"You'd be surprised. There are some nice streams there. And upstate New York and places like Vermont aren't that far away."

"Umm," Pete said.

"Have you taught your daughter to fly-fish? Or isn't she interested?"

Pete glanced at her. "Not interested. At least so far."

"That's too bad."

They split a Tarte Tatin which was carmelized apple pie in puff pastry. When the waitress brought the check, Eve didn't snatch it as she'd done at The Manitou. Instead, she let him pay just like the old days when a respectable woman would rather be trapped between converging alligators than to call a man and invite him to dinner.

Outside the restaurant, Eve leaned against her SUV and looped her arms around his neck and drew him close. Her body meshed against his and she moved just enough that he found his thoughts shifting to soft music and wood fires and more wine. She nibbled at his neck and her mouth found his and their tongues intermingled. He unzipped the top of her jacket and reached in and cupped one of her breasts. She leaned back with her eyes closed.

A couple came out of the restaurant and he quickly removed his hand. They stood gazing at each other while the couple got in their car and drove away. Eve leaned forward and bit his ear and whispered, "If you don't put your hand back where it was, I'm going to have to kill you right here in the parking lot."

He reached in again and squeezed her breast gently and brushed his hand back and forth across her nipple. She closed her eyes, and after a while, opened them and looked at him. "Doesn't this make you feel like a teenager again?" she said.

"Kind of, but the thing about adulthood is that you gives you better choices. Crackling fires . . ."

"Mmm," she murmured. "Do you have any oldies that might get a lady in the mood if we were to share a fire?"

"I'd have to check, but with two hundred CDs to choose from, I'm sure I could come up with something."

"We have a dinner coming up, remember? If you don't get me too tired slaving in the kitchen to feed you."

"I promise to go easy on you. I'll even bring McDonald's if that will ease the burden."

Their bodies separated a few inches and he felt her hand move toward his belt. Now it was his turn to close his eyes.

When she was gone, Pete stood in the brisk April night for a moment, then got in his Range Rover and headed home. He listened to a Drifters CD as he drove along the narrow road. And wondered how Eve knew he had a daughter.

THIRTY-SEVEN

arry had insisted that Pete use a spare desk at *The Northern Sentinel* while his office was being repainted. When he walked in, Harry was already slurping coffee and working on the content of his next issue. His broad face broke into a grin.

"It's kind of nice to have someone else around for a couple of days to bounce things off of," Harry said. "Coffee's ready." He motioned toward his new coffee machine.

"You have Marian and Justin," Pete said. He was referring to the *Sentinel's* advertising manager and the young stringer Harry employed, neither of whom were in the office yet.

"Sure and they're both top-notch people. But they aren't on the same level as guys like you and me. We have that perspective and breadth of knowledge that comes from experience."

"Graybeards."

Harry furled his brow and said, "I don't think of myself as a graybeard. Experienced, maybe."

Pete set his briefcase on the desk that would be his base of operations for the next two days and walked over to the coffee machine and waited as it gurgled and filled his mug. It was a step up from the glass pot and hot plate Harry had used for years and produced memorably awful sludge. Pete hadn't slept well again the night before and needed a jolt. He sipped from his mug while he scanned the copy of *The Wall Street Journal* he'd picked up at his office on the way over.

"Aren't you going to tell me about your big date last night?" Harry asked.

"It was nice. We went to La Becasse. Good food, nice ambiance."

"Better food than they serve at the Bay Grille?"

Pete had already accepted that his two days as Harry's guest weren't likely to be very productive given the editor's penchant for chatter about a myriad of subjects. He took another sip of his coffee and said, "I don't know if it was better, but it's pretty darn good. Eve liked it."

"She's a classy woman, isn't she? I know you weren't hot to ask her out at first, but I'll bet you're glad you did, huh?"

"I didn't ask her out. She asked me."

Harry digested that for a moment. "It's not like the old days, is it? Modern women don't wait around to be asked. They want what they want when they want it."

Pete let that pearl of wisdom pass and asked something that had been on his mind since the previous evening. "Have you ever mentioned Julie in your conversations with her?"

Harry appeared to ponder the question. After a minute, he said, "No, I'm sure I haven't."

"You almost blurted something out that night the four of us had drinks."

"Yeah, but you cut me off, remember? Then you lectured me for an hour about saying anything about your personal life or things that have been happening to you. Like it's a big secret that you have a daughter and everything."

"It's not a big secret, but when someone is stalking you and sticking knives in her dorm room door, you get a little sensitive about having personal information bandied around."

"The incidents have been all over the newspapers anyway. Not the *Sentinel* of course, but other newspapers. Good old Harry McTigue lets other papers scoop him and just sits back out of deference to his friend."

"Not all of the incidents have been in the newspapers," Pete said.

"Maybe not *all* of them, but the most important one has. That's how everyone knows about your door."

"The most *important* one is what happened to my daughter," Pete replied, suddenly feeling snarly. He shot Harry a look, but was immediately sorry for using a sharp tone with his friend. His temper was always close to boiling over these days.

"I know that," Harry said. "That's why the only thing you see in the *Sentinel* is yesterday's news as far as this story is concerned. And not word one about Julie."

"I know and I appreciate it. It's just . . ."

"That's the way it'll be until you find this guy who's after you."

"Thanks." He knew he risked offending Harry again, but he had to know. "Are you absolutely positive you've never said anything to Eve about Julie? Either before or after our conversation that night?"

"Before your sermon, I told her a few things about you, like how you like oldies music, how you practiced law in Chicago for twenty years, how old you are, that kind of stuff. But nothing about Julie, I'm sure of that. She didn't ask whether you had children and I didn't volunteer anything."

"Okay."

Harry studied him and said, "Is something on your mind?"

"Eve knows a lot about me. I was wondering whether she'd been pumping you, that's all."

"She's probably a typical woman who wants to know all about the man she's dating. A guy I know went through that with the woman who's now his wife. She checked him out every which way from Sunday. Internet and all of the social networking sites, professional directories, everything. The FBI wouldn't have been more thorough. She laughs about it now."

Pete's cell phone burred. It was Joe Tessler.

"I forgot to tell you because of everything that's been going on," he said, "but when our forensics team was out to Heavenly Meadows to look at where that third alpaca was killed, they found several footprints in the soil around the animal's body. About a man's size nine narrow. The prints couldn't have been made by the two ladies who run the place because they both wear shoes three sizes smaller. The footprints had to have been made by the perp."

"That's something."

"When the techs tested the carpet fiber in your office, they also found residue that matches the soil at the farm. That pretty much establishes that the perp who killed the alpaca is the same one who messed up your office."

"If there was ever any doubt."

"Yeah, if there was any doubt."

"Any conclusions from this?"

"Nothing definitive. But it's the first time the perp has left evidence of his presence. If we identify a suspect, we might be able to match his shoes and the footprints and tie him to the scene that way."

Pete thanked Tessler for vouching for him when Dennis Sheets called and filled him in on the results of the meeting, including how Rifenberrick and the others all denied that Robyn Fleming had asked any of them to pass information to anyone on the outside. He also told Tessler about his telephone conversation with the banker and asked if he could verify that none of the funds in Robyn's account had been used.

"Probably," Tessler said.

Pete promised to get copies of some of Robyn's hate letters to him in case he needed background. Before they got off the telephone, he asked Tessler for the names of Robyn's mother and sister who had visited her in prison since he hadn't written them down earlier. The mother's name was Shirley Lambert. The sister's was Evelyn Beth Lambert.

He stared at the names for a minute and then began his search for Ashton Feeney. He tried directory service in the northern Michigan area first, but was told that there was no telephone listing for him. Then he bit the bullet and paid to use the locator service he'd used several times in the past. Since he had no address, telephone number, Social Security number, or driver's license information, he purchased an upper Midwest search based solely on the name.

Twenty minutes later, a list appeared on his screen. One hundred fifty-seven men with the name Ashton Feeney were on it, proving again that in a country of over three hundred million citizens, even an unusual name had been selected by parents numerous times. He wondered how many people would have popped up if he'd requested a national search.

He used Harry's printer to print out the list and then began the laborious task of identifying the Ashton Feeney that made sense. None were listed for the northern Michigan area, which was consistent with what he'd learned earlier from the operator. Playing the percentages, he crossed off those men who were from small towns and other out-of-the-way places. That left him with thirty-three names. He further narrowed the list by crossing off the Ashton Feeneys who didn't live in Chicago, where Robyn Fleming had lived for a spell, or in Detroit or Indianapolis. He began to work the telephone using the *Sentinel's* WATS line.

In an hour, he'd eliminated Indianapolis which had the fewest Ashton Feeneys. After going to Ebba's Bakery with Harry for a sandwich, he started on Detroit. Three frustrating hours later, during which he had to constantly fight with long distance operators over the fact that he didn't have the street addresses, he'd pretty much determined that none of the names on that list for that city was the Ashton Feeney he was looking for.

He moved on to Chicago. Harry, who periodically looked at him as if he were nuts, was uncharacteristically silent as Pete did battle with the information operators. When one couldn't or wouldn't help him, he hung up and dialed the information number again. By late afternoon, Pete's voice was hoarse from the endless haggling and his right ear was so tender from the phone that he flinched every time he made a new call.

Pete decided to hang it up for the day. He begged off Harry's suggestion that they have dinner at Rona's and took the scenic route home along the lake. The weather had warmed in the last few days and the days were long enough that there was still an hour of daylight. The choppy water glistened in the low sunlight and offered promise of the spring to come.

There was nothing of note in the mail. Most importantly, there were no new hate letters from Robyn. On the drive out, he'd decided to call Irma and find out whether she'd seen Kurt Romer around recently. He figured had the best chance of catching her sober if he called early.

"Hello, Irma speaking." It sounded like he was an hour or two late because she was already slurring her words.

"Irma, this is Pete Thorsen. How are you?"

Silence, then, "Pete Thorsen. We must be telegraphic friends or something. I been needing to talk to you for a week, but I couldn't find your card. Then here you call me. Ain't that something?"

"It can only be telepathic as you say. How have you been?"

"So, so, Pete. My leg hurts. My granddad had arthritis real bad and I'm wondering if I might be getting the same thing. The good news is that it gets better as the day goes on. By nighttime, I'm ready to rock and roll again."

"That's good. You're too young to be sidelined with a bad leg."

"You're a real smooth talker, aren't you? I been thinking about you every night since the last time we were together. I'm still saving that wine. Is that the reason you're calling?"

"Well, I do like wine, but mostly I thought it would be nice to hear your voice."

"I don't know why the good Lord don't make more men like you. You got that way about you, you know? You know how to make a woman feel special."

Before she could lapse into telephone sex, he said, "Irma, I was wondering, has Kurt Romer been around recently?"

Silence again, then in a voice so low he could barely hear her, "That's what I wanted to talk to you about. That and the dinner we planned."

"Has something happened?"

In the same low voice, she said, "I'm in The Nighthawk. I'm afraid someone might hear me talking."

"I could drive over. We could get a table and talk where nobody could hear."

"It ain't safe," she hissed into the phone. "Why don't we meet at my place instead? I could make us that dinner and tell you all about it."

Pete rolled his eyes and searched for something he could say to get the information about Romer he wanted without venturing into Irma's love nest.

"Maybe you were thinking the same thing I was about getting together," she said hopefully. "You'd have to bring a corkscrew for that wine, though. I can't find mine."

"Can't you give me a hint about what's happened with Kurt Romer?"

"I tell you, it ain't safe. I could leave right now so I can pick up a little something for us to snack on. Then we'd be all set when you get here." She gave him her address.

THIRTY-EIGHT

On the way to Thompsonville, Pete was tempted about twelve times to turn around and return to the lake. He didn't for the very good reason that if Irma had information about Romer, he wanted to know it.

Irma lived in a manufactured housing development just outside Thompsonville. The sign at the entrance proclaimed "Country Club Park" even though it looked nothing like a country club and he saw no evidence of a park. The streets were lined with an array of double wide and single wide manufactured homes with a sprinkling of mobile homes mixed in. Irma's house was a small place with pale green vinyl siding. Pete walked up to the front door, took a deep breath, and knocked.

The door swung open almost immediately and a wave of floral perfume rolled out and assaulted his nostrils. "You must be eager for my food," Irma said. "I hardly had time to freshen up."

Pete resisted the temptation to fan the air and tried not to flinch when she planted a sloppy kiss on his mouth.

She grabbed his hand and led him inside. "This is the living room," she said as they passed through a small room with clear plastic covers on the sofa and stuffed chairs. "Here's the kitchen and dining area. And this here's the bedroom," she said grandly, sweeping a hand toward an open door. "The bedroom is the biggest because that's where everything happens." She gave him a knowing wink.

"I brought the corkscrew," he said awkwardly, pulling the tool from his pocket and waving it in the air.

"Oh, goody!" she squealed. "You do the honors and we'll have a glass while I finish dinner."

The small table in the dining alcove was already set with stoneware plates, stainless steel flatware, and folded paper napkins. A bottle of wine sat grandly in the middle. He was pleasantly surprised to see that it was a very drinkable Merlot. He popped the cork, but blanched when he saw the coat of dust on the heavy stemmed goblets. He swiped at the goblets with one of the paper napkins when Irma wasn't looking and filled each a third full. He carried them to the living room and handed one to Irma. He dropped into a stuffed chair across from her.

"Don't be so bashful, young man," Irma said. "You can sit over here by me." She patted the plastic next to her.

"I'll move in a minute. I need to unwind first."

"You lawyers are always working, aren't you? That's reputation all of you have. Work, work, work. If it'll help, I can give you a backrub."

"Thanks, I just need to relax for a few minutes."

"Well, you take your time. It's so nice to have a man around the house I can do things for." She sat there with a crazy grin on her face shaking her head in wonderment. Her straight gray hair looked like she hadn't fussed with it and the dress she wore reminded him of a Hawaiian muumuu.

"So what's the big news about Kurt Romer?" he asked casually.

"Just a minute. I need to check on the food. I know you men like to eat early these days."

She left for the kitchen and after a minute the microwave oven began grinding away. He looked at his watch. Then he heard some rattling around in the kitchen. The microwave started again. Irma appeared in the living room door and asked, "Do you want lasagna with meat sauce or lasagna with meat sauce?"

She laughed crazily at her joke and ducked into the dining alcove and scooped up the dinner plates and disappeared into the kitchen. In a minute, she returned with the plates. "Almost on," she said giddily. She lit a fat candle and positioned it in the center of the table, then lit two more candles on the small sideboard. She admired her work for a moment, then went into the kitchen and turned out the lights. "Dinner is served," she announced grandly.

Pete noticed that Irma had moved the place settings and chairs so they were adjacent rather that across as they'd been when he first arrived. She stood by one of the chairs and Pete finally realized she was waiting for him to pull it out for her. Like a regular high society lady. Pete pulled the chair away from the table, then helped push it in after she sat down. He sat down himself and poured more wine.

"Bon appetit," she said, clinking her goblet against his.

He cut a piece of lasagna and put it in his mouth. He chewed for a moment and said, "Umm, that's good."

"That's a man's meal," she said, grinning happily. "I've never met a man yet who didn't like Italian. These Stouffer's dinners have thirty percent more food than the average dinner, too."

He took another bite and said, "All right, I'm dying of curiosity. You've got to tell me what the story is with Kurt Romer."

She looked at him and moved her knee against his. She poked her fork his way and said, "Are you ready for this?"

Pete nodded.

"He's back in jail," she whispered as though someone might be lurking outside her double wide eavesdropping on her.

"You're kidding."

"Nope. That's why I wanted to talk to you in private. That and for us to get together, of course."

"When did this happen?"

"I can tell you exactly because I knew you'd want to know." She went back to the kitchen and returned with a calendar. She pointed at a date. "That's the exact date they came for him. Right there."

Pete looked at the calendar. If Irma was right, Romer was jailed again at least four days before his office was trashed.

"What happened? I mean, why was he sent back to prison?"

Irma cocked an eyebrow in a knowing way and looked at him with her hawkish face and whispered, "Drugs."

"He was back to producing meth."

"That's what they say, darlin'."

He remembered their telephone conversation and asked, "When we talked on the telephone you were in The Nighthawk and said you couldn't talk because it was too dangerous. What did you mean?"

"I was scared someone might hear us."

"Like a friend of Kurt's?"

"That or Bonni," she whispered. "She might tell him."

"But he's in jail. What could he do?"

"Them people have ways," she said, cocking that eye again. "You don't know how they are. Kurt and Bonni talked to me before the government took him away and threatened me if I ever said anything about them."

"Umm," Pete murmured.

"But why don't we just have a nice evening rather than talk about them two." Her knee was against his again and she was stroking his left hand so aggressively that he thought she might wear the skin off. When he finally extricated himself from her clutches, he felt like he'd been pummeled by a den of irascible black bears.

George Strait was crooning some country favorite about a woman who had done him wrong when Pete walked into The Nighthawk. Bonni was working the bar in her trademark outfit. The wattage of her smile amped up when she saw him.

"As I live and breathe, a genuine George Strait fan. Where y'been, stranger?"

"Busy. But it's great to be back." He ordered a Coors Light.

"You've switched."

He nodded. "Variety."

Bonni served two other customers who'd just walked in and then came back and leaned toward Pete with the familiar pose that ensured he would have a good view. "So what have you been up to?" she asked.

"I've been here and there. Taking in a George Strait concert or two."

Her eyes widened. "Where?" She sounded like her breath had suddenly been squeezed from her body.

"Just kidding. I'm not much of a concert goer. Plus he's not touring anymore, I understand."

"You'd be a concert goer if you ever went to one of George Strait's. I don't know how many of his concerts I've gone to. Must be ten at least. When he sings about some of the love he's lost, I just melt and want to take him in my arms." She closed her eyes and a dreamy expression engulfed her face.

"I understand your boyfriend Kurt ran into some problems."

Her eyes lost their dreamy state. "Why do you say 'boyfriend'?"

"Wasn't he? I thought the two of you were living together."

"You've been talking to that whore Irma again. I let Kurt stay at my apartment while he was looking for a place of his own. We both continued our separate lives."

"Okay, it's none of my business anyway. What was it, drugs that got him into trouble again?"

Bonni leaned farther across the bar and lowered her voice. "Before I agreed to take him in — our relationship was something like renter-rentee — I made him swear that he wasn't making that stuff anymore. The bastard *lied* to me, Pete. He *lied*. He almost got me in trouble along with him. I don't have anything to do with drugs, never have. But the government questioned me, Bonni Calhoun, just because I knew the man. What a creep!"

Pete nodded sympathetically.

"Are you dating anyone, Pete? I mean seriously? I'd enjoy getting together with you sometime if you're not."

"I'm seeing someone at the moment, but who knows? Sometimes these things don't work out."

THIRTY-NINE

Pete called Joe Tessler the next morning to let him know that Kurt Romer was in prison again for violating the terms of his parole and, quite likely, was facing new charges for manufacturing and selling meth. That eliminated him from his suspect list, Pete said, because he was back in custody at the time his office was trashed. He also mentioned that he was having trouble tracking down Ashton Feeney since he didn't have his address or any other information.

"I might be able to help you with Feeney," Tessler said.

"Really? How?"

"When people visit the prison, they're required to sign in with their names and addresses."

"Do they have to give their telephone numbers, too?"

"No, for some reason they don't ask for that."

Pete felt disgusted with himself that he hadn't thought to check with Tessler before spending half the day irritating every AT&T information operator in the Midwest. "Did you write down the addresses?" Pete asked.

"I did. Just a minute while I find my notes of the conversation." Pete heard papers rustling as Tessler searched his desk. "Here it is," he said. He gave him Feeney's address. It was in Chicago.

"How about the mother and sister?"

"I have that, too. Both ladies gave the same address in Trenton, New Jersey." He gave him that address as well.

When he was off the phone with Tessler, Harry said, "I couldn't help but overhear your conversation about Romer. I guess we can all breathe easier now, huh?"

"I guess," Pete said, having mixed feelings because it meant one more name was off his suspect list."

"If I'd known this, maybe I would have saved some money and not had that alarm installed."

"Are you arming the system every night?"

"Most nights. Sometimes we forget."

"I'd make it part of your bedtime routine. Romer being in jail again means he couldn't have been the one who trashed my office, but nothing else. The fact that the stalker went after my daughter suggests that others I'm close to could become targets, too. Joe Tessler agrees."

"Now you've made me nervous again."

"I didn't mean to. But reality is reality."

Pete didn't relish another long drive, but now that he had Ashton Feeney's address, he thought it would be better to size him up personally instead of just trying to talk to him on the telephone. He also made a dinner date with Angie for that night. He was getting nervous that they hadn't heard from Judge Rosenberg yet.

He drove west on Peterson Avenue on Chicago's northwest side looking for the address Tessler had given him. The street number he'd written down appeared prominently below a sign that identified the large brick and glass building as *The New Era Rehabilitation Center*. It spanned most of the block and looked new. He circled around on side streets and got back on Peterson and continued to watch the numbers. Even if he'd written down one digit of the address incorrectly, there was no other address on the block that resembled what he was looking for.

He parked in one of the *Center's* visitor slots. The reception area was a high-ceiling atrium constructed of wood and glass with green plants everywhere. He asked at the reception desk for Ashton Feeney.

"Are you a member of Mr. Feeney's family?"

"No, I'm Pete Thorsen. Mr. Feeney and I have a mutual friend—Robyn Fleming—and since I was in the area, I thought I'd stop and say hello."

The receptionist called and after chatting briefly, said, "Mr. Feeney said you can go up. Third floor, second door on your right as you get off the elevator."

Pete found Feeney's room, which had his name on a brass plate next to the handicap-accessible door. He rapped, and when he walked in, he found himself face-to-face with a double-amputee in a wheelchair. Feeney stared at him for a few moments, then his expression softened and he extended his right hand. "Ashton Feeney," he said. "I've heard your name before, Mr. Thorsen."

Pete tried to act casual and nodded and said, "Robyn Fleming."

"Yes," Feeney said, continuing to size him up. "You don't look like a bad guy. Of course, looks can be deceiving."

"Robyn thinks I'm pretty bad as I think you're aware, but fortunately she's got it wrong. How do you know Robyn?"

"I spend summers in Harbor Springs at the old family cottage. I was in a support group up there with Robyn for several years. You know, when you lose the use of your legs, you need all of the support you can get."

When Pete didn't say anything, Feeney smiled thinly and said, "That was supposed to be a joke. A bad one admittedly."

"I know what happened to Robyn. How about you?"

"Two words. If an acronym counts as one word. Iraq. IED."

Pete grimaced and asked, "Are you getting by okay?"

"Oh, sure," Feeney said sarcastically, "my time in the hundred meters dipped below ten seconds last week."

Pete wanted to express sympathy, but sensed that anything he could say would sound condescending and be a mistake. Instead he said, "You were down to the prison in Indiana to see Robyn a while back."

"I was. I thought the visit might boost both our spirits. But I found that it's not very uplifting to listen to someone rail about how her lawyer screwed her the entire time."

"I didn't do what she claims."

Feeney shrugged and said, "Why don't you tell her then?"

"I have. The problem is that her perception of me is as twisted as the crazy scheme she concocted that got her ex-boyfriend paralyzed in the first place."

Feeney looked down and finally said, "She seems like a different person than the one I used to know."

"She is. She's the queen of hate now, blaming me for her circumstances."

"You almost got another letter. I refused to deliver it."

"Did she ask you to deliver anything else?"

"Just the letter. Maybe she *intended* to ask me to deliver something else, I don't know. My refusal on the letter could have put her off."

"She hasn't had many visitors. Her mother a couple of times, her sister."

"She's turned on them, too. Not like you, but they can't do anything right either. The mother is dead now. I don't know whether that gets her off the hook or not. Maybe Robyn still wants to spit on her grave."

Pete thought about the tragedy of it all. "Well," he said, "I'm going to be on my way. Anything I can do for you?"

Feeney sized him up. "A successful lawyer like you ought to be able to contribute to the Wounded Warrior Project."

"I've been a regular contributor for several years and plan to continue in the future. You have my card, Ash. Let me know if there's anything else I can do."

"He seems like a tragic figure," Angie DeMarco said, surveying the dining room at Gibsons.

"He is and he isn't. It's hard to conceive of anything more devastating than having your legs blown off by a terrorist's bomb, but he didn't seem that bitter. On my way out, a nurse told me that he walks with artificial limbs and is relentless with his work in the pool. He's apparently determined to get to the point where he can function like he did before he was injured."

"And you don't think that he's had anything to do with what's been happening to you. Acting as an intermediary or anything."

"I absolutely don't. He's a West Point graduate and is working like a man possessed to get his life together. He didn't say so directly, but he seems to have washed his hands of Robyn after the prison visit. He's the antithesis of what she's become."

"Where does that leave you with Robyn?"

"I have a couple of other suspects on my radar, but I can't shake the feeling that she's the one responsible for all of this. I'm just baffled about how she's doing it. But enough of that. So you don't read anything into the fact that we haven't heard anything yet from Judge Rosenberg?"

"I really don't. It's rare that I get into family court so I don't have a feel for him. Maybe he's the type who likes to let things simmer before he makes a decision."

"Like Solomon would do."

"Yeah."

Pete sat glumly. "I guess it's easy to be patient if your personal interests aren't at stake," he said.

She placed a hand over his.

"I take it you haven't had any contact with Larry Helms?"

"Nothing."

Pete split the remainder of the wine between his glass and Angie's.

She squeezed his hand and said, "You're doing everything right. All of this will be over soon."

Harry had said the same thing, but he didn't believe it then and he didn't believe it now.

FORTY

Before heading north to the lake the following morning, Pete made a stop at River North Spa & Fitness. He asked to see the manager, telling the woman at the reception desk that he was interested in becoming a member. In due course, a man with closely cropped dark hair wearing black nylon Adidas athletic pants and a tight black tee shirt came out. Apparently black was *the* color in the world of fitness.

The manager gave him a brief tour of the facilities. He pointed out the equipment and other accoutrements that he claimed were superior to anything the East Bank Club offered, and explained the fee structure and options available to prospective members. Pete asked about personal trainers. The manager showed him a list with a dozen or so names and how much each charged.

"I met a guy at a party recently," Pete said. "He's a member here and raved about the personal trainer he uses. I believe her name is Eve Bayles. I don't see her on your list."

The manager's bristly black eyebrows knit together and he studied his list. "Are you sure you have the name right?"

"I think so," Pete said. He pulled out his wallet and unfolded a slip of paper. "Yes," he said, showing it to the manager. "I could have written the name down wrong. Maybe it has an 'i' rather than an 'e.' But I'm certain the rest of it is right."

The manager shook his head. "We don't have anyone by that name."

"Could she have left?"

The manager shook his head again. "I don't think so. I've been here since the center opened and I personally vet every personal trainer who works here because I want to be sure we only hire the most qualified people."

"That's strange," Pete said.

"Just a minute, I'll confirm my recollection."

He dialed an extension and asked, "Have we ever had someone named Eve Bayles working here as one of our personal trainers?" He spelled the name.

After a couple of minutes, he said, "Okay, thanks." He confirmed to Pete that they'd never had anyone by that name working for them and then went on to profile some of personal trainers they *did* have on staff and assured Pete that he'd be pleased with any of them.

Pete took the application form and a selection of River North's marketing materials and thanked the manager for his time. The nagging thought that had been forming in his mind began crystallize.

Harry was fine-tuning the next issue of *The Northern Sentinel* when Pete walked in. He stopped what he was doing and wanted to know if he'd found Ashton Feeney. Pete told him the story, including that Feeney was an Iraq War casualty who once been in a support group with Robyn Fleming and others.

"So he's out, huh?" Harry asked.

"Almost definitely. Feeney said he washed his hands of Robyn after he visited her in prison."

"Too much hate and self-pity."

"That's the impression I got."

Harry told him that while he was in Chicago, Higgie Brown and Sunshine Warrick had stopped to see him. They were in mourning again over the loss of their third alpaca and also had heard about his office. Pete made a mental note to pay a courtesy call on them.

"Have you been to the fitness center lately?" Pete asked.

"Yesterday as a matter of fact. I'm hoping to go again tomorrow. Want to join me? After another fancy dinner at Gibsons with Angie, you probably need to work off a couple of pounds."

"I might," Pete said. He gazed out at the street for a moment, then asked, "How did you happen to start working with Eve?"

"I'm not sure I know what you're getting at. She's one of the personal trainers at the center."

"I know that. But did you select her from among the group of personal trainers or what?"

"No, as a matter of fact. She'd seen me in the center working out all the time and approached me one day. She said I'd benefit from working with a personal trainer and offered her services at fifty percent off her normal rate for the first six sessions." He grinned. "Being a Scot, I negotiated fifty percent off for the first *ten* sessions."

"Living up to your reputation as a cheapskate."

"Living up to my reputation as a man who appreciates value when he can get it."

"But the bottom line is that she approached you."

"Yeah, I just told you that. And I told you why. She thought I was the kind of guy she'd like to work with to help me get to the next level of fitness."

Pete digested that for a few moments and said, "That day you brought her over and introduced her to me, was that her idea or yours?"

"What's the matter, did you come back all depressed after you discovered that that Feeney guy is a double-amputee and now you're looking for me to pump you up so you feel like some kind of a chick magnet?"

Pete just looked at him.

"Okay Mr. Viking stud, she said she'd like to meet you. But you know what? That's just the kind of lady she is. She suggested the four of us have drinks, too. You know why? She wanted to meet Rona, that's why. Because of our relationship. It's her holistic approach to personal training. Getting to know the entire man."

Pete nodded and said, "Makes sense." He looked at the wall clock and added, "I'm going to drive out and see the alpaca ladies and give them my condolences. Want to come?"

Harry shook his head. "Can't. I have to sign off on the next issue so the printing presses can roll tonight. Do you want to look at the issue in advance to make sure I haven't violated your personal privacy in any way?"

Pete grinned. "I trust you."

"How about dinner after you get back from the farm? We can't have you wasting away so the ladies around town won't be tempted to give you a squeeze now and then, can we?"

The sun was low in the sky when Pete pulled into Heavenly Meadows. There were signs of spring everywhere. Green shoots were sprouting from the ground and the buds on the lilac bushes looked like they were ready to burst from their winter shackles as soon as the weather warmed another ten degrees.

He went straight to the barn where he was certain Higgie and Sunshine would still be tending to their alpacas. They were feeding them when he walked in. Higgie walked over to greet him and give him the *de rigueur* hug.

"I'm sorry about your latest alpaca."

"George," she said.

"I understand he was killed out in the pasture like the other two."

"She," she corrected him. Higgie must have noticed the puzzled look on his face because she said, "Our baby was named for George Eliot, the Victorian author. He was really a she. All of our babies are named after the great figures of literature. Jane took her name from Jane Austen.

Virgil was named after the ancient Roman poet. We believe that naming our babies in this way connects them with universal life."

Pete wanted to comment, but felt anything he would say might diminish the meaning they ascribed to the naming ritual.

"They were repainting your office when Sunshine and I stopped by. We talked to Harry and he told us that the man who trashed it was the same one who smeared our babies' life fluids on your door."

"*Likely* the same one," Pete corrected her.

"Anything you can tell us about the investigation?" she asked hopefully.

"They've made progress I understand," he said, going out on a limb. "It's important that they keep everything connected with the investigation secret, though, so I'm afraid there isn't much I can add."

She stared into his eyes for a long time, then said, "You're such a good man, Mr. Thorsen."

"Thank you, but please call me Pete."

"We were forced to do a terrible thing, Pete."

His eyebrows moved up as he waited for her to continue.

"Remember how we used to let our babies come and go as they wish? For their own safety, we've put closures across the door to restrict them at night." She pointed to a lattice-like gate of the kind parents with toddlers use to block stairs. "We've prayed that doing this won't cause more trauma in their minds, but what choice did we have? We couldn't bring ourselves to close the doors altogether."

As Pete drove back to town, he thought about what he could do next to resolve the questions in his mind about Eve Bayles. He also thought about the brutal way the alpacas had been butchered and how their blood had been used to send him messages. The image caused a shudder to ripple down his spine.

FORTY-ONE

Pete's office was fresh but with a sterile feeling. He propped the outer door open a foot to let the paint fumes escape and moved his desk and credenza so they were in approximately the same place they'd been in before the office had been trashed. He glanced at the mangled framed photographs of Julie and his late-wife, Doris, both lying flat on the credenza, but abandoned the notion of doing anything with them. They had to be reframed after the blood was professionally removed.

The paintings were a different matter because many of them hadn't been damaged. Whoever was responsible obviously was most intent on defacing the things that were personal to him. He straightened the frames of a couple of paintings and hung them to make the space look less depressingly barren.

Julie called, but only had thirty seconds to talk. She needed money. After arranging a transfer to her account, Pete walked down to *The Northern Sentinel* where he found Harry huddled with his advertising manager. Pete waited until they finished and then said to Harry, "Can you trace an obituary for me? The death occurred in Trenton, New Jersey."

"Do you have some compensation in mind?"

"Dinner again, maybe? With the dessert of your choice? The woman's name is Shirley Lambert. She died about a year-and-a-half ago."

"Should I check city-wide or do you have the name of some suburban paper?"

"Both." He gave him Lambert's address. "I'm going across the street to get a breakfast sandwich from Ebba's. Do you think you can have something by the time I get back?"

"No problem. If she's dead and there was an obit, I should be able to find it."

As Pete was going out the door, Harry called, "Could you pick up something for me, too? Maybe the same breakfast sandwich you're having. And a small doughnut. No frosting or glaze or anything. Just something plain."

"How about if we skip the doughnut? You're in training, remember?"

"I guess you're right," he said thoughtfully. "But everything on the sandwich. Not the scaled-down version that you always order for yourself."

Pete took his time getting the food, and when he got back, Harry was eyeing the bags as soon as he walked in. He tendered the two sheets of paper in his hand and extended the other hand for a bag, as if it were a barter transaction. He ripped the paper apart and began to munch away. Pete read the obituaries while he ate his breakfast sandwich.

"So who's this Shirley Lambert?" Harry asked through a mouthful of sandwich.

"Robyn Fleming's mother."

"Mmm," Harry murmured as he took another bite.

Both obituaries said that Shirley was survived by two daughters, Robyn Fleming and Evelyn Beth Lambert, and by a son, Martin E. Lambert. The obituary in the suburban paper was more expansive that the one in the *Times of Trenton* and said Shirley's activities during her life included membership in the Presbyterian church, the local garden club, and three different book clubs. It also said she was well known in the community for her collection of Elizabethan porcelain figurines.

The obituary gave the location of both daughters as Trenton, which Pete knew was untrue in Robyn's case at least, and the location of her son Martin as Alameda, California.

"It looks like you're focusing on Robyn as the one who's behind everything," Harry said as he licked his fingers.

"Like I told Joe Tessler, I'm trying to be thorough. If Robyn is responsible, I want to figure out how she's doing it from prison."

"Maybe she's paying someone. You hear stories about that happening with mob figures and the gangs."

"I've thought of that," Pete said, trying not to sound testy about the obvious. "Robyn has had exactly five visitors during the entire time she's been in prison. I've met three of them and don't believe any of them is the intermediary between Robyn and someone on the outside. One of the others, her mother, is dead."

"So who does that leave?"

"Evelyn Beth Lambert, the sister, who visited Robyn twice. Now I find there's a brother, too, but he isn't on the list of prison visitors Tessler gave me. So I don't know."

"Do you know where the sister and brother live?"

"According to this," he said, waving the obits in the air, "the sister lives in New Jersey and the brother lives in California."

"That's a long way in both cases."

"If they really live there."

"You're going to check, right?" Harry asked.

"I'm going to try. Tessler also talked to the bank Robyn used to use and verified that her account has been inactive since she went to prison, which is the same information I got. You need to pay a person if you want him to do your bidding and there's no evidence that she has."

Harry gazed out the window and looked like he was deep in thought.

"Can I use your telephone and impersonate one of your reporters again?"

"I guess so," Harry replied, instantly looking wary. His eyes followed Pete as he walked over to the desk he'd used while his office was being repainted and dialed a number.

When the operator answered, he asked for Trenton, New Jersey and the telephone number for Evelyn Beth Lambert. He gave her the street address. A minute later the operator said, "We have no listing for that person at that address. We did have a listing for a Shirley Lambert at the subject address, but service in her name has been discontinued."

"When was it discontinued?"

"I can't tell you that, sir. I don't have that information."

Pete hung up and called directory service for Alameda, California. The operator reported two listings for Martin E. Lambert. He talked her into giving him both numbers.

He glanced at the wall clock. With the three-hour time difference, it was shortly before 7:00 a.m. in California. He dialed the first Martin Lambert, and when a woman answered, he asked for Mr. Lambert.

"This is Martin Lambert," a voice said a minute later.

"Mr. Lambert, my name is Pete Thorsen. I'm a reporter for *The Northern Sentinel* in Michigan. I'm working on a story and wonder if you'd mind talking to me for a few minutes."

"What about? I'm just leaving for the office."

"It's about a woman who was sent to prison a few years ago. We have information that the case is about to be reopened because new evidence has come to light. You're Ms. Fleming's brother, right?"

Silence, then, "I have no interest in talking to you." The line went dead.

Pete sat with the receiver in his hand, thinking. The phone started to chirp and he hung up.

Harry had been watching him carefully and said, "How do you come up with these cockamamie stories you always use?"

Pete half heard him, but was thinking about whether to call the number back and see if the wife would talk or wait until evening and take another run at Martin Lambert. He opted to try the wife, but decided to wait an hour.

He walked up to his office to kill time and then returned to *The Northern Sentinel*. Harry was conferring with his staff of two. Pete said good morning to the others and went back to his desk and dialed the Lambert's number a second time.

"Mrs. Lambert," he said when she answered, "I spoke to your husband earlier this morning, but he had to leave for work. I wonder if I could talk to you for a minute?"

"You're the reporter, right?"

"Yes. Like I told Mr. Lambert, I'm working on a story about his sister's case being reopened. I'm trying to get some general information for my story. It wouldn't be for attribution or anything. That's when a person talks to a reporter—"

"I know what it means," Mrs. Lambert said, sounding irritated. "I was a journalism major in college."

"No kidding?" Pete said. "Did you work at a newspaper or for a news magazine?"

"Just a suburban paper. Then I got my master's degree in children."

"That's wonderful. How many do you have?"

"Four, ranging from an eleven-year-old down to two."

"Wow, *that* must keep you busy. I have one and sometimes feel like I don't have time for anything else."

"How old is she? Or he?"

"She," Pete said, doing his best to bond with Mrs. Lambert. "She's sixteen going on twenty-nine," he added, using his well-honed line.

She laughed. "My day is coming."

"Maybe your kids will be perfect and skip right over the teen years."

"Don't I wish," she said, sighing deeply.

"Getting back to the reason for my call, shall we have an understanding that *everything* you say will be off the record unless you specifically say that I can quote you on something?"

She was silent for a moment. "I don't know if I should talk about anything. It's Marty's side of the family and I think he should decide what to tell you or not tell you."

"I understand, but I'm not going to ask you for any deep, dark family secrets. I just want some off-the-record stuff to use as background for my story."

"Still . . ."

"Let's do it this way. I'll ask a couple of questions where I need to verify information I already have. If you feel uncomfortable at any point, just tell me. And as I said a minute ago, everything is off the record unless we agree otherwise."

Silence, then, "Would Marty have to know that I talked to you?"

"Only if you want to tell him. It doesn't matter to me either way."

"I don't want to get him mad at me."

"And I certainly don't want to cause friction between you two."

Silence again, then, "What's your first question?"

"The obituaries I've seen have both of Marty's sisters living with your mother-in-law. I know that isn't the case with Robyn. How about Evelyn?"

"That's easy. None of them got along and the sisters haven't lived with their mother for like, forever."

"That's kind of what I thought. You said that they didn't get along. Can you add anything to that?"

"Looking at it as an outsider," Mrs. Lambert said, "I think the problem started as a giant case of sibling rivalry and grew from there. Then when Evie got arrested, things got worse because Robyn started to play the holier-than-thou big sister."

"What did she get arrested for?"

"Burglary."

"Umm," Pete murmured. "Did Marty see much of them?"

"Heavens no," she said. "We saw the sisters at Shirley's funeral. That was the first time he'd seen them in eighteen years. Neither one came to our wedding."

"That's too bad. What's that language from the Tolstoy novel?"

"That's one of my favorite quotes. It's from *Anna Karenina*. 'All happy families are alike; each unhappy family is unhappy in its own way.' World lit was my minor."

"Great quote," Pete said. "I take it that Evie as you call her was never married because the obituaries referred to her as Evelyn Beth Lambert."

"Only twice," Mrs. Lambert said derisively. "That we know of."

"There's a lot of divorce going around these days," Pete commented sagely. "Did Evie always keep her maiden name when she got married as so many women do these days?"

"Are you kidding? Her name was Bayles or something like that the first time she got married. Next it was Marcuss. Then she switched back to Lambert. When Marty talks about her, he always refers to her sarcastically as 'Whatever her name is today'."

The fact that Eve Bayles was Robyn's sister didn't come as a surprise to him because all of the signs had been pointing that way.

"What kind of person is Evie?"

"Do you want my opinion?"

"Of course. Off the record of course."

"Three words. Bitchy. Conniving. Cold."

"That's certainly direct."

"It's the truth."

"Where is she now?"

"We heard that she might be in Chicago, but we don't know for sure."

Pete talked to her for another fifteen minutes and asked her other questions to cover his story that he was a reporter. Before they hung up, she pressed him to repeat his earlier pledge that everything she'd told him was off the record and that he wasn't to say anything to Marty about the fact that they'd talked.

FORTY-TWO

"How did you get onto her?" Tessler asked.

"Eve mentioned my daughter when we were having dinner. I knew I'd never said anything to her about Julie, and I checked with Harry and he swore he hadn't either. That got me thinking and I used the information you gave me about Robyn's prison visitors to track down her brother. He wouldn't talk to me, but I called back and got the sister-in-law who told me a lot of things, including that one of Evelyn Beth Lambert's married names was Bayles."

Tessler nodded his head several times, but didn't say anything.

"I put that together with everything else I knew—she'd obviously been using Harry to get close to me, she didn't have the employment background she said she did, she apparently had cat burglar charges against her a few years ago—and suddenly it all fit."

"Any thoughts on what we do next?" Tessler asked.

"That's what I've been sitting here thinking about."

"I could run out and question her I suppose."

"You could," Pete said, "but isn't there a risk that that would cause her to take off? She'd know we were onto her and she has no ties to this area except to do me in if I'm right about her motives."

Tessler looked thoughtful. "I doubt if we can arrest her. Being Robyn Fleming's sister, cozying up to you, knowing you have a daughter, none of those things is a crime. The only evidence we have that she might have been involved in the incident in your office is the footprint by the last alpaca that was killed."

"We need more evidence."

Tessler laughed. "Okay, Sherlock, tell me where it is and I'll go pick it up."

"With the other suspects off the table, we can concentrate on Eve. We should be able to come up with something."

"Frank will enjoy hearing what you just said. Are the Seitz brothers off the table, too?"

· "Probably."

"He's never going to let you forget it you know."

Pete didn't say anything.

"That still—"

"Short term, I can think of three things we can do. One is run the names Eve Bayles and Evelyn Beth Lambert through your national data bases to see if either one shows up. According to her sister-in-law, she's been arrested for burglary at least once."

"No problem with that. I can run the names this afternoon."

Then I think you and I should drive down to the prison in Indianapolis. I'm wondering whether the relationship between Robyn and Eve Bayles is really as strained as the sister-in-law made it out to be."

"That's back to the theory that Robyn is pulling the strings from inside the prison."

"Yes."

"When were you thinking of going down to the prison?"

"Tomorrow?"

Tessler shook his head. "Tomorrow is my day off. I was planning to do some things."

"Watch the soaps? I know you like *As the World Turns*."

"A lot of people joke about that show, but it really isn't bad," Tessler said defensively. "One segment I watched had this babe in a dress that would be illegal in most countries climbing all over the detective. I swear, I had to take a cold shower after it was over."

"Fantasizing that the detective was you, huh?"

Tessler grinned. "We *are* sex symbols, you know."

"You can record tomorrow's episode so you won't miss a thing. I also think you should set up our visit this afternoon. If we have to wait for visiting day, we're probably looking at two weeks from now."

"Any ideas what I can say when I call?"

He thought about the line he used with Mrs. Lambert and said, "You might mention to the warden that you're looking into reopening Robyn's case because new evidence has come to light and that you need to talk to her."

"Another lie."

Pete shrugged. "If it works . . ."

"Let me see what I can do. And your third point?"

"Eve is supposed to cook dinner for me some night soon at her place. I'll try to get a look at her footwear."

Tessler looked at him blankly for a few moments. "Are you planning to go through with the dinner now that we know who she is?"

"She hasn't given me a specific date yet."

"I think you're crazy if you accept her invitation in these circumstances. We should be able to come up with some other way to get what we want."

"As I said, I'm waiting for a date."

When Tessler was gone, Pete sat in his office and went through everything again. His thoughts kept getting interrupted by images of a black-clad figure slicing an alpaca's throat and draining its blood into a plastic bag and of a switchblade stuck into a door.

He called Julie to chat for a few minutes and then checked in with Rae Acton.

Tessler had offered to drive, for which Pete was thankful, and on the way to Indianapolis filled him in on the results of his criminal database search. Ten years earlier, Evelyn Beth Lambert had been arrested on charges that she was a cat burglar operating in Trenton and some of the surrounding towns. Her lawyer worked out a deal whereby she pleaded no contest to the charges and was given a six-month suspended sentence. Four years later, she was questioned by the police in Columbus, Ohio about similar incidents in that city but was never charged. She was then using the name Eve Bayles, but the police noted her previous arrest under the name Evelyn Beth Lambert.

"Your source was right about her criminal past," Tessler said.

"Her burglary background might also explain how she got into Julie's dorm and my office without leaving a trace."

"One more piece of the puzzle."

"But not a smoking gun."

Tessler nodded. "Circumstantial, though."

They cleared the Indianapolis suburbs and suddenly the prison loomed before them like a Medieval fortress that had sprouted from the flat countryside. Red brick walls soared twenty feet in the air and guard towers that rose even higher occupied the corners of the prison like stern sentries. Each tower had wraparound windows, presumably bulletproof, that afforded visibility in all directions and was equipped with multiple search lights and loud speakers. A hundred feet outside the walls, a high chain link fence with razor wire that jutted up like menacing teeth encircled the complex.

As they approached the main gate, boldly lettered red and yellow signs that were posted every hundred feet served warning that all vehicles, official or otherwise, were required to stop at the guard house. The signs said that vehicle occupants had to present sufficient identification and submit to whatever search the guards deemed appropriate. *Absolutely No Exceptions.*

Tessler pulled up to the striped arm that blocked the road at the guard house and stopped. They got out of the car when requested to do so and each of them presented identification and submitted to a pat-down search. They watched as the guards poked around the trunk of Tessler's car and looked under the hood and rifled through the contents of Pete's briefcase. Satisfied that they were clean and on the list of scheduled visitors, the arm blocking the road raised and a guard waved them through. Closer to the prison, another guard directed where they should park.

Inside the prison walls, they passed through a metal detector and submitted to additional questions. Then they were told to wait in a seating area with worn plastic chairs that were bolted securely to the floor. Pete's eyes flicked around as he waited with Tessler. Four senior ladies, none sitting close to the others and all staring at the floor as though concerned that someone might recognize them, were presumably there to see their inmate daughters.

The lone male besides Pete and Tessler was a young man in a striped three-piece suit who sat bolt upright with his arms folded on a briefcase that rested on his knees. He had an earnest, determined look on his face. Pete thought back to twenty years earlier when he'd visited the Joliet Correctional Center outside Chicago to interview an indigent criminal defendant his law firm had been assigned to represent on appeal. He wondered if he'd looked the same that day.

In due course, a guard came to take them to a room where lawyers met with their inmate clients. Each time they passed through a security zone and the bars clanged shut behind them, Pete's heart beat a little faster and the memories of his visit to Joliet came rushing back. It reminded him of why he'd gone into corporate law and not criminal defense work.

A thick glass slab that rose nearly to the ceiling divided the interview room. A counter-level metal shelf twelve inches wide was mounted on each side of the glass, and telephones to facilitate communication sat on the shelves on either side. Like the waiting area, the chairs were bolted to the floor.

"Are you straight on our story?" Pete whispered. "We're looking for signs that Eve may be doing Robyn's bidding."

Tessler nodded. He looked more relaxed than Pete felt.

Five minutes later, a door on the other side of the glass opened and a female guard who looked like she could control the place all by herself pushed a wheelchair through the opening. Pete was shocked by Robyn's appearance. In the ten years he'd known her, she'd always been meticulous in her grooming, but that had changed. She must have lost thirty pounds since she went to prison and her hair was unkempt and now almost completely gray. She stared straight ahead, expressionless. The guard adjusted her wheelchair so she faced them and handed her the telephone on her side of the glass. The guard nodded at them and disappeared through the door again.

Robyn looked at Tessler first and when she shifted to Pete, her vacant eyes came alive and fixed on him and remained there. Pete tried not to show his discomfort and after a minute he said, "Hello Robyn" in the hopes of relieving the tension.

Tessler said, "Let me tell you why we're here, Ms. Fleming. Someone approached us on a confidential basis and claims he has evidence that Evan Smoots, the man who was convicted at the same time you were, acted alone. The source claims that Smoots implicated you because you repeatedly rebuffed his advances and were trying to get back together with your former boyfriend, Sean. According to him, Smoots was motivated by insane jealousy."

"What's scumbag doing here?" Robyn asked. Her eyes continued to sear Pete.

"I asked Mr. Thorsen to come along because he's a special consultant to our department and is helping us investigate. He —"

"You lying bastard!" Robyn screamed, jabbing her finger at Pete. Her voice rose to a shriek. "Get him out of here! Get him out of here!"

"I think you should hear about Mr. Thorsen's conversation with your sister first."

"I don't have a sister!"

"Evie?" Tessler asked tentatively.

"She's dead! She died when my mother died! She was like the rest of the scum in this world! Now she's dead!"

"We have information that Evie's been here to see you twice."

"She snuck in with my mother! Like scumbag Thorsen just did! But she's dead now! Dead! Dead! Dead! Did you hear me? She's dead! Why are you talking about her?"

"Ms. Fleming—"

"Guard! Make them leave! Make them leave." She threw the phone toward them. It ricocheted off the glass and hung dangling by the cable.

Pete had moved his phone away from his ear when she began to rant, but he could still hear her voice as plain as if she were sitting next to him.

The guard stormed into the room. "Settle down," she admonished Robyn, kicking the stops off the wheelchair and heading for the door. "And you two—one of you press your buzzer. Your visit is terminated!"

Before she disappeared through the door, Robyn turned her head and screamed at them, "You're scum, Thorsen! I'm going to write to that man who did your door and tell him to cut your guts out!" The door closed behind them and Pete could hear screams tail off as the guard pushed her down the corridor.

Their guard came to escort them out. They went through the exit procedure, and when Tessler turned onto the state highway and headed north again, he glanced at Pete and said, "That didn't exactly go according to script, did it?"

Pete said grimly, "She's gone over the edge."

Tessler shook his head.

A few miles farther up the road, Pete turned to Tessler and said, "Notice how she didn't even want to talk about the new evidence we said we had?" Pete gestured with two fingers when he said 'evidence'."

"Of course, we really don't *have* any new evidence."

"She doesn't know that. A normal person would have wanted to hear us out even if she didn't completely believe us."

"You'd think so."

"She's gone completely over the edge."

"That's the second time you've said that," Tessler said. "Are you leading up to something?"

"In her present state of mind, Robyn isn't capable of orchestrating anything from prison other than the hate letters she periodically sends me."

"I have to ask you again then—are you still convinced that Eve what's-her-name is the stalker?"

"I'm convinced. She must have some motivation we don't understand."

"What do you propose doing?"

"The only thing we can do. Wait to see what her next move is."

FORTY-THREE

After Tessler dropped him off at his cottage, he checked his telephone messages and saw that Eve Bayles had called. He listened to her sultry voice as she made a few quips and reminded him of her promise to cook dinner for them at her house. She gave him a choice of the following night or the night after and ended with a suggestive innuendo.

Pete listened to the message a second time. He stared at the phone as her soothing voice purred from the speaker. Only days earlier, he'd been excited about the prospect of having dinner with her and drinking wine and seeing where the evening would lead. Now the thought unnerved him.

He glanced at the time and called Rae Acton on her cell phone. She assured him that everything was quiet around Julie's dorm and promised to give him another report in the morning. He turned off the lamps downstairs and went up to his bedroom.

From his window, he saw a sliver of moon rising over the lake. It was so thin and its luminescence so dim that it didn't cast a sheen on the water. The surrounding cottages were hardly visible unless you knew where they were. He stared out for a long time.

He turned on the outside flood lights and lay in bed staring at the macabre patterns created on the walls and ceiling from the artificial light that filtered through the slits along the sides of the shades. An hour later, he was still awake.

Thinking that Eve had a plan and wouldn't be skulking around that night, he got up and turned off the outside lights again and returned to bed. As the moon continued its orbit, a strip of barely perceptible light moved across his ceiling with glacial slowness.

After tossing and turning for most of the night, Pete was up before first light. He finished in the bathroom and looked around outside his cottage for signs he'd had a visitor again. Seeing none, he went back inside and made some hot chocolate and paced around his cottage and thought about what he should say when he called Eve back.

Pete drove to his office and was sitting with his feet propped up on his desk, eating a bagel, when Eve called a second time. He let the phone ring and go to voicemail. He needed more time to think.

He finished his bagel and walked down the street to *The Northern Sentinel* where Harry waved him in. "I was looking for a dinner companion last night," he said, "but you'd gone silent on all of your phones. Were you out with Eve again?"

He shook his head. "In Cadillac," he lied. "An issue came up involving the Colonel's old company. They called me because I'm the only person with an institutional memory about the business. It was late when I got back."

"Umm," Harry murmured. "I know what the Colonel did and all, but I still miss the guy. The three of us had some good times."

"He killed the Janiceks' daughter, Harry. Or at least he was responsible for having her killed."

"I know," Harry said looking out the window. "I guess I was thinking more on a personal level."

"How much more personal can you get than to kill someone because she wouldn't go along with your twisted scheme to bomb public sites in Chicago and lay the blame on other people?"

Harry looked at him with a cocked eyebrow. "Did you get up on the wrong side of the bed this morning? You seem awfully edgy. All I was trying to do was divorce the good from the bad in the man."

"The good was just camouflage for what he was really doing."

"Okay," Harry sighed, "I get the message."

"I get tired of hearing that every slimeball who does terrible things has this wonderful sunny side and deserves nomination as Person of the Year. A monster is still a monster."

"Can we drop it?" Harry asked. He studied Pete for a few moments and said, "Would it improve your outlook on life if your oldest and best friend invited you to dinner tonight? My treat?"

"Maybe," Pete said, forcing a grin. "If I can bring along a couple of my favorite sermons about good and evil."

"Bring whatever you like as long as you balance things out by also bringing a copy of the Orvis guide to fly-fishing. It's that time of the year again, partner."

"You say the sweetest things. What time?"

"The usual."

"Does that mean 6:30 p.m. going on 7:00 p.m.?"

"You should talk, hotshot. After what you did a few days ago?"

"I just forgot I wasn't on Harry McTigue time." Before he left he asked, "Have you visited the fitness center this week?"

Harry stared at him blankly. "Are you implying I should only have a salad without dressing or croutons tonight?"

"No, I was wondering how your workout program is going."

"I had a real good session two days ago. I'm trying to set up another appointment with my personal trainer, but she seems distracted. Must have too many clients she's juggling or something. Or has a new boy-friend she's obsessed with." He grinned.

Or figuring out a plan to dispose of me, Pete thought as he walked back to his office.

Pete dialed Eve's cell phone number and she answered almost imme-diately. "Well, Lazarus has returned from the dead," she said. "I was beginning to think you were having second thoughts about my cooking."

He forced a chuckle. "Sorry for not returning your calls. I had a business meeting out of the area yesterday, and by the time I got back, I thought you might be tucked in for the night. I wasn't in the office yet when you called again this morning."

"So it's not my cooking you're trying to avoid?" she purred.

"Not knowingly. What's on the menu?"

"Secret. Does that mean we're on for tonight?"

"I'm afraid it'll have to be tomorrow night. If that isn't a problem."

"What do you have going tonight? Another business meeting? Or is it a date with one of your other three women?"

Pete forced another chuckle. "Neither. I committed to have dinner with a friend tonight and don't want to cancel. I already cancelled on him another time recently."

"Any friend I know?"

"Maybe. Does tomorrow night still work for you?"

She confirmed that it did and they agreed on 7:00 p.m. She gave him her address, which he already knew, and told him not to bring anything except himself.

As soon as he hung up, he called Harry.

"Eve is cooking dinner for me tomorrow night at her place. If you talk to her, confirm that we're having dinner tonight. I told her I can-celled out on you once recently and didn't want to do it again. Let's keep our stories consistent."

Harry was immediately suspicious about what was going on, but Pete begged off on explaining and said he had a reason for his request.

FORTY-FOUR

Pete drove into the fitness center parking lot and circled around the building to the section in back that was reserved for staff. He recognized Eve's Ford Escape parked in one of the slots. Satisfied that she wouldn't be home, he exited the lot and got back on the highway to Benzonia. He passed through the small village until he came to Michaels Road.

Eve's house was a gray ranch about a half-mile out that was perched atop a gentle hill on several acres of property. The house was set back from the road and the surrounding trees gave it an aura of seclusion. A realtor's sign announced that the property was for sale, which was consistent with Eve's comment that she was renting the house until the owner found a buyer.

He didn't see any other cars so he pulled in the driveway and surveyed the house for a few moments, which told him absolutely nothing. He resisted the urge to get out of his Range Rover and peer in a window or test the doors to see if one was unlocked. He rolled down the dirt driveway again toward Michaels Road and headed for the restaurant where he'd agreed to meet Joe Tessler for lunch.

The Sugar Moon Café was almost directly across the street from the Crystal Crate & Cargo, Harry McTigue's favorite shopping place when he needed to pick up a gift for Rona that would keep her floating on air for a week. There were only a handful of people in the restaurant and he selected an out-of-the-way table in the corner. Tessler arrived five minutes later.

"You're determined to go through with this, huh?" Tessler asked after he was finished perusing the menu.

"Do have another suggestion?"

"You could wait until she makes some other move. She might make a mistake."

"How many mistakes has she made so far? None. Zero. It's time to bring this to a head."

"She left some footprints by the last alpaca she killed," Tessler argued.

"Is that enough to charge her with a crime?"

Tessler paused for a moment, then said, "By itself, probably not. But if we get something else on her . . ."

"We're not going to, Joe. I've made up my mind. But I'm not stupid. I need your help."

"You're venturing into her lair. That seems to me to be pretty stupid."

"Give me an alternative for crissakes!"

Pete's voice must have been louder than he intended because he noticed a couple having lunch at a table near the window glance their way.

Pete lowered his voice again. "Let's assume that she intends to do me harm. How would she approach it?"

Tessler appeared to think for a moment. "Well, she's got you out there in an isolated area. She could have an accomplice lurking out of sight and they could jump you."

Pete digested that. When Tessler didn't continue, Pete asked, "Anything else?"

The detective thought some more. "She could slip you something to disable you. Then you'd be in real trouble."

Pete pushed Tessler for more information. "What would she slip me and how would she do it?"

"Special K, Roofies, that kind of thing. She could—"

"Date-rape drugs."

"Right. Date-rape drugs. She could put some in your wine as one possibility. I don't know about food. She's cooking you dinner, right?"

"That's what she says."

"I would say the wine. That makes the most sense."

"What are the effects of those drugs? I know that they're supposed to make a person compliant and unaware of what's going on."

"Loss of consciousness is what you'd have to worry about. Assuming she's planning something, she'd probably want to knock you out."

He tried not to show his nervousness and said, "Let's say I came up with some excuse and brought a bottle of wine and watched to make sure she didn't slip anything in it. That would avoid the problem, right?"

"Sure. But think about it for a moment. If she can't put you out and do whatever to you, what have you gained by serving as a piece of bait in the first place? We wouldn't have any more on her after the night is over than we have now. And you'd still be taking a risk."

"I'd get to see the inside of her house and maybe look around. I'm looking for alternatives."

Tessler shook his head and said, "I think our best shot is to hit her with the footprints and match them to her shoes or boots. Then we could hassle her about her various names and confront her with the fact we know that she's Robyn Fleming's sister. We could also lay on her the fact we know she doesn't have the background she's been telling everyone she has. You know, employment-wise. Make her look like a liar."

"We talked about that, remember? She might disappear."

"If she does, she does. At least she'd be away from here."

Pete had already considered the pros and cons of that. If she did take off, he knew he'd be looking over his shoulder for years. Maybe the rest of his life. He had Julie to worry about, too.

"Is she strong enough to over-power you without the use of drugs?" Tessler asked.

Pete roused himself from his private thoughts. "She's a personal trainer and can bench press as much as you or I could. She's also a black belt. If she had a knife . . ."

"All the more reason to reconsider all of this. I think you should beg off the dinner. Call and tell her you're sick or something."

"Based on what we presently have, would Frank let you hassle her like you suggested if we decide to go that route?"

Tessler appeared to think again. "I can't say," he said. "He might. You heard him at your office that day. He wants me to get to the bottom of this."

"But you don't know for sure."

Tessler shook his head. "I can't give you an ironclad, no."

Pete didn't say anything.

"I could visit her myself and not tell Frank," Tessler suggested.

"Couldn't that blow up in your face if our analysis is wrong for some reason and Frank finds out about what you've done? If Eve went to him and complained, for instance. I'm not exactly the sheriff's favorite person, remember."

"It could."

Pete walked into the Bay Grille promptly at 6:30 p.m. and was surprised to see Harry already there holding court at the bar with Rona and the chef.

"You're one minute late," Harry said ebulliently.

Pete shrugged. "No one's perfect."

When they were seated at their customary table, Harry babbled on about every topic under the sun while Pete tried to listen politely. His mind was on his dinner with Eve the following night. Before he came, he'd called Tessler and told him he'd decided to go forward with the dinner, but with precautions they worked out.

They'd also discussed what Pete should look for when he was inside Eve's house. Gauging her shoe size was the obvious thing. Tessler also suggested that he try to find out whether she had a printer that could have been used to print out the messages that had been left for him. They agreed that he couldn't expect to find blood-stained clothes lying around or a knife with blood residue on it.

"Here's something that will blow your mind," Harry said as he reached into his briefcase and withdrew a copy of *Sports Afield*. "We were just talking about the trout season, so what happens? This arrived in today's mail." He waved the hunting and fishing magazine. "And what do I see on page thirty and the next six pages? A color spread on the Brule River. *Our* Brule River. We gotta plan a trip." He pulled out a pocket calendar and went through a day-by-day recitation of when he was available for the rest of April and during May.

Their food came. The waitress had barely put their plates on the table when Harry sawed off a piece of steak and popped it into his mouth and flushed it down with a healthy swallow of Merlot. Pete picked at his grilled walleye and steamed asparagus.

Harry said through a half-full mouth, "Eve called this afternoon just as you predicted and asked if I was having dinner with you tonight."

Pete looked at him with raised eyebrows. "Did you stick with our script?"

Harry winked at him. "Oh yeah, right down the line. But you know me. I'm something of an expert on telling when a woman is checking up on a guy. I sensed that she was worried you might be out with another woman."

Pete forced a smile. "You think so?"

"I do." Harry repeated his story about the wife of a friend who checked him out so thoroughly when they were dating and then told him ten similar stories.

"It's a fine art with women," he said, sounding like the world's foremost authority on the opposite gender.

Pete half listened to him, but he had a different take on Eve's inquiry. She might have an inkling that he was onto her. His mind worked overtime to recall every nuance of their past conversations.

FORTY-FIVE

The clock moved maddeningly slow all day, and as Pete's anxiety built, he drove through the fitness center lot twice to see if Eve's Ford Escape was there. The second time, around 4:00 p.m., it was gone. He continued on to Benzonia and went past her house and saw her SUV parked in front. He drove around the side roads for a half hour, and when he passed Eve's house again, her SUV was still the only vehicle in sight.

He went home and changed clothes and looked at himself in a full-length mirror. Maybe he was overly conscious of it, but the emergency call device Tessler had given him seemed to create a bulge in his pants pocket. He switched to khakis that were a bit more generous through the thighs and checked himself in the mirror again. Better, he thought.

He wandered around the cottage, straightening magazines and watering a plant. Finally it was time to leave.

Darkness was settling in when he pulled into Eve's driveway. He parked his Range Rover so it was facing out. The call device felt like an anvil in his pocket as he walked to the door carrying a bottle of Pinot Noir in a festive gift bag. He had an explanation ready in case she scolded him for bringing wine in spite of her instructions to bring only himself.

Eve greeted him with a kiss on the lips and a warm embrace. She wore a neat white apron over a black outfit that was accessorized by a bold necklace with chunky turquoise stones mounted on a silver chain. Her hair was down in the usual look he found so tantalizing. He stepped inside and tried to look relaxed. Through a connecting arch to the dining room, he saw candles already flickering.

She looked at the bag in his hand and a thin smile tugged at the corners of her mouth. "You don't follow instructions very well, do you?"

Pete shook his head contritely. "Sorry, I just couldn't help myself."

"Let's see what you brought." She was still smiling.

He pulled out the bottle of Pinot Noir and waggled it back and forth in front of her.

She said, "Too bad I already have wine decanted. I'll put this away and we can drink it another night."

"*Or,* we can put a stopper in your decanter and drink this. I was assured by the fellow who sold it to me that this wine contains a magic elixir."

"Is this the same man who sells you those addictive oldies?"

They both laughed although Pete thought he detected a hint of irritation in her eyes. She took him by the hand and led him into the kitchen where she pulled a corkscrew from a drawer and handed it to him.

"Wine glasses are on the table. Do your opening duties and bring me a glass. I have to finish dinner."

He expelled air from his lungs as he walked to the dining room. *That didn't go so bad,* he thought. He took his time opening the bottle and glanced over his shoulder once to see if she was watching. She wasn't. He took one of the wine glasses from the small dining room table, and after glancing toward the kitchen again, held it up to the light emitted by one of the candles. He quickly swabbed the glass with a napkin from one of the place settings, thinking he'd probably elevated paranoia to new heights.

He poured the wine and carried the glasses to the kitchen where Eve was straining broccoli. He waited for her to finish and slipped the glass he hadn't wiped into her hand. They clinked glasses and he offered a toast. They both took sips.

"That's good," Eve murmured. "You'll have to disobey my instructions more often. And next time, you can always forget and bring a diamond necklace." She leaned forward and kissed him on the lips again.

Without being obvious about it, he glanced at her feet. Not surprising for a woman who was five-feet ten, they weren't exactly tiny. They looked narrow as well. He looked around the kitchen, as if checking out the appliances, and then glanced at her feet again. They could be a woman's size nine, but he wasn't sure. Maybe he'd see a pair of her shoes around the house and have a chance to check the size without her noticing.

He wandered into the living room while she continued her cooking chores and looked at a couple of the paintings on the wall. He glanced toward the kitchen again and walked casually down the short hallway that led to the bedrooms. Both rooms were dark except for the light filtering down the hall from the living room, but they looked immaculate. He debated whether to click on the lights in one of them so he could see better.

"Are you checking on my housekeeping?"

He jumped when he heard the voice and he turned to see Eve a few feet behind him.

"Did I startle you?" She had the thin smile on her face again.

"No, no," he said. "I was just giving myself a short tour while you finished dinner. I know the place is for sale. I hope I'm not a presumptuous guest."

"Not as long as you give me a passing grade on my housekeeping."

"You get an A-plus."

"You've earned your dinner, then. C'mon, we're on."

Dinner was Cornish hens with broccoli and wild rice. He helped her carry the food to the dining room table and watched as she lit three more candles on the sideboard. She excused herself and went back to the kitchen. Moments later the kitchen went dark and then the living room lights dimmed as well. Eve walked into the dining room again like an apparition in black with the candle light shimmering around her.

The apron was gone and the turquoise necklace nestling in her cleavage glinted in the soft light. She sat down adjacent to him. He wanted to reach over and move the necklace to the side so he'd have an unobstructed view, but had to remind himself that in spite of all of her charm and femininity, the woman sitting next to him was most probably a psycho bent on doing him harm.

They talked about Chicago, the place they had in common besides northern Michigan, and Pete asked some questions about River North Spa & Fitness to test her. She handled the questions smoothly. They chatted about their army days and Pete asked her some more questions about her experience as a Best Warrior judge.

Pete sipped more of his wine and wondered again as he had periodically during the day whether he should have taken Tessler's advice and begged off the dinner. He'd managed to neutralize the wine issue, which had been on his mind constantly since his conversation with Joe Tessler about date-rape drugs, but he wondered what her plan "B" was. It was almost like she was playing with him.

"Harry told me that your last lady friend died in an automobile accident on the Leelanau Peninsula."

Every time she came out with something like her last comment, he wondered whether she'd heard it from Harry, as she often claimed, or whether it was the product of her probe into his past. He wasn't inclined to tell her the entire tortured story behind Lynn's death, so he just said, "Yes."

"Have you gotten over it yet?"

He shrugged. "I didn't know her very long."

"Longer than me?"

"Yes," he said, "longer than you."

The conversation turned to other things and they finished dinner. Pete made the *de rigueur* raves about her cooking and helped clear the dishes. After that, they returned to the dining room table and talked some more. Pete tried not to show his distraction. His hand brushed the outside of his pants pocket with the alert device. He was thankful that it was in the opposite pocket rather than in the one next to her where she might feel it. He began to think of plausible excuses to leave early.

"What's your legal practice like these days?" Eve asked. Her knee brushed his.

"I don't practice much anymore as I think I told you."

"But you do take on some matters you said. Are your clients individuals as well as companies?"

"In this area, you don't have a choice. If you want to practice, you take both. In my case, though, I can be selective. I've segued, as they say."

"Having fewer clients must make it easier to juggle your responsibilities. Like keeping one client's secrets secure from someone else."

The red flag in Pete's mind was flapping again. *Was she finally getting to it?* He fingered the device in his pocket again.

"That's never been a problem," he said casually. "It isn't for most lawyers."

"Mmm," she murmured. "I thought it might be."

Pete didn't say anything.

"So what was your most exciting case?" she asked.

"You mean legal case?"

"No Sherlock. I mean the cases you've developed a reputation for getting involved in."

"For the tenth time, that's been overblown. People start gossiping and all of a sudden it's all blown out of proportion. I'm a lawyer, not a detective. Law is what I do. When I'm not writing or fly-fishing or doing something else that interests me."

"I think you're too modest." She reached for the wine bottle. It slipped out of her hand and flopped on its side.

Pete's arms were frozen as he watched the wine trickle onto the table.

FORTY-SIX

"Damn!" she said, scrambling to her feet. She began to mop the spilled wine with her napkin.

Pete set the bottle upright again and saw that it was nearly empty. Eve went to the kitchen and returned with a handful of fresh napkins and he helped her finish cleaning up.

"What a klutz," she said disgustedly. She took the wine bottle and checked to see how much remained and split the few drops between their glasses. "I'll be back," she said. She disappeared into the kitchen again with the soiled napkins and the empty bottle. She returned a minute later with a fresh glass of wine in one hand and the wine decanter and an empty glass in the other.

She set the empty glass in front of him and said, "A clean glass for when you're ready for my inferior stuff. Aren't you lucky I had the foresight to decant a reserve bottle ahead of time?" She nudged him with her hip and smiled seductively.

He stared at the decanted wine and wondered how he was going to avoid drinking some of it without tipping off his suspicions. His glass was a quarter full. He needed to come up with an exit strategy before it was gone. The fact that Eve came out of the kitchen with her own glass full instead of pouring it at the table fueled his anxiety.

"We were talking about your reputation as a sleuth. Why are you so reluctant to talk about it? A lot of women find it exiting when their man has an adventuresome side." She took a sip of her wine and began caressing his arm with the back of her hand.

"Adventuresome? Me?"

"C'mon, Mr. Modesty. Can't you tell me at least *one* little story? There's so little excitement up here. You don't have to worry about confidentiality because the cases are over, right?" She continued to rub his arm and when he looked at her, her eyes seemed predatory rather than warm. Or was it just the candlelight? Or his imagination?

He tried to get her off the subject by telling her a sanitized version of what happened after they found Cara Lane's body in the lake.

"I heard that's how you got close to the detective in the sheriff's office. From the case you just told me about."

Pete eyed her and said, "I wouldn't say I'm *close* to Joe Tessler. I know him obviously."

"You were with him that day I saw you at Ebba's Bakery."

"That's because the sheriff's people were all there on account of my trashed office. Tessler is the lead detective and had some questions for me. Neither of us had had breakfast, so we decided to eat while we finished talking."

Eve filled the empty glass in front of him from the decanter. "Well, *I* heard that the two of you *are* close. You feed Joe information and he feeds you information. Kind of a mutual bargain."

Pete screwed up his face and looked at her and said, "Where do you get all of this stuff?"

"I work with a lot of people at the fitness center. Some of them like to talk."

He sipped from his nearly-empty glass and tried to be attentive to his conversation with Eve while his mind cranked overtime to decipher hidden meaning in her questions. He found it difficult not to sneak an occasional glance at the full glass of wine in front of him. He remembered Tessler telling him that the drugs were essentially odorless and tasteless when mixed with wine or other alcoholic drinks. He didn't know if the wine had been doctored, but he wasn't about to test it.

The voice inside him that had been hammering away all day was at it again. *What the hell was he doing there anyway?* He'd been in some tight scrapes in recent years, but there was something about being alone with this woman in an isolated house with candles all around that put him on edge. Sometimes when he looked at her, he saw a hardness in her eyes until they softened when she realized he was looking at her.

He passed a hand over the outside of his khakis and felt the emergency call device in his pocket again. That morning, they'd tested it at four hundred feet to confirm that it worked. *How about five hundred feet?* he wondered. *Or six hundred feet?* Would trees affect the transmission? Were there other factors? The devices must be dependable because seniors relied on them to call for help in emergencies. But questions kept creeping into his mind.

"A quarter for your thoughts," she said. "It used to be a penny, but with inflation . . ." Her knee brushed against his.

"I was just thinking about the outline for an article that I promised to e-mail to a magazine editor tomorrow."

"Is it the one about Viking helmets with horns versus no horns?"

"No," he said, chuckling, "a different one. I'm saving the horns story for Harry's paper."

"I'm sure it'll be a big hit. You're not drinking your wine." Her lower lip curled in a pout.

"I've been feeling queasy all day and don't know if I should drink anymore. Maybe it's something I ate last night."

She smiled at him. "You're not too queasy for dessert are you?"

"Depends. What's on the menu?"

Eve got up from her chair and stood behind him so her breasts pressed against his shoulders. She brushed his ear with her lips and nibbled and used her tongue. She put her cheek against his and murmured,

"Well, I have some key lime pie we could thaw. Or . . ." She nibbled at his ear again. "If you're not too queasy, that is."

He turned his head and kissed her on the cheek. "Mmm, what a choice."

Her tongue probed his ear some more and she whispered, "We can take our wine and get comfortable. That might help you decide." Her hand began to stroke his leg.

Pete decided that now was the time. He kissed her on the cheek again and said, "How about ten rain checks I can use when I'm feeling better." He took her face in his hands and kissed her on the mouth and then on the eyes.

She didn't move and looked at him with the familiar thin smile. "You're really feeling that bad, huh?"

"Not terrible. I'm just not at the top of my game."

"You're queasy," she said. The smile was still there.

"For lack of a better word."

"Do you want to call it a night, then?"

"I think I'd better. Can I help you clean up before I go?"

"Thanks, I can handle it. I wouldn't want you to get sick on my kitchen floor." Still smiling.

He retrieved his jacket from the coat tree and kissed her on the lips. "Sleep well." Her smile was beginning to unnerve him.

He closed the door behind him and walked to his Range Rover. *God, that was clumsy*, he thought. He turned the key in the ignition and breathed out audibly as he headed out the drive. He turned right on Michaels Road toward Benzonia, and a hundred feet in front of him, a vehicle flashed its headlights. He was startled at first, but then realized it was Joe Tessler. Pete pulled up head-to-tail alongside his unmarked Acura and lowered his window. "Follow me into town and I'll tell you what happened."

They parked in a strip mall and Tessler got into the front seat of Pete's Range Rover. Pete told him about the evening, concluding by saying, "It was awkward at the end, but I decided to get out of there."

"She didn't try anything I take it."

"She didn't pull a knife on me if that's what you mean. But she seemed different than the other times I've been with her."

"How so?"

Pete thought about it and said, "As I look back, I always had the feeling that she was playing with me. Tonight was different. Maybe it was my paranoia because of everything we've learned, but I couldn't shake the feeling that she was eager to get on with it."

Tessler nodded, but didn't say anything.

"One time when I thought she was cooking, I walked down the hall toward the bedrooms, hoping I'd see something we could use. A pair of her shoes so I could check the size, a computer and printer. Suddenly she was five feet behind me. It scared the hell out of me. The hall floor is bare wood and I didn't hear a thing."

"How did you explain poking around in her house?"

"I made some stupid comment about knowing the place was for sale and was just looking around."

"Plausible."

"Plausible, but I don't think I convinced her. She kept smiling at me. Like she knew that I know."

"Creepy."

Pete's mind flashed back to when she knocked over his wine bottle and then brought out the decanter. She'd been smooth as silk until that time. She must have improvised when things didn't go according to script.

"At least you stayed away from her wine."

"How could I help it? You had me so damn spooked I was afraid to be in the same room with it."

"Better safe than sorry."

"You know," Pete said, "sitting here in the safety of my car it's easy to make light of some of these things. But we can't lose sight of what a sicko she really is. The way she butchered the alpacas and the rest of it . . ."

"We should get together in the morning and talk about it after a good night's sleep. Maybe something will come to us."

"I'm ahead of you. I think the option you outlined is the best one. If you feel you need to talk to Frank first, do it right away in the morning and then get out to question her just as soon as possible. If necessary, you need to figure out a way to hold her until we can build the rest of our case."

Tessler appeared to think about it. "I'll need you there to support me with Frank. You have a better command of the facts than I do."

"I'll be there. I just want this over with." He paused and then said, "It's embarrassing to admit, but when she got out of her chair and stood behind me and started to rub on me and proposition me, I came close to pressing the button while I still could."

FORTY-SEVEN

After he got home, Pete spent two hours outlining the case against Eve Bayles, including that her shoe size seemed consistent with the prints found near the dead alpaca and everything else they'd discovered. Some of the points might not pass muster in a court of law, but presented together, they made a persuasive narrative.

He ripped the pages from his legal pad and recopied the presentation in a more legible form with some of the material rearranged. A jolt of adrenaline shot through his body as he read the revised presentation. Tomorrow he was finally going on offense against the psycho who'd been terrorizing him and his daughter.

He went through his nightly ritual of checking the doors and windows and arming his alarm system, then turned off the downstairs lights and went up the steps to the second floor. He set his alarm clock for 6:00 a.m. to be sure he had time for his morning routine before he met Tessler for breakfast to go over their script prior to descending on the sheriff. He got into bed and clicked off the bedside lamp and stretched out, feeling his muscles relax. When his eyes adjusted to the inky darkness, he watched the faint sliver of moonlight that seemed to be barely moving across the ceiling.

Sleep didn't come easily. He kept replaying the evening in his mind and thought about the meeting with Sheriff Richter in the morning. He tossed and turned and rolled over and finally went to the bathroom for a glass of water and some aspirin. When he got back in bed, he squeezed his eyes closed and willed himself to sleep.

A meadow with a white house on the far side loomed before him. A figure appeared in the doorway and beckoned, then disappeared inside again. Pete ran toward the house with little Julie in tow. Their legs churned furiously, but they didn't get any closer so they ran faster. He heard the wind behind them, howling, gusting. He scooped Julie into his arms and ran faster still. It was like he was on a demonic treadmill with the belt moving in reverse. The angry black cloud descended like an unseen hand was pushing it to earth. It was right behind them. The figure appeared in the doorway and beckoned again. He clutched Julie tighter and continued to run . . . .

Pete's eyes snapped open and he rolled over onto his back. He was breathing heavily and his tee shirt was damp. When he touched his forehead, he felt beads of sweat. He drew air into his lungs and breathed out. The sliver of moonlight had worked its way farther across the ceiling.

Pete sensed that he wasn't alone. He lay completely still and resisted the impulse to sit up and peer into the darkness or call out. Near the foot of his bed, he could make out a shadowy mass. His heart hammered in his chest cavity. He tried to distinguish the mass from the surrounding blackness and his mind raced. He thought of the Louisville Slugger bat next to his bed.

"Bad dreams Pete?" a soft voice asked.

He tried to calm himself so his voice wouldn't quiver. Breathe in, breathe out. Breathe in, breathe out. Don't show fright. Finally he forced out, "What are you doing here, Eve?"

"I came to check up on you," she said softly. "You said you were feeling queasy."

Pete didn't say anything. He tried to relax his body so he wouldn't shake.

"Does the kitty have your tongue, Pete?"

He slid toward the head of his bed a few inches in an uncontrollable reflex to put more distance between Eve and himself.

"No, no, Pete, that's a bad thing to do when you're queasy. You have to lie very still. It's better for your queasiness. If you disobey, Dr. Eve will have to give you something to keep you still."

The bat! He needed to reach the bat! His left arm was under the blanket and he moved his hand an inch toward the edge of the bed.

"You aren't a very good conversationalist, Pete."

He didn't say anything again, but moved his hand another inch.

"I thought you were rude tonight. You ate the dinner I cooked, but rejected my wine and dessert. A woman doesn't like to be rejected, Pete."

He remained silent and tried to focus his thoughts. He moved his hand another inch.

"If I were a suspicious person, Pete, I might wonder if you were nervous about being alone with me."

Keep her talking, he thought. *Buy some time.* "We know who you are, Eve," he said, hoping that his voice hadn't quivered. He moved his hand another inch.

"Really, Pete? I told you who I am. I'm Eve Bayles, Harry's personal trainer."

His hand moved another inch toward the edge of the bed. *Rattle her*, he thought. *Let her know that she'd been found out.*

"Also known as Evie Lambert, Robyn Fleming's sister," he said.

"Wow! You *are* smart, Pete. It's easy to see how you earned your reputation as a super sleuth."

See if you can reason with her. Tell your side of the story.

"Robyn's lying if she told you I turned her in. I didn't tell anybody about our conversation. The man she hired to sabotage her former boyfriend's hang gliding wing is the one she should be blaming. He tried to cut a deal with the prosecuting attorney and fingered her as a bargaining chip." Pete moved his hand another inch to the left.

"My sister doesn't lie to me."

"She lied, Eve. Or should I call you Evie?"

"You lawyers are all the same. You double-down when you're caught in a lie."

He wished he could see her hands. Then he'd know what he was dealing with. A gun would be worst. At less than ten feet, he'd have no chance if she had a gun. More likely it was a knife. That's what she'd used to slaughter the alpacas and pin the note to Julie's door. The image of the wicked switchblade sticking in the door flashed through his mind. He tried to calm himself. He moved his hand another inch.

"It's not a lie, Eve." He moved his hand an inch more.

"You shouldn't say bad things about my sister."

This was his chance! Shake her up! Tell her things she doesn't want to hear!

"Robyn hates you," he said. "She told me herself. She claims that you're dead."

"She doesn't hate me, scumbag!"

She pounded her fist into his bed. He jumped but used the outburst to move his hand several inches closer to the bat. He couldn't tell whether the impact was just from her fist or whether she'd plunged a knife into the mattress.

Maybe he was pushing her too hard. No, he was playing it right. Continue to upset her. She might let her guard down.

He slid his hand another two inches to the left.

"Face it, Eve. Your sister despises you. Your *own* sister. You're all alone now." His fingers felt the bat. He hoped she couldn't see his hand outside the blanket.

Silence for a moment, then she said in a voice that was calm again, "When I tell her how I took care of you, Pete, she'll love me again."

"You're delusional, Eve." His fingers curled around the handle of the bat.

"I'll tell her you lost your ability to walk before you died. Just like her. She'll appreciate that. Now why don't you turn over on your stomach please. Very slowly."

His heart pounded wildly.

"Turn over, Pete."

"Why?"

"Because it's time," she said softly. "Time for Dr. Eve to relieve your queasiness."

"No," he said after a moment. His fingers tightened on the bat's handle.

A blur of motion erupted and in two seconds he felt a cold blade against his neck. "I asked you politely, Pete. This isn't like dessert you can turn down or accept. You have no choice." The blade pressed harder.

"I'll turn over," he said.

He felt the blade move away.

FORTY-EIGHT

He started to follow Eve's instructions, then violently reversed direction and swung the bat as hard as he could toward where he thought she might be standing. His left arm wasn't as strong as his right, but felt the bat strike some part of her body. A gasp followed by a soft moan came from the darkness. He frantically rolled the other way and landed on his feet with his back to the wall and switched the bat to his right hand.

He heard another moan and then saw the black mass move. *She was coming at him!* For just a nanosecond, a sliver of moonlight glinted off metal. He braced himself, then stepped forward and swung the bat with all of the strength he could muster. The bat hissed through the air like a venomous snake about to strike and struck a window. But no flesh! The glass exploded and shards cascaded into the room.

She was still coming! He got the bat around just in time to use the end as a foil. It caught her in the middle of her body and the impact knocked him backward. He jabbed viciously with the bat a second time, his primordial survival instincts raging. It struck her body again and he heard another gasp. He stepped back when she began to move again, but slammed into the bedroom wall. He swung the bat with a backhand motion. It struck her with a glancing blow. *Get out of the corner!* he told himself.

He placed a hand on the bed to vault over and felt something rake his left arm. He scrambled across the bed and saw the outline of the doorway ahead! He started for it, but when he glanced left, he thought he saw Eve again. He whirled and stepped toward her and swung the bat with a wild swing. Her shriek pierced the darkness and she moaned in pain. He thought he saw her sink to the floor and took another overhand swing with the bat. He heard a muffled *Thump!* as the bat struck the rug covering the wood floor. His hands and arms tingled from the impact and he heard moans coming from the darkness. His heart pounded wildly as he decided what to do. He bolted for the open bedroom door.

He bounded down the steps two at a time, relying on familiarity since he couldn't see. His bare feet slipped on the wood and his feet shot out from under him. He landed on the edge of a step and numbing pain shot through his spinal system. He looked up the stairs and didn't see Eve. He rubbed his lower back and then forced himself to get back on his feet and continue to the first floor.

He stood plastered to a kitchen wall, body throbbing. For the first time, he became conscious that his left hand was wet and sticky. He listened for sounds of Eve coming down the stairs. He heard nothing, but remembered how silently she moved. Like a predatory cat. The window shades in the kitchen were up and he took a chance and moved quickly to a band of moonlight and looked at his hand. Blood streamed from the long cut on his arm where Eve had slashed him with her knife. *How much blood could he lose before he began to feel lightheaded?* He felt his way to one of the kitchen drawers and pulled out a clean dish towel and wrapped it around his arm.

His mind raced. Calling the sheriff's office wasn't an option. If she came up behind him while he was on the phone, it was over. Making a dash for his Range Rover was out, too, because the keys were in his bedroom dresser drawer along with his wallet.

A light appeared from upstairs! He flattened himself against the wall again. She was obviously off the floor and moving around even though he'd heard nothing. *Maybe he hadn't hurt her as badly as he thought.* He felt the blood soak the towel wrapped around his arm. Light filtered down the stairway and illuminated the wall across from where he was standing. *He had to move!*

He saw the emergency call device that he'd left on the kitchen counter earlier. The light upstairs was still on. He tucked the bat under his towel-wrapped left arm and moved silently across the kitchen floor, cringing when he stepped into the light, and grabbed the device and moved back again.

The upstairs light went off! That meant she was still up there. *He knew the house better than she did,* he thought. *That was an advantage.* He also knew he had to get out of the kitchen because it was only a matter of time before she came after him and that was the most exposed area. He still heard no sounds on the stairs.

He moved through the short hallway to the mudroom, being careful not to hit a wall with the end of the bat and tip Eve to his location. His left hand continued to feel wet and sticky and he clamped his arm to his side in order to make the towel tighter and try to stanch the bleeding. The bat impeded that, and he switched the call device to his left hand, momentarily taking his finger off the button that he'd been pressing since he left the kitchen, and grabbed the bat with his right hand.

He felt exposed and nestled deeper among the long snowmobile suits that hung from wall pegs. He depressed the call device button again and held it. *One one-thousand, two one-thousand, three one-thousand . . .* He squeezed his eyes closed for a moment and prayed that Tessler had taken the device's receiver inside his house when he'd gone home. And that the device could effectively transmit a signal from miles away.

He took his finger off the button and listened for sounds that Eve was downstairs. He heard nothing. He remembered the duct tape and other materials he kept on a shelf. He moved to his left and felt along the shelf. His fingers touched the roll.

He moved back among the snowmobile suits and listened again. Hearing nothing, he leaned the bat against his thigh and used the heavy suits to muffle the sound as he stripped tape off the roll. Even with his hands buried in the suits, it sounded like an ambulance siren as it unraveled. He bit the tape to start the tear and again used the coats as a sound muffler. He wrapped the length of duct tape around the blood-soaked towel on his arm.

"I know you're down here, Pete. Why not make this easy on yourself?"

His heart jumped like it was about to catapult from his body. Her voice came from nearby. He hadn't heard a sound, but she was in the kitchen. He didn't say anything. He didn't dare tear off any more of the duct tape. He slipped the roll over a coat peg behind him and held the bat close to his right thigh and strained to hear more sounds.

"You know I'll find you, Pete."

Eve's voice sounded farther away. The living room maybe? His fingers opened and closed on the bat handle. *He needed a plan*. It was a matter of time until she checked the mudroom. A plan, he thought desperately. Some plan.

The mudroom's door opened outside. All he had on was a tee shirt and boxers and the outside temperature was near freezing. Maybe he should grab one of the snowmobile suits and bolt for the door. *No, by the time he got it on, she'd be on top of him!*

"We should talk, Pete. It'll be better that way."

Her voice sounded more distant. *The corridor leading to the downstairs bedrooms?* He leaned the bat against his thigh again and wiped his left palm on his shorts. He could tell that his arm was still bleeding.

From even farther away, he heard, "If we aren't able to settle this, it's going to be very bad for that little girl of yours. You can't pay that private detective to watch her for the next fifty years."

Rage welled up in Pete, and he wanted to run down the hallway and beat her to death with his bat! *Breathe deeply*, he told himself. *In and out. In and out.* He heard glass breaking.

"Oops, so sorry, Pete. I seem to have dropped the picture of you and little sweetie building that quaint sand castle on the beach. I'm *so* sorry."

Pete's hand tightened on the bat handle, then loosened and tightened again.

He stepped across the mudroom to the door leading outside. The lock clicked when he turned it but he was confident she wouldn't hear the soft sound. He eased the inner door open, then clicked on the outside bug light and opened the outer door six inches and let the spring close it. The sound of the door snapping shut reverberated through the cottage. He quickly moved back to the coats and nestled into them again. He gripped the bat with both hands and held it above his head. And waited, his heart thumping wildly. *He was going to end it now!*

His shoulder muscles ached from the strained position, but he didn't dare move. He felt the blood from the cut on his arm reverse directions and begin to trickle down his shoulder to his tee shirt. *Don't move,* he told himself. *Don't move. Where was she?* He didn't hear her voice and heard no footsteps. He second guessed himself a thousand times in a matter of seconds. Maybe rolling the dice wasn't a smart thing to do. Maybe she saw through his maneuver and was waiting him out.

He saw a faint shadow cross the mudroom floor. He waited, fear squeezing his organs like a vise. The shadow became more pronounced. Then Eve was in the mudroom, looking at the inner door that was half open. The dim luminosity from the bug light glinted off her knife.

His heart hammered louder as he let her get a step into the room. Then two steps. And three. He tightened his grip on the bat and swung as though he was about to crush a Pedro Martinez fastball over the fence at Yankee Stadium in the ninth inning. The bat caught her below the shoulder blades and air *whooshed* from her body. She stood upright for a moment, then pitched forward and her knife skittered across the floor.

His chest heaved and sweat ran down his face as he stared at the prone body. He wiped his forehead with the sleeve of his tee shirt. The blow hadn't sated the rage that had been building in him. He eyed the back of her head and raised the bat again as he listened to the spasmodic moans that came from her body. Her arm moved a few inches and her fingers opened and closed as though she was trying to find something.

This is for what you tried to do to my daughter and me! He brought the bat down with an overhead chop that hit the floor six inches from her head. Her body jumped, as though prodded with electrodes. He raised the bat again and pounded the floor in the same place.

He stepped over Eve's body and continued to eye her. Her right hand right hand still groped around the floor. He nudged the hand with his foot and it twitched. He raised the bat and brought it down with another savage swing. The bones in her hand snapped like a handful of dry wishbones being pulled apart and her body jumped again. Pete heard another moan as her left hand reached feebly for the right one. He leaned against the wall and closed his eyes.

He wasn't aware of Joe Tessler's presence until he appeared in the door, crouched, gun drawn and extended with both hands in the classic ready position. Tessler looked at the black-clad body sprawled on the floor, then up at Pete who was still leaning against the wall in only his underwear with his left arm dripping blood from the kitchen towel.

"Is she dead?" Tessler asked.

"I don't think so."

"How about a weapon?"

"Click that light switch," Pete muttered, gesturing toward the door.

The light came on and they both blinked in the sudden brightness.

"Over there," Pete said. He pointed to the knife under a small stand next to the wall.

Tessler squatted and examined the knife without picking it up.

Two more uniformed deputies came in with guns drawn. They stood just inside the door with open mouths as they looked first at Pete and then the woman lying on the floor. Blood ran from her battered hand, which was already turning purple, and convulsive moans came from her body.

"I assume you cold-cocked her with that bat."

Pete shrugged. "It's all I had."

"That's hardly a contest," Tessler said. "A Louisville Slugger versus a black belt with an eight-inch switchblade."

Pete didn't say anything, but he felt tears running down his cheeks and he wiped them away. He rested his head against the wall again.

Tessler and the deputies went through their standard crime scene routine while they waited for the ambulance to arrive. The two EMTs who came out stared in disbelief, as the deputies had before them, and then finally became engaged and loaded Eve onto a stretcher and pushed it into the back of their boxy vehicle.

"I'm glad your emergency call device worked," Pete said wearily.

Tessler looked at him blankly. "What do you mean?"

"Isn't that how you knew I was in trouble?"

Tessler looked puzzled. "I couldn't sleep when I got home. I finally got up and decided to drive by your place to make sure no one was prowling around."

Pete shook his head and gave a little grunt, but couldn't think of anything to say.

"You need to get that arm attended to," Tessler said.

Pete stared at the ambulance as the EMTs closed the door. "I know the way to the hospital," he muttered. He was afraid that if he were in the same space with Eve Bayles, or Evelyn Beth Lambert or whatever her name was, he'd do something he'd later regret.

Tessler must have read his mind. He said, "You're not driving. You're being chauffeured in a smoke-free Acura." He appeared to study Pete for a moment. Choosing his words carefully, he added, "Do you have a robe or something you could put on? And maybe you should leave that bat here."

Pete realized he was still holding the Louisville Slugger. He looked down at the splintered handle and said, "This was the bat I used all the way through high school."

"Didn't you use metal bats?" Tessler asked.

"Not where I went to school."

FORTY-NINE

"All rise for the Honorable Solomon Rosenberg."

The judge took his seat on the bench. Pete sat with Angie DeMarco. White Flag Cummings had "another commitment" and couldn't be there. Across the aisle, Larry Helms huddled with Wayne Sable and Maureen Fesko. All three looked anxious.

"I'm pleased that everyone on both sides could be here," the judge intoned, "and I appreciate your patience. I'm going to tell you what I've decided because I don't want you to think I'm needlessly keeping you in suspense while I make my other remarks.

"I've decided to maintain the *status quo*. Mr. Sable will continue to have legal custody of Julie, and Mr. Thorsen will continue to have the same liberal visitation rights he's enjoyed up to now."

Pete expelled air in relief.

Maureen Fesko jumped to her feet and said, "That's wrong, Judge! That man is going to get my niece killed! I—"

Larry helms tugged on her arm, obviously trying to get her to sit down. Even Wayne Sable looked at his sister with a bewildered expression.

The judge banged his gavel and said, "Ms. Fesko, if you don't take your seat and remain quiet, I'm going to have you removed from this courtroom. We heard quite enough from you during the hearing on the motions." Rosenberg glared at her.

Maureen looked stunned by the judge's admonition.

When quiet reigned again, Rosenberg continued and said, "I came to that decision for two reasons. Julie will be of majority age in another year and then she can make her own decisions regarding who she wants to live with or see. And second, neither party came to this court with exactly what I'd consider clean hands."

The judge proceeded to lecture Wayne Sable about his wanton ways and failing to see Julie on a regular basis and care enough to inquire about where her support was coming from and step up and provide financial help himself. Then he unloaded on Pete for the things he'd been involved in that led to Sable's motion in the first place.

As they walked out of the courtroom, Angie whispered to Pete, "Satisfied?"

"Yes," he whispered back. "But I feel like a boy who was caught with his hand in the cookie jar and then lied to his mother about how many ginger snaps he'd eaten."

"I think that story about the knife in Julie's door really caught his attention."

"It's over."

"That's what you told me on the telephone. It was Robyn Fleming's sister, huh?"

Pete nodded.

"I remember Robyn when you were representing her small business *pro bono*. What was going on between the sisters that led to this?"

"I don't know. The only thing I know for sure is that Eve thought that by doing me in, she could get back in her sister's good graces."

"And she was going to sever your hamstrings."

"I guess so. She wanted to tell Robyn that I knew what it was like to be unable to walk before she killed me."

"That's sick."

Pete still shuddered when he thought about it. "They're both nuts," he said. "And psychopaths."

"What's going to happen to Eve now?"

"She's going away for a long time, that much I know. They have her on an attempted murder charge and seven other lesser charges. Tessler told me they're also looking at reopening the cat burglar cases in various cities if the statutes of limitations haven't run. That night at my place, they found her SUV parked two cottages over, and when they searched it, they found a device to manipulate my alarm system and a full set of burglar tools."

"How did she expect to get away with it?"

Pete shook his head. "From what I can gather, she was pretty good at dropping out of sight. Her vehicle was stuffed with her things. She apparently planned to take off as soon as she took care of me."

Angie looked at him and asked, "How did you get onto her?"

"Various things. Eventually Joe Tessler and I pieced it together."

"She must have made *some* mistake."

"She went after my daughter."

ABOUT THE AUTHOR

Robert Wangard is a crime-fiction writer who splits his time between Chicago, where he practiced law for many years, and northern Michigan. *Stalked* is the fifth in the Pete Thorsen Mystery series. The first four, *Target, Malice, Deceit* and *Payback* were widely-acclaimed by reviewers and *Payback* was named by ForeWord Reviews as a 2014 INDIEFAB Book of the Year Finalist. Wangard is also the author of *Hard Water Blues*, an anthology of short stories. He is a member of Mystery Writers of America, the Short Mystery Fiction Society, and other writers' organizations.

Readers: Did you enjoy *Stalked* or one of my other novels?
If so, I'd appreciate it if you would post a review on the appropriate book pages on Amazon.com, BN.com and Goodreads.com. Thanks.

www.rwangard.com